T0109879

CLASSIC FANTASY STORIES

More short stories available
from Macmillan Collector's Library

Enchanted Tales
Classic Love Stories
Classic Dog Stories
Classic Cat Stories
Classic Stories of the Sea
Classic Hallowe'en Stories
Classic Science Fiction Stories
Classic Locked Room Mysteries
Round About the Christmas Tree
Ghost Stories by Charles Dickens
Complete Ghost Stories by M. R. James
Best Short Stories by W. Somerset Maugham
Prelude & Other Stories by Katherine Mansfield
The Awakening & Other Stories by Kate Chopin
In the Ravine & Other Stories by Anton Chekhov
The Third Man & Other Stories by Graham Greene
The Happy Prince & Other Stories by Oscar Wilde
The Best of Sherlock Holmes by Arthur Conan Doyle
Tales of Mystery and Imagination by Edgar Allan Poe
A Glove Shop in Vienna & Other Stories
by Eva Ibbotson
Standing Her Ground: Classic Short Stories
by Trailblazing Women
Sleepily Ever After: Bedtime Stories for Grown Ups
Tales and Poems by Edgar Allan Poe
Just So Stories by Rudyard Kipling
Dubliners by James Joyce

CLASSIC FANTASY STORIES

Selection and introduction by
FARAH MENDLESOHN

MACMILLAN COLLECTOR'S LIBRARY

This collection first published 2024 by Macmillan Collector's Library
an imprint of Pan Macmillan
The Smithson, 6 Briset Street, London ECIM 5NR
EU representative: Macmillan Publishers Ireland Ltd, 1st Floor,
The Liffey Trust Centre, 117–126 Sheriff Street Upper,
Dublin 1, DO1 YC43
Associated companies throughout the world
www.panmacmillan.com

ISBN 978-1-0350-2643-2

Introduction and author biographies copyright © Farah Mendlesohn
Selection and arrangement copyright © Macmillan Publishers International Ltd. 2024

The Permissions Acknowledgements on p. 401 constitute an extension of
this copyright page.

1 3 5 7 9 8 6 4 2

A CIP catalogue record for this book is available from the British Library.

Casing design and endpaper pattern by Andrew Davidson
Typeset in Plantin by Jouve (UK), Milton Keynes
Printed and bound in China by Imago

Visit **www.panmacmillan.com** to read more
about all our books and to buy them.

Contents

Introduction vii

WASHINGTON IRVING 1
Rip Van Winkle: A Legend of the Kaatskill Mountains

ELIZABETH GASKELL 32
The Old Nurse's Story

CHRISTINA ROSSETTI 71
Goblin Market

CHARLES DICKENS 95
The Magic Fishbone

FRANK R. STOCKTON 113
The Griffin and the Minor Canon

SARAH ORNE JEWETT 139
The Gray Man

OSCAR WILDE 151
The Happy Prince

RICHARD GARNETT 167
The Demon Pope

H. P. BLAVATSKY 184
The Ensouled Violin

E. NESBIT 233
The Dragon Tamers

WILLIAM MORRIS 257
The Folk of the Mountain Door

ARTHUR MACHEN 279
The Bowmen

REGINA MIRIAM BLOCH 286
The Swine-Gods

RABINDRANATH TAGORE 301
Once There Was a King

W. E. B. DU BOIS 316
The Princess of the Hither Isles

MAY SINCLAIR 325
The Nature of the Evidence

VERNON LEE 346
The Doll

E. M. FORSTER 362
The Celestial Omnibus

AVRAM DAVIDSON 390
The Golem

Permissions Acknowledgements 401

Introduction

FARAH MENDLESOHN

Fantasy is the fiction of the impossible and the unexplainable. It is also the fiction of the unbelievable and the *unbelieved in*. This helps us to think about when fantasy started. Although many myths and legends are the source material for much fantasy today, at the time such myths and legends emerged they were believed in, if not as real, then as a realist understanding of the world. Greek gods legends, Navajo creation stories, the Genesis, are not fantasy because they are all written with some kind of belief behind them. Within all these traditions there are, of course, plenty of tales that are acknowledged as stories, such as 'Sinbad the Sailor' from *The Arabian Nights*, Coyote and Anansi stories, and the 'Epic of Gilgamesh', but they were still told within a tradition in which they were *possible*.

The growing distinction between the believable and the unbelievable that emerged in the Renaissance produced stories clearly written as fantastical, as tales of the impossible. These stories have led many fantasy scholars to choose the Renaissance as the genre's starting point, identifying Shakespeare's

The Tempest (a story about a wizard-scientist), or Margaret Cavendish's *The Blazing World* (in which the author finds a hidden race who can be reached through a hole in the North Pole), or John Bunyan's *The Pilgrim's Progress* and its sequel (in which people go on epic quests to find salvation and a making over of the world) as originating texts.

The modern fantastic, with its sub-genres and tropes, can be located in the eighteenth century with the rise of the Enlightenment and the contemporaneous rise of literary and artistic realism. Fantasy was not simply a continuation of earlier forms of storytelling, it was part of a conscious revolt against the ideas of people like the utilitarian philosopher John Stuart Mill, ideas that Charles Dickens, for example, put in the mouth of one of his walk-on characters in *Hard Times*: '"Ay, Ay, Ay! But you mustn't fancy," cried the gentleman, quite elated by coming so happily to his point. "That's it! You are never to fancy."'

The art of the fantastic is not just in the content but also in the conjuration of the fantastic through imaginative and fanciful writing. Three of the most influential twentieth-century fantasy writers, J. R. R. Tolkien, Michael Moorcock and Diana Wynne Jones, all emphasized that how you wrote the fantastic was as important as the fantastical idea. This idea helps us to understand how fantasy consists of multiple and overlapping kinds (or genres) of fantasy, whether the otherworldly epic, the domestic chaos of the fairy in the hearth, the haunting or the paranormal romance. Each is written differently, each tries to impress on the reader the sense of something other.

This collection has tried to represent a broad swathe of the strands that have gone into the making of modern fantasy with the exception of epic fantasy, which doesn't lend itself to the short-story form.

Fairy stories are one of the most important threads in the modern fantastic. Charles Perrault, the creator of many of the fairy tales we know today, collected his stories in the French countryside in the seventeenth century and repackaged them for the court; in the eighteenth century, Jacob and Wilhelm Grimm collected the German *Märchen*, or folk tales, for the middle classes. By the nineteenth century, it was becoming more common for people to write their own tales, using the forms they had learned. One of the first new authors was Washington Irving. In Washington Irving's 'Rip Van Winkle' (1819), the elves have migrated to America, and when a man stumbles into their mountain, his life is changed forever. Both Charles Dickens and Oscar Wilde are represented in this collection by fairy stories.

Dickens sets his tale in a fairy court but one that is curiously mundane. It also functions as a 'club story', a story told within a story, which is a form that fantasy writers love. Wilde's 'The Happy Prince' (1888) is a different kind of urban fantasy. It captures the power of the fantastic to address, with pathos, the cruelty of the world. It is allegorical but it is also mimetic, and challenges the idea that the fantastic is escapist. Making the mundane fantastical is a technique that in the twentieth century became a staple of stories in the American 'slick' magazines, as demonstrated by Frank Stockton's 'The Griffin and the Minor Canon' (1887) and author and editor Avram Davidson's story, 'The Golem' (1955).

One of fantasy's powers lies in its allegorical possibilities. The middle of the nineteenth century saw a growing interest in medievalism led by the pre-Raphaelite Brotherhood. The most famous story of this period is neither by a 'brother', nor is it prose. Christina Rossetti's 'Goblin Market' (1862) is a lush conjuration of the fantastic that takes the traditional story of fairy folk tempting mortals and layers it with passion and pleasure. It has been repeatedly illustrated through the years and many writers have paid homage to it. The socialist William Morris and the critic and author John Ruskin both experimented with the pastoral and fantastical mode, which combined folk tales with moral messages. In his story 'The Folk of the Mountain Door' William Morris expresses his longing for a different England. W. E. B. Du Bois, writing just after the First World War, uses the same form in 'The Princess of the Hither Isles' (1920) to question who that vision is for and to challenge some of its inherent pro-colonialist assumptions.

One of the major strands in modern fantasy is the Gothic. *The Castle of Otranto*, published by Horace Walpole (1764) as a 'found story' (itself a common trope in fantastic fiction) set off a craze for evil monks, wild romance and overblown kidnappings with veiled hints of rape. In 'The Old Nurse's Story' (1852), Elizabeth Gaskell combines her attentiveness to the experiences of women of different classes with a ghost story, redolent with all the tropes of the new Gothic: the old house, the orphan and a terrible secret. Told by the observant nurse, the story is in part about the restrictions placed on women and the resentment and evil it generates.

The Gothic offered several threads to the fantastical genres. Weird fiction, now most strongly associated with H. P. Lovecraft and William Hope Hodgson, allowed authors to express the sense of seething danger in the world around them. The example in this collection, 'The Swine-Gods' by Regina Miriam Bloch, shows off the emphasis on language to create the uncanny.

By the mid-nineteenth century, folk tales of ghostly apparitions were being transformed into the literary ghost story. At the end of the century and into the middle of the first half of the twentieth century, this became one of the dominant forms of the fantastic. It is here that we find many women and queer writers: the threat of the disrupter to heterosexual norms could be expressed well in a ghost story such as Vernon Lee's 'The Doll'.

The Great War had a particular effect on the zeitgeist: seances became a cultural phenomenon. In the face of so much loss, the presence of the ghost seemed intensely close. One of the best-known stories to emerge from the period is Arthur Machen's 'The Bowmen' (1914). This story, written about the retreat at Mons, and inspired by Rudyard Kipling's 'The Lost Legion' (1893), in which British troops in Afghanistan are aided by ghosts, was published in the *Evening News*, and quickly entered folklore with soldiers insisting that they had seen the angels described.

The widespread Victorian suspicion of the fantastical means that many of the great names of nineteenth-century fantasy either wrote for children (under the age of twelve) or were labelled children's authors. The result is that the classic names of fantasy from the mid-to-late nineteenth century, and a majority of the ones still in print, are fantasies labelled as children's stories such as George Mac-Donald's Christian fantasies, *At the Back of the North Wind* (1868) and *The Princess and the Goblin* (1872), Charles Kingsley's Christian socialist fable, *The Water Babies* (1863), and Lewis Carroll's *Alice's Adventures in Wonderland* (1866). Representing the children's fiction strand here are Charles Dickens with 'The Magic Fishbone' (1863), Christina Rossetti's poem 'Goblin Market', which with its both overtly Christian and overly hedonistic imagery has a fair claim on being the first young adult fantasy, and the hugely influential Edith Nesbit with 'The Dragon Tamers', a story about bringing the fantastic under control.

The stories in this volume have been selected both to draw attention to the tropes of the fantastic and also to the language used to render a story fantastical. In some, the fantasy is obvious; in others, how the story is told is what tells us we are in a fantasy. Today we recognize these tones immediately as signals of genre – we may even buy a book because its voice tells us immediately that it is the kind of fantasy we love – but when these stories were first written, they were all highly experimental, each author asking the question: 'How do I make my readers feel a sense of wonder?'

CLASSIC FANTASY STORIES

WASHINGTON IRVING

Washington Irving (1783–1859) was one of the very first fantasy writers in the United States. An essayist and folk story collector, he spent time in Germany and was influenced by the tradition of *Märchen* (folk tales). His time in Spain, as an American minister, led to two bestsellers – a biography of Christopher Columbus (1828) and *Tales of the Alhambra* (1832). His greatest achievement was the creation of an American folklore and he in turn influenced American authors as disparate as John Bellers and L. Frank Baum, and British writers such as Mary Shelley and Charles Dickens. His best-known fantasy stories are 'The Legend of Sleepy Hollow' and 'The Headless Horseman' – the latter has become a ghost story so famous that many people don't realize it has an author.

Rip Van Winkle: A Legend of the Kaatskill Mountains

By Woden, God of Saxons,
From whence comes Wensday, that is Wodensday,
Truth is a thing that ever I will keep
Unto thylke day in which I creep into
My sepulchre——

CARTWRIGHT.

A POSTHUMOUS WRITING OF DIEDRICH KNICKERBOCKER.

[The following Tale was found among the papers of the late Diedrich Knickerbocker, an old gentleman of New York, who was very curious in the Dutch history of the province, and the manners of the descendants from its primitive settlers. His historical researches, however, did not lie so much among books as among men; for the former are lamentably scanty on his favorite topics; whereas he found the old burghers, and still more their wives, rich in that legendary lore, so invaluable to true history. Whenever, therefore, he happened upon a genuine Dutch family, snugly shut up in its low-roofed farm-house, under a spreading sycamore, he looked upon it as a little clasped volume of black-letter, and studied it with the zeal of a book-worm.

The result of all these researches was a history of the province during the reign of the Dutch governors, which he published some years since. There have been various opinions as to the literary character of his work, and, to tell the truth, it is not a whit better than it should be. Its chief merit is its scrupulous accuracy, which indeed was a little questioned, on its first appearance, but has since been completely established; and it is now admitted into all historical collections, as a book of unquestionable authority.

The old gentleman died shortly after the publication of his work, and now that he is dead and gone, it cannot do much harm to his memory to say, that his time might have been much better employed in weightier labors. He, however, was apt to ride his hobby his own way; and though it did now and then kick up the dust a little in the eyes of his neighbors, and grieve the spirit of some friends, for whom he felt the truest deference and affection; yet his errors and follies are remembered "more in sorrow than in anger," and it begins to be suspected that he never intended to injure or offend. But however his memory may be appreciated by critics, it is still held dear by many folk, whose good opinion is well worth having; particularly by certain biscuit-bakers, who have gone so far as to imprint his likeness on their new-year cakes; and have thus given him a chance for immortality, almost equal to the being stamped on a Waterloo Medal, or a Queen Anne's Farthing.]

★

Whoever has made a voyage up the Hudson must remember the Kaatskill mountains. They are a dismembered branch of the great Appalachian family, and are seen away to the west of the river, swelling up to a noble height, and lording it over the surrounding country. Every change of season, every change of weather, indeed every hour of the day, produces some change in the magical hues and shapes of these mountains, and they are regarded by all the good wives, far and near, as perfect barometers. When the weather is fair and settled, they are clothed in blue and purple, and print their bold outlines on the clear evening sky, but sometimes, when the rest of the landscape is cloudless, they will gather a hood of gray vapors about their summits, which, in the last rays of the setting sun, will glow and light up like a crown of glory.

At the foot of these fairy mountains, the voyager may have descried the light smoke curling up from a village, whose shingle-roofs gleam among the trees, just where the blue tints of the upland melt away into the fresh green of the nearer landscape. It is a little village, of great antiquity, having been founded by some of the Dutch Colonists, in the early times of the province, just about the beginning of the government of the good Peter Stuyvesant, (may he rest in peace!) and there were some of the houses of the original settlers standing within a few years, built of small yellow bricks brought from Holland, having latticed windows and gable fronts, surmounted with weathercocks.

In that same village, and in one of these very houses (which, to tell the precise truth, was sadly time-worn and weather-beaten), there lived many years since, while the country was yet a province of Great Britain, a simple good-natured fellow, of the name of Rip Van Winkle. He was a descendant of the Van Winkles who figured so gallantly in the chivalrous days of Peter Stuyvesant, and accompanied him to the siege of Fort Christina. He inherited, however, but little of the martial character of his ancestors. I have observed that he was a simple good-natured man: he was, moreover, a kind neighbor, and an obedient hen-pecked husband. Indeed, to the latter circumstance might be owing that meekness of spirit which gained him such universal popularity; for those men are most apt to be obsequious and conciliating abroad, who are under the discipline of shrews at home. Their tempers, doubtless, are rendered pliant and malleable in the fiery furnace of domestic tribulation, and a curtain lecture is worth all the sermons in the world for teaching the virtues of patience and long-suffering. A termagant wife may, therefore, in some respects, be considered a tolerable blessing; and if so, Rip Van Winkle was thrice blessed.

Certain it is, that he was a great favorite among all the good wives of the village, who, as usual with the amiable sex, took his part in all family squabbles; and never failed, whenever they talked those matters over in their evening gossipings, to lay all the blame on Dame Van Winkle. The children of the village, too, would shout with joy whenever he approached. He assisted at their sports, made their playthings, taught them to fly kites and shoot marbles, and told them long stories of ghosts, witches, and Indians. Whenever he went dodging about the village, he was surrounded by a troop of them, hanging on his skirts, clambering on his back, and playing a thousand tricks on him with impunity; and not a dog would bark at him throughout the neighborhood.

The great error in Rip's composition was an insuperable aversion to all kinds of profitable labor. It could not be from the want of assiduity or perseverance; for he would sit on a wet rock, with a rod as long and heavy as a Tartar's lance, and fish all day without a murmur, even though he should not be encouraged by a single nibble. He would carry a fowling-piece on his shoulder for hours together, trudging through woods and swamps, and up hill and down dale, to shoot a few squirrels or wild pigeons. He would never refuse to assist a neighbor even in the roughest toil, and was a foremost man at all country frolics for husking Indian corn, or building stone-fences; the women of the village, too, used to employ him to run their errands, and to do such little odd jobs as their less obliging husbands would not do for them. In a word, Rip was ready to attend to anybody's business but his own; but as to doing family duty, and keeping his farm in order, he found it impossible.

In fact, he declared it was of no use to work on his farm; it was the most pestilent little piece of ground in the whole country; every thing about it went wrong, and would go wrong, in spite of him. His fences were continually falling to pieces: his cow would either go astray, or get among the cabbages; weeds were sure to grow quicker in his fields than anywhere else; the rain always made a point of setting in just as he had some out-door work to do; so that though his patrimonial estate had dwindled away under his management, acre by acre, until there was little more left than a mere patch of Indian corn and potatoes, yet it was the worst-conditioned farm in the neighborhood.

His children, too, were as ragged and wild as if they belonged to nobody. His son Rip, an urchin begotten in his own likeness, promised to inherit the habits, with the old clothes of his father. He was generally seen trooping like a colt at his mother's heels, equipped in a pair of his father's cast-off galligaskins, which he had much ado to hold up with one hand, as a fine lady does her train in bad weather.

Rip Van Winkle, however, was one of those happy mortals, of foolish, well-oiled dispositions, who take the world easy, eat white bread or brown, whichever can be got with least thought or trouble, and would rather starve on a penny than work for a pound. If left to himself, he would have whistled life away in perfect contentment; but his wife kept continually dinning in his ears about his idleness, his carelessness, and the ruin he was bringing on his family. Morning, noon, and night, her tongue was incessantly going, and every thing he said or did was sure to produce a torrent of household eloquence. Rip had but one way of replying to all lectures of the kind, and that, by frequent use, had grown into a habit. He shrugged his shoulders, shook his head, cast up his eyes, but said nothing. This, however, always provoked a fresh volley from his wife; so that he was fain to draw off his forces, and take to the outside of the house—the only side which, in truth, belongs to a hen-pecked husband.

Rip's sole domestic adherent was his dog Wolf, who was as much hen-pecked as his master; for Dame Van Winkle regarded them as companions in idleness, and even looked upon Wolf with an evil eye, as the cause of his master's going so often astray. True it is, in all points of spirit befitting an honorable dog, he was as courageous an animal as ever scoured the woods—but what courage can withstand the ever-during and all-besetting terrors of a woman's tongue? The moment Wolf entered the house his crest fell, his tail drooped to the ground or curled between his legs, he sneaked about with a gallows air, casting many a sidelong glance at Dame Van Winkle, and at the least flourish of a broomstick or ladle, he would fly to the door with yelping precipitation.

Times grew worse and worse with Rip Van Winkle as years of matrimony rolled on; a tart temper never mellows with age, and a sharp tongue is the only edged tool that grows keener with constant use. For a long while he used to console himself, when driven from home, by frequenting a kind of perpetual club of the sages, philosophers, and other idle personages of the village; which held its sessions on a bench before a small inn, designated by a rubicund portrait of His Majesty George the Third. Here they used to sit in the shade through a long, lazy summer's day, talking listlessly over village gossip, or telling endless sleepy stories about nothing. But it would have been worth any statesman's money to have heard the profound discussions that sometimes took place when by chance an old newspaper fell into their hands from some passing traveller. How solemnly they would listen to the contents, as drawled out by Derrick Van Bummel, the schoolmaster, a dapper, learned little man, who was not to be daunted by the most gigantic word in the dictionary; and how sagely they would deliberate upon public events some months after they had taken place.

The opinions of this junto were completely controlled by Nicholas Vedder, a patriarch of the village, and landlord of the inn, at the door of which he took his seat from morning till night, just moving sufficiently to avoid the sun and keep in the shade of a large tree; so that the neighbors could tell the hour by his movements as accurately as by a sun-dial. It is true, he was rarely heard to speak, but smoked his pipe incessantly. His adherents, however, (for every great man has his adherents), perfectly understood him, and knew how to gather his opinions. When any thing that was read or related displeased him, he was observed to smoke his pipe vehemently, and to send forth short, frequent, and angry puffs, but when pleased, he would inhale the smoke slowly and tranquilly, and emit it in light and placid clouds; and sometimes, taking the pipe from his mouth, and letting the fragrant vapor curl about his nose, would gravely nod his head in token of perfect approbation.

From even this stronghold the unlucky Rip was at length routed by his termagant wife, who would suddenly break in upon the tranquillity of the assemblage and call the members all to naught; nor was that august personage, Nicholas Vedder himself, sacred from the daring tongue of this terrible virago, who charged him outright with encouraging her husband in habits of idleness.

Poor Rip was at last reduced almost to despair; and his only alternative, to escape from the labor of the farm and clamor of his wife, was to take gun in hand and stroll away into the woods. Here he would sometimes seat himself at the foot of a tree, and share the contents of his wallet with Wolf, with whom he sympathized as a fellow-sufferer in persecution. "Poor Wolf," he would say, "thy mistress leads thee a dog's life of it; but never mind, my lad, whilst I live thou shalt never want a friend to stand by thee!" Wolf would wag his tail, look wistfully in his master's face, and if dogs can feel pity I verily believe he reciprocated the sentiment with all his heart.

In a long ramble of the kind on a fine autumnal day, Rip had unconsciously scrambled to one of the highest parts of the Kaatskill mountains. He was after his favorite sport of squirrel shooting, and the still solitudes had echoed and re-echoed with the reports of his gun. Panting and fatigued, he threw himself, late in the afternoon, on a green knoll, covered with mountain herbage, that crowned the brow of a precipice. From an opening between the trees he could overlook all the lower country for many a mile of rich woodland. He saw at a distance the lordly Hudson, far, far below him, moving on its silent but majestic course, with the reflection of a purple cloud, or the sail of a lagging bark, here and there sleeping on its glassy bosom, and at last losing itself in the blue highlands.

On the other side he looked down into a deep mountain glen, wild, lonely, and shagged, the bottom filled with fragments from the impending cliffs, and scarcely lighted by the reflected rays of the setting sun. For some time Rip lay musing on this scene; evening was gradually advancing; the mountains began to throw their long blue shadows over the valleys; he saw that it would be dark long before he could reach the village, and he heaved a heavy sigh when he thought of encountering the terrors of Dame Van Winkle.

As he was about to descend, he heard a voice from a distance hallooing, "Rip Van Winkle! Rip Van Winkle!" He looked round, but could see nothing but a crow winging its solitary flight across the mountain. He thought his fancy must have deceived him, and turned again to descend, when he heard the same cry ring through the still evening air: "Rip Van Winkle! Rip Van Winkle!"—at the same time Wolf bristled up his back, and giving a low growl, skulked to his master's side, looking fearfully down into the glen. Rip now felt a vague apprehension stealing over him; he looked anxiously in the same direction, and perceived a strange figure slowly toiling up the rocks, and bending under the weight of something he carried on his back. He was surprised to see any human being in this lonely and unfrequented place, but supposing it to be some one of the neighborhood in need of his assistance, he hastened down to yield it.

On nearer approach he was still more surprised at the singularity of the stranger's appearance. He was a short, square-built old fellow, with thick bushy hair, and a grizzled beard. His dress was of the antique Dutch fashion—a cloth jerkin strapped round the waist—several pairs of breeches, the outer one of ample volume, decorated with rows of buttons down the sides and bunches at the knees. He bore on his shoulder a stout keg, that seemed full of liquor, and made signs for Rip to approach and assist him with the load. Though rather shy and distrustful of this new acquaintance, Rip complied with his usual alacrity; and mutually relieving one another, they clambered up a narrow gully, apparently the dry bed of a mountain torrent. As they ascended, Rip every now and then heard long rolling peals, like distant thunder, that seemed to issue out of a deep ravine, or rather cleft, between lofty rocks, toward which their rugged path conducted. He paused for an instant, but supposing it to be the muttering of one of these transient thunder-showers which often take place in mountain heights, he proceeded. Passing through the ravine, they came to a hollow, like a small amphitheatre, surrounded by perpendicular precipices, over the brinks of which impending trees shot their branches, so that you only caught glimpses of the azure sky and the bright evening cloud. During the whole time, Rip and his companion had labored on in silence; for though the former marvelled greatly what could be the object of carrying a keg of liquor up this wild mountain, yet there was something strange and incomprehensible about the unknown, that inspired awe and checked familiarity.

On entering the amphitheatre, new objects of wonder presented themselves. On a level spot in the centre was a company of odd-looking personages playing at nine-pins. They were dressed in a quaint outlandish fashion; some wore short doublets, others jerkins, with long knives in their belts, and most of them had enormous breeches, of similar style with that of the guide's. Their visages, too, were peculiar; one had a large beard, broad face, and small piggish eyes; the face of another seemed to consist entirely of nose, and was surmounted by a white sugar-loaf hat, set off with a little red cock's tail. They all had beards, of various shapes and colors. There was one who seemed to be the commander. He was a stout old gentleman, with a weather-beaten countenance; he wore a laced doublet, broad belt and hanger, high-crowned hat and feather, red stockings, and high-heeled shoes, with roses in them. The whole group reminded Rip of the figures in an old Flemish painting, in the parlor of Dominie Van Shaick, the village parson, and which had been brought over from Holland at the time of the settlement.

What seemed particularly odd to Rip was, that though these folks were evidently amusing themselves, yet they maintained the gravest face, the most mysterious silence, and were, withal, the most melancholy party of pleasure he had ever witnessed.

Nothing interrupted the stillness of the scene but the noise of the balls, which, whenever they were rolled, echoed along the mountains like rumbling peals of thunder.

As Rip and his companion approached them, they suddenly desisted from their play, and stared at him with such fixed, statue-like gaze, and such strange, uncouth, lack-lustre countenances, that his heart turned within him, and his knees smote together. His companion now emptied the contents of the keg into large flagons, and made signs to him to wait upon the company. He obeyed with fear and trembling; they quaffed the liquor in profound silence, and then returned to their game.

By degrees Rip's awe and apprehension subsided. He even ventured, when no eye was fixed upon him, to taste the beverage, which he found had much of the flavor of excellent Hollands. He was naturally a thirsty soul, and was soon tempted to repeat the draught. One taste provoked another; and he reiterated his visits to the flagon so often that at length his senses were overpowered, his eyes swam in his head, his head gradually declined, and he fell into a deep sleep.

On waking, he found himself on the green knoll whence he had first seen the old man of the glen. He rubbed his eyes—it was a bright sunny morning. The birds were hopping and twittering among the bushes, and the eagle was wheeling aloft, and breasting the pure mountain breeze. "Surely," thought Rip, "I have not slept here all night." He recalled the occurrences before he fell asleep. The strange man with a keg of liquor—the mountain ravine—the wild retreat among the rocks—the woebegone party at nine-pins—the flagon—"Oh! that flagon! that wicked flagon!" thought Rip—"what excuse shall I make to Dame Van Winkle?"

He looked round for his gun, but in place of the clean, well-oiled fowling-piece, he found an old fire-lock lying by him, the barrel incrusted with rust, the lock falling off, and the stock worm-eaten. He now suspected that the grave roysterers of the mountain had put a trick upon him, and having dosed him with liquor, had robbed him of his gun. Wolf, too, had disappeared, but he might have strayed away after a squirrel or partridge. He whistled after him and shouted his name, but all in vain; the echoes repeated his whistle and shout, but no dog was to be seen.

He determined to revisit the scene of the last evening's gambol, and if he met with any of the party, to demand his dog and gun. As he rose to walk, he found himself stiff in the joints, and want-ing in his usual activity. "These mountain beds do not agree with me," thought Rip, "and if this frolic should lay me up with a fit of the rheumatism, I shall have a blessed time with Dame Van Winkle." With some difficulty he got down into the glen: he found the gully up which he and his companion had ascended the preceding evening; but to his astonishment a mountain stream was now foaming down it, leaping from rock to rock, and filling the glen with babbling murmurs. He, however, made shift to scramble up its sides, working his toilsome way through thickets of birch, sassafras, and witch-hazel, and sometimes tripped up or entangled by the wild grape-vines that twisted their coils or tendrils from tree to tree, and spread a kind of network in his path.

At length he reached to where the ravine had opened through the cliffs to the amphitheatre; but no traces of such opening remained. The rocks presented a high impenetrable wall, over which the torrent came tumbling in a sheet of feathery foam, and fell into a broad deep basin, black from the shadows of the surrounding forest. Here, then, poor Rip was brought to a stand. He again called and whistled after his dog; he was only answered by the cawing of a flock of idle crows, sporting high in air about a dry tree that overhung a sunny precipice; and who, secure in their elevation, seemed to look down and scoff at the poor man's perplexities. What was to be done? the morning was passing away, and Rip felt famished for want of his breakfast. He grieved to give up his dog and gun; he dreaded to meet his wife; but it would not do to starve among the mountains. He shook his head, shouldered the rusty firelock, and with a heart full of trouble and anxiety, turned his steps homeward.

As he approached the village he met a number of people, but none whom he knew, which somewhat surprised him, for he had thought himself acquainted with every one in the country round. Their dress, too, was of a different fashion from that to which he was accustomed. They all stared at him with equal marks of surprise, and whenever they cast their eyes upon him, invariably stroked their chins. The constant recurrence of this gesture induced Rip, involuntarily, to do the same, when, to his astonishment, he found his beard had grown a foot long!

He had now entered the skirts of the village. A troop of strange children ran at his heels, hooting after him, and pointing at his gray beard. The dogs, too, not one of which he recognized for an old acquaintance, barked at him as he passed. The very village was altered; it was larger and more populous. There were rows of houses which he had never seen before, and those which had been his familiar haunts had disappeared. Strange names were over the doors—strange faces at the windows—every thing was strange. His mind now misgave him; he began to doubt whether both he and the world around him were not bewitched. Surely this was his native village, which he had left but the day before. There stood the Kaatskill mountains—there ran the silver Hudson at a distance—there was every hill and dale precisely as it had always been—Rip was sorely perplexed—"That flagon last night," thought he, "has addled my poor head sadly!"

It was with some difficulty that he found the way to his own house, which he approached with silent awe, expecting every moment to hear the shrill voice of Dame Van Winkle. He found the house gone to decay—the roof fallen in, the windows shattered, and the doors off the hinges. A half-starved dog that looked like Wolf was skulking about it. Rip called him by name, but the cur snarled, showed his teeth, and passed on. This was an unkind cut indeed—"My very dog," sighed poor Rip, "has forgotten me!"

He entered the house, which, to tell the truth, Dame Van Winkle had always kept in neat order. It was empty, forlorn, and apparently abandoned. This desolateness overcame all his connubial fears—he called loudly for his wife and children—the lonely chambers rang for a moment with his voice, and then all again was silence.

He now hurried forth, and hastened to his old resort, the village inn—but it too was gone. A large rickety wooden building stood in its place, with great gaping windows, some of them broken and mended with old hats and petticoats, and over the door was painted, "The Union Hotel, by Jonathan Doolittle." Instead of the great tree that used to shelter the quiet little Dutch inn of yore, there now was reared a tall, naked pole, with something on the top that looked like a red night-cap, and from it was fluttering a flag, on which was a singular assemblage of stars and stripes—all this was strange and incomprehensible. He recognized on the sign, however, the ruby face of King George, under which he had smoked so many a peaceful pipe: but even this was singularly meta-morphosed. The red coat was changed for one of blue and buff, a sword was held in the hand instead of a sceptre, the head was decorated with a cocked hat, and underneath was painted in large characters, GENERAL WASHINGTON.

There was, as usual, a crowd of folk about the door, but none that Rip recollected. The very charac-ter of the people seemed changed. There was a busy, bustling, disputatious tone about it, instead of the accustomed phlegm and drowsy tranquillity. He looked in vain for the sage Nicholas Vedder, with his broad face, double chin, and fair long pipe, uttering clouds of tobacco smoke instead of idle speeches; or Van Bummel, the schoolmaster, doling forth the contents of an ancient newspaper. In place of these, a lean, bilious-looking fellow, with his pockets full of handbills, was haranguing vehemently about rights of citizens—elections—members of Congress—liberty—Bunker's Hill—heroes of seventy-six—and other words, which were a perfect Babylonish jargon to the bewildered Van Winkle.

The appearance of Rip, with his long grizzled beard, his rusty fowling-piece, his uncouth dress, and an army of women and children at his heels, soon attracted the attention of the tavern politicians. They crowded round him, eyeing him from head to foot with great curiosity. The orator bustled up to him, and, drawing him partly aside, inquired "on which side he voted?" Rip stared in vacant stupidity. Another short but busy little fellow pulled him by the arm, and, rising on tiptoe, inquired in his ear, "whether he was Federal or Democrat?" Rip was equally at a loss to comprehend the question: when a knowing, self-important old gentleman in a sharp cocked hat, made his way through the crowd, putting them to the right and left with his elbows as he passed, and planting himself before Van Winkle, with one arm akimbo, the other resting on his cane, his keen eyes and sharp hat penetrating, as it were, into his very soul, demanded, in an austere tone, "what brought him to the election with a gun on his shoulder, and a mob at his heels, and whether he meant to breed a riot in the village?" "Alas! gentlemen," cried Rip, somewhat dismayed, "I am a poor quiet man, a native of the place, and a loyal subject of the king, God bless him!"

Here a general shout burst from the bystanders—"A tory! a tory! a spy! a refugee! hustle him! away with him!" It was with great difficulty that the self-important man in the cocked hat restored order; and, having assumed a tenfold austerity of brow, demanded again of the unknown culprit, what he came there for, and whom he was seeking? The poor man humbly assured him that he meant no harm, but merely came there in search of some of his neighbors, who used to keep about the tavern.

"Well, who are they? Name them."

Rip bethought himself a moment, and inquired, "Where's Nicholas Vedder?"

There was a silence for a little while, when an old man replied, in a thin, piping voice, "Nicholas Vedder! why, he is dead and gone these eighteen years! There was a wooden tombstone in the churchyard that used to tell all about him, but that's rotten and gone too."

"Where's Brom Dutcher?"

"Oh, he went off to the army in the beginning of the war; some say he was killed at the storming of Stony Point—others say he was drowned in a squall at the foot of Antony's Nose. I don't know—he never came back again."

"Where's Van Bummel, the schoolmaster?"

"He went off to the wars too, was a great militia general, and is now in Congress."

Rip's heart died away at hearing of these sad changes in his home and friends, and finding himself thus alone in the world. Every answer puzzled him too, by treating of such enormous lapses of time, and of matters which he could not understand: war—Congress—Stony Point;—he had no courage to ask after any more friends, but cried out in despair, "Does nobody here know Rip Van Winkle?"

"Oh, Rip Van Winkle!" exclaimed two or three, "Oh, to be sure! that's Rip Van Winkle yonder, leaning against the tree."

Rip looked, and beheld a precise counterpart of himself, as he went up the mountain: apparently as lazy, and certainly as ragged. The poor fellow was now completely confounded. He doubted his own identity, and whether he was himself or another man. In the midst of his bewilderment, the man in the cocked hat demanded who he was, and what was his name?

"God knows," exclaimed he, at his wit's end; "I'm not myself—I'm somebody else—that's me yonder—no—that's somebody else got into my shoes—I was myself last night, but I fell asleep on the mountain, and they've changed my gun, and every thing's changed, and I'm changed, and I can't tell what's my name, or who I am!"

The by-standers began now to look at each other, nod, wink significantly, and tap their fingers against their foreheads. There was a whisper, also, about securing the gun, and keeping the old fellow from doing mischief, at the very suggestion of which the self-important man in the cocked hat retired with some precipitation. At this critical moment a fresh, comely woman pressed through the throng to get a peep at the gray-bearded man. She had a chubby child in her arms, which, frightened at his looks, began to cry. "Hush, Rip," cried she, "hush, you little fool; the old man won't hurt you." The name of the child, the air of the mother, the tone of her voice, all awakened a train of recollections in his mind. "What is your name, my good woman?" asked he.

"Judith Gardenier."

"And your father's name?"

"Ah! poor man, Rip Van Winkle was his name, but it's twenty years since he went away from home with his gun, and never has been heard of since—his dog came home without him; but whether he shot himself, or was carried away by the Indians, nobody can tell. I was then but a little girl."

Rip had but one question more to ask; but he put it with a faltering voice:

"Where's your mother?"

"Oh, she too had died but a short time since; she broke a blood-vessel in a fit of passion at a New England peddler."

There was a drop of comfort, at least, in this intelligence. The honest man could contain himself no longer. He caught his daughter and her child in his arms. "I am your father!" cried he—"Young Rip Van Winkle once—old Rip Van Winkle now! Does nobody know poor Rip Van Winkle?"

All stood amazed, until an old woman, tottering out from among the crowd, put her hand to her brow, and peering under it in his face for a moment, exclaimed, "Sure enough! it is Rip Van Winkle—it is himself! Welcome home again, old neighbor. Why, where have you been these twenty long years?"

Rip's story was soon told, for the whole twenty long years had been to him but as one night. The neighbors stared when they heard it; some were seen to wink at each other, and put their tongues in their cheeks: and the self-important man in the cocked hat, who, when the alarm was over, had returned to the field, screwed down the corners of his mouth, and shook his head—upon which there was a general shaking of the head throughout the assemblage.

It was determined, however, to take the opinion of old Peter Vanderdonk, who was seen slowly advancing up the road. He was a descendant of the historian of that name, who wrote one of the earliest accounts of the province. Peter was the most ancient inhabitant of the village, and well versed in all the wonderful events and traditions of the neighborhood. He recollected Rip at once, and corroborated his story in the most satisfactory manner. He assured the company that it was a fact, handed down from his ancestor the historian, that the Kaatskill mountains had always been haunted by strange beings. That it was affirmed that the great Hendrick Hudson, the first discoverer of the river and country, kept a kind of vigil there every twenty years, with his crew of the *Half-moon*; being permitted in this way to revisit the scenes of his enterprise, and keep a guardian eye upon the river, and the great city called by his name. That his father had once seen them in their old Dutch dresses playing at nine-pins in a hollow of the mountain; and that he himself had heard, one summer afternoon, the sound of their balls, like distant peals of thunder.

To make a long story short, the company broke up, and returned to the more important concerns of the election. Rip's daughter took him home to live with her; she had a snug, well-furnished house, and a stout, cheery farmer for a husband, whom Rip recollected for one of the urchins that used to climb upon his back. As to Rip's son and heir, who was the ditto of himself, seen leaning against the tree, he was employed to work on the farm; but evinced an hereditary disposition to attend to anything else but his business.

Rip now resumed his old walks and habits; he soon found many of his former cronies, though all rather the worse for the wear and tear of time; and preferred making friends among the rising generation, with whom he soon grew into great favor.

Having nothing to do at home, and being arrived at that happy age when a man can be idle with impunity, he took his place once more on the bench at the inn door, and was reverenced as one of the patriarchs of the village, and a chronicle of the old times "before the war." It was some time before he could get into the regular track of gossip, or could be made to comprehend the strange events that had taken place during his torpor. How that there had been a revolutionary war—that the country had thrown off the yoke of old England—and that, instead of being a subject of His Majesty George the Third, he was now a free citizen of the United States. Rip, in fact, was no politician; the changes of states and empires made but little impression on him; but there was one species of despotism under which he had long groaned, and that was—petticoat government. Happily that was at an end; he had got his neck out of the yoke of matrimony, and could go in and out whenever he pleased, without dreading the tyranny of Dame Van Winkle. Whenever her name was mentioned, however, he shook his head, shrugged his shoulders, and cast up his eyes; which might pass either for an expression of resignation to his fate, or joy at his deliverance.

He used to tell his story to every stranger that arrived at Mr. Doolittle's hotel. He was observed, at first, to vary on some points every time he told it, which was, doubtless, owing to his having so recently awaked. It at last settled down precisely to the tale I have related, and not a man, woman, or child in the neighborhood, but knew it by heart. Some always pretended to doubt the reality of it, and insisted that Rip had been out of his head, and that this was one point on which he always remained flighty. The old Dutch inhabitants, however, almost universally gave it full credit. Even to this day they never hear a thunder-storm of a summer afternoon about the Kaatskill, but they say Hendrick Hudson and his crew are at their game of nine-pins; and it is a common wish of all hen-pecked husbands in the neighborhood, when life hangs heavy on their hands, that they might have a quieting draught out of Rip Van Winkle's flagon.

NOTE.

The foregoing Tale, one would suspect, had been suggested to Mr. Knickerbocker by a little German superstition about the Emperor Frederick *der Rothbart*, and the Kypphaüser mountain: the subjoined note, however, which he had appended to the tale, shows that it is an absolute fact, narrated with his usual fidelity:

"The story of Rip Van Winkle may seem incredible to many, but nevertheless I give it my full belief, for I know the vicinity of our old Dutch settlements to have been very subject to marvellous events and appearances. Indeed, I have heard many stranger stories than this, in the villages along the Hudson; all of which were too well authenticated to admit of a doubt. I have even talked with Rip Van Winkle myself, who, when I last saw him, was a very venerable old man, and so perfectly rational and consistent on every other point, that I think no conscientious person could refuse to take this into the bargain; nay, I have seen a certificate on the subject taken before a country justice and signed with a cross, in the justice's own handwriting. The story, therefore, is beyond the possibility of doubt.

"D. K."

ELIZABETH GASKELL

Elizabeth Gaskell (1810–1865), usually known as Mrs Gaskell, was an English novelist, biographer and short story writer. She grew up in the Midlands, which in the nineteenth century was the centre of the industrial revolution and of many radical ideas. Her work is overwhelmingly 'realist', focusing on the lives of women in early nineteenth-century rural England. The daughter of a unitarian minister, she was also connected through her mother to radical industrial families such as the Wedgwoods, Martineaus and Darwins, and married a unitarian minister, settling in Manchester, which was then the centre of the cotton trade. Gaskell travelled to Europe in 1841 and maintained a correspondence and social life with writers such as Charles Dickens and John Ruskin. Fantasy was not her usual choice of fiction but she, like her contemporaries, was experimenting with form and subject matter.

The Old Nurse's Story

You know, my dears, that your mother was an orphan, and an only child; and I dare say you have heard that your grandfather was a clergyman up in Westmoreland, where I come from. I was just a girl in the village school, when, one day, your grandmother came in to ask the mistress if there was any scholar there who would do for a nurse-maid; and mighty proud I was, I can tell ye, when the mistress called me up, and spoke to my being a good girl at my needle, and a steady honest girl, and one whose parents were very respectable, though they might be poor. I thought I should like nothing better than to serve the pretty young lady, who was blushing as deep as I was, as she spoke of the coming baby, and what I should have to do with it. However, I see you don't care so much for this part of my story, as for what you think is to come, so I'll tell you at once. I was engaged and settled at the parsonage before Miss Rosamond (that was the baby, who is now your mother) was born. To be sure, I had little enough to do with her when she came, for she was never out of her mother's arms, and slept by her all night long; and proud enough was I sometimes when missis trusted her to me. There never was such a baby before or since, though you've all of you been fine

33

enough in your turns; but for sweet, winning ways, you've none of you come up to your mother. She took after her mother, who was a real lady born; a Miss Furnivall, a granddaughter of Lord Furnivall's, in Northumberland. I believe she had neither brother nor sister, and had been brought up in my lord's family till she had married your grandfather, who was just a curate, son to a shopkeeper in Carlisle—but a clever, fine gentleman as ever was—and one who was a right-down hard worker in his parish, which was very wide, and scattered all abroad over the Westmoreland Fells. When your mother, little Miss Rosamond, was about four or five years old, both her parents died in a fortnight—one after the other. Ah! that was a sad time. My pretty young mistress and me was looking for another baby, when my master came home from one of his long rides, wet, and tired, and took the fever he died of; and then she never held up her head again, but just lived to see her dead baby, and have it laid on her breast before she sighed away her life. My mistress had asked me, on her death-bed, never to leave Miss Rosamond; but if she had never spoken a word, I would have gone with the little child to the end of the world.

The next thing, and before we had well stilled our sobs, the executors and guardians came to settle the affairs. They were my poor young mistress's own cousin, Lord Furnivall, and Mr. Esthwaite, my master's brother, a shopkeeper in Manchester; not so well to do then, as he was afterwards, and with a large family rising about him. Well! I don't know if it were their settling, or because of a letter my mistress wrote on her death-bed to her cousin, my lord; but somehow it was settled that Miss Rosamond and me were to go to Furnivall Manor House, in Northumberland, and my lord spoke as if it had been her mother's wish that she should live with his family, and as if he had no objections, for that one or two more or less could make no difference in so grand a household. So, though that was not the way in which I should have wished the coming of my bright and pretty pet to have been looked at—who was like a sunbeam in any family, be it never so grand—I was well pleased that all the folks in the Dale should stare and admire, when they heard I was going to be young lady's maid at my Lord Furnivall's at Furnivall Manor.

But I made a mistake in thinking we were to go and live where my lord did. It turned out that the family had left Furnivall Manor House fifty years or more. I could not hear that my poor young mistress had ever been there, though she had been brought up in the family; and I was sorry for that, for I should have liked Miss Rosamond's youth to have passed where her mother's had been.

My lord's gentleman, from whom I asked as many questions as I durst, said that the Manor House was at the foot of the Cumberland Fells, and a very grand place; that an old Miss Furnivall, a great-aunt of my lord's, lived there, with only a few servants; but that it was a very healthy place, and my lord had thought that it would suit Miss Rosamond very well for a few years, and that her being there might perhaps amuse his old aunt.

I was bidden by my lord to have Miss Rosamond's things ready by a certain day. He was a stern proud man, as they say all the Lords Furnivall were; and he never spoke a word more than was necessary. Folk did say he had loved my young mistress; but that, because she knew that his father would object, she would never listen to him, and married Mr. Esthwaite; but I don't know. He never married at any rate. But he never took much notice of Miss Rosamond; which I thought he might have done if he had cared for her dead mother. He sent his gentleman with us to the Manor House, telling him to join him at Newcastle that same evening; so there was no great length of time for him to make us known to all the strangers before he, too, shook us off; and we were left, two lonely young things (I was not eighteen), in the great old Manor House. It seems like yesterday that we drove there. We had left our own dear parsonage very early, and we had both cried as if our hearts would break, though we were travelling in my lord's carriage, which I thought so much of once. And now it was long past noon on a September day, and we stopped to change horses for the last time at a little smoky town, all full of colliers and miners. Miss Rosamond had fallen asleep, but Mr. Henry told me to waken her, that she might see the park and the Manor House as we drove up. I thought it rather a pity; but I did what he bade me, for fear he should complain of me to my lord. We had left all signs of a town, or even a village, and were then inside the gates of a large wild park—not like the parks here in the south, but with rocks, and the noise of running water, and gnarled thorn-trees, and old oaks, all white and peeled with age.

The road went up about two miles, and then we saw a great and stately house, with many trees close around it, so close that in some places their branches dragged against the walls when the wind blew; and some hung broken down; for no one seemed to take much charge of the place;—to lop the wood, or to keep the moss-covered carriage-way in order. Only in front of the house all was clear. The great oval drive was without a weed; and neither tree nor creeper was allowed to grow over the long, many-windowed front; at both sides of which a wing projected, which were each the ends of other side fronts; for the house, although it was so desolate, was even grander than I expected. Behind it rose the Fells, which seemed unenclosed and bare enough; and on the left hand of the house, as you stood facing it, was a little, old-fashioned flower-garden, as I found out afterwards. A door opened out upon it from the west front; it had been scooped out of the thick dark wood for some old Lady Furnivall; but the branches of the great forest trees had grown and overshadowed it again, and there were very few flowers that would live there at that time.

When we drove up to the great front entrance, and went into the hall I thought we should be lost—it was so large, and vast, and grand. There was a chandelier all of bronze, hung down from the middle of the ceiling; and I had never seen one before, and looked at it all in amaze. Then, at one end of the hall, was a great fire-place, as large as the sides of the houses in my country, with massy andirons and dogs to hold the wood; and by it were heavy old-fashioned sofas. At the opposite end of the hall, to the left as you went in—on the western side—was an organ built into the wall, and so large that it filled up the best part of that end. Beyond it, on the same side, was a door; and opposite, on each side of the fire-place, were also doors leading to the east front; but those I never went through as long as I stayed in the house, so I can't tell you what lay beyond.

The afternoon was closing in and the hall, which had no fire lighted in it, looked dark and gloomy, but we did not stay there a moment. The old servant who had opened the door for us bowed to Mr. Henry, and took us in through the door at the further side of the great organ, and led us through several smaller halls and passages into the west drawing-room, where he said that Miss Furnivall was sitting. Poor little Miss Rosamond held very tight to me, as if she were scared and lost in that great place, and as for myself, I was not much better. The west drawing-room was very cheerful-looking, with a warm fire in it, and plenty of good, comfort-able furniture about. Miss Furnivall was an old lady not far from eighty, I should think, but I do not know. She was thin and tall, and had a face as full of fine wrinkles as if they had been drawn all over it with a needle's point. Her eyes were very watchful to make up, I suppose, for her being so deaf as to be obliged to use a trumpet. Sitting with her, working at the same great piece of tapestry, was Mrs. Stark, her maid and companion, and almost as old as she was. She had lived with Miss Furnivall ever since they both were young, and now she seemed more like a friend than a servant; she looked so cold and grey, and stony, as if she had never loved or cared for any one; and I don't suppose she did care for any one, except her mistress; and, owing to the great deafness of the latter, Mrs. Stark treated her very much as if she were a child. Mr. Henry gave some message from my lord, and then he bowed good-bye to us all,—taking no notice of my sweet little Miss Rosamond's out-stretched hand—and left us standing there, being looked at by the two old ladies through their spectacles.

I was right glad when they rung for the old foot-man who had shown us in at first, and told him to take us to our rooms. So we went out of that great drawing-room, and into another sitting-room, and out of that, and then up a great flight of stairs, and along a broad gallery—which was something like a library, having books all down one side, and win-dows and writing-tables all down the other—till we came to our rooms, which I was not sorry to hear were just over the kitchens; for I began to think I should be lost in that wilderness of a house. There was an old nursery, that had been used for all the little lords and ladies long ago, with a pleasant fire burning in the grate, and the kettle boiling on the hob, and tea things spread out on the table; and out of that room was the night-nursery, with a little crib for Miss Rosamond close to my bed. And old James called up Dorothy, his wife, to bid us welcome; and both he and she were so hospitable and kind, that by and by Miss Rosamond and me felt quite at home; and by the time tea was over, she was sitting on Dorothy's knee, and chattering away as fast as her little tongue could go. I soon found out that Dorothy was from Westmoreland, and that bound her and me together, as it were; and I would never wish to meet with kinder people than were old James and his wife. James had lived pretty nearly all his life in my lord's family, and thought there was no one so grand as they. He even looked down a little on his wife; because, till he had married her, she had never lived in any but a farmer's household. But he was very fond of her, as well he might be. They had one servant under them, to do all the rough work. Agnes they called her; and she and me, and James and Dorothy, with Miss Furnivall and Mrs. Stark, made up the family; always remembering my sweet little Miss Rosamond! I used to wonder what they had done before she came, they thought so much of her now. Kitchen and drawing-room, it was all the same. The hard, sad Miss Furnivall, and the cold Mrs. Stark, looked pleased when she came fluttering in like a bird, playing and pranking hither and thither, with a continual murmur, and pretty prattle of gladness. I am sure, they were sorry many a time when she flitted away into the kitchen, though they were too proud to ask her to stay with them, and were a little surprised at her taste; though to be sure, as Mrs. Stark said, it was not to be wondered at, remembering what stock her father had come of. The great, old rambling house, was a famous place for little Miss Rosamond. She made expeditions all over it, with me at her heels; all, except the east wing, which was never opened, and whither we never thought of going. But in the western and northern part was many a pleasant room; full of things that were curiosities to us, though they might not have been to people who had seen more. The windows were darkened by the sweeping boughs of the trees, and the ivy which had overgrown them: but, in the green gloom, we could manage to see old China jars and carved ivory boxes, and great heavy books, and, above all, the old pictures!

Once, I remember, my darling would have Dorothy go with us to tell us who they all were; for they were all portraits of some of my lord's family, though Dorothy could not tell us the names of every one. We had gone through most of the rooms, when we came to the old state drawing-room over the hall, and there was a picture of Miss Furnivall; or, as she was called in those days, Miss Grace, for she was the younger sister. Such a beauty she must have been! but with such a set, proud look, and such scorn looking out of her handsome eyes, with her eyebrows just a little raised, as if she wondered how any one could have the impertinence to look at her; and her lip curled at us, as we stood there gazing. She had a dress on, the like of which I had never seen before, but it was all the fashion when she was young: a hat of some soft white stuff like beaver, pulled a little over her brows, and a beautiful plume of feathers sweeping round it on one side; and her gown of blue satin was open in front to a quilted white stomacher.

"Well, to be sure!" said I, when I had gazed my fill. "Flesh is grass, they do say; but who would have thought that Miss Furnivall had been such an out-and-out beauty, to see her now?"

"Yes," said Dorothy. "Folks change sadly. But if what my master's father used to say was true, Miss Furnivall, the elder sister, was handsomer than Miss Grace. Her picture is here somewhere; but, if I show it you, you must never let on, even to James, that you have seen it. Can the little lady hold her tongue, think you?" asked she.

I was not so sure, for she was such a little sweet, bold, open-spoken child, so I set her to hide herself;

43

and then I helped Dorothy to turn a great picture, that leaned with its face towards the wall, and was not hung up as the others were. To be sure, it beat Miss Grace for beauty; and, I think, for scornful pride, too, though in that matter it might be hard to choose. I could have looked at it an hour, but Dorothy seemed half frightened at having shown it to me, and hurried it back again, and bade me run and find Miss Rosamond, for that there were some ugly places about the house, where she should like ill for the child to go. I was a brave, high-spirited girl, and thought little of what the old woman said, for I liked hide-and-seek as well as any child in the parish; so off I ran to find my little one.

As winter drew on, and the days grew shorter, I was sometimes almost certain that I heard a noise as if some one was playing on the great organ in the hall. I did not hear it every evening; but, certainly, I did very often; usually when I was sitting with Miss Rosamond, after I had put her to bed, and keeping quite still and silent in the bed-room. Then I used to hear it booming and swelling away in the distance. The first night, when I went down to my supper, I asked Dorothy who had been playing music, and James said very shortly that I was a gowk to take the wind soughing among the trees for music: but I saw Dorothy look at him very fearfully, and Bessy, the kitchen-maid, said something beneath her breath, and went quite white. I saw they did not like my question, so I held my peace till I was with Dorothy alone, when I knew I could get a good deal out of her. So, the next day, I watched my time, and I coaxed and asked her who it was that played the organ; for I knew that it was the organ and not the wind well enough, for all I had kept silence before James. But Dorothy had had her lesson I'll warrant, and never a word could I get from her. So then I tried Bessy, though I had always held my head rather above her, as I was evened to James and Dorothy, and she was little better than their servant. So she said I must never, never tell; and if I ever told, I was never to say *she* had told me; but it was a very strange noise, and she had heard it many a time, but most of all on winter nights, and before storms; and folks did say, it was the old lord playing on the great organ in the hall, just as he used to do when he was alive; but who the old lord was, or why he played, and why he played on stormy winter evenings in particular, she either could not or would not tell me. Well! I told you I had a brave heart; and I thought it was rather pleasant to have that grand music rolling about the house, let who would be the player; for now it rose above the great gusts of wind, and wailed and triumphed just like a living creature, and then it fell to a softness most complete; only it was always music, and tunes, so it was nonsense to call it the wind. I thought at first, that it might be Miss Furnivall who played, unknown to Bessy; but, one day when I was in the hall by myself, I opened the organ and peeped all about it and around it, as I had done to the organ in Crosthwaite Church once before, and I saw it was all broken and destroyed inside, though it looked so brave and fine; and then, though it was noon-day, my flesh began to creep a little, and I shut it up, and ran away pretty quickly to my own bright nursery; and I did not like hearing the music for some time after that, any more than James and Dorothy did. All this time Miss Rosamond was making herself more, and more beloved. The old ladies liked her to dine with them at their early dinner; James stood behind Miss Furnivall's chair, and I behind Miss Rosamond's all in state; and, after dinner, she would play about in a corner of the great drawing-room, as still as any mouse, while Miss Furnivall slept, and I had my dinner in the kitchen. But she was glad enough to come to me in the nursery afterwards; for, as she said, Miss Furnivall was so sad, and Mrs. Stark so dull; but she and I were merry enough; and, by-and-by, I got not to care for that weird rolling music, which did one no harm, if we did not know where it came from.

That winter was very cold. In the middle of October the frosts began, and lasted many, many weeks. I remember, one day at dinner, Miss Furnivall lifted up her sad, heavy eyes, and said to Mrs. Stark, "I am afraid we shall have a terrible winter," in a strange kind of meaning way. But Mrs. Stark pretended not to hear, and talked very loud of something else. My little lady and I did not care for the frost; not we! As long as it was dry we climbed up the steep brows, behind the house, and went up on the Fells, which were bleak, and bare enough, and there we ran races in the fresh, sharp air; and once we came down by a new path that took us past the two old gnarled holly-trees, which grew about half-way down by the east side of the house. But the days grew shorter, and shorter; and the old lord, if it was he, played away more, and more stormily and sadly on the great organ. One Sunday afternoon,—it must have been towards the end of November—I asked Dorothy to take charge of little Missey when she came out of the drawing-room, after Miss Furnivall had had her nap; for it was too cold to take her with me to church, and yet I wanted to go. And Dorothy was glad enough to promise, and was so fond of the child that all seemed well; and Bessy and I set off very briskly, though the sky hung heavy and black over the white earth, as if the night had never fully gone away; and the air, though still, was very biting and keen.

"We shall have a fall of snow," said Bessy to me. And sure enough, even while we were in church, it came down thick, in great large flakes, so thick it almost darkened the windows. It had stopped snowing before we came out, but it lay soft, thick and deep beneath our feet, as we tramped home. Before we got to the hall the moon rose, and I think it was lighter then,—what with the moon, and what with the white dazzling snow—than it had been when we went to church, between two and three o'clock. I have not told you that Miss Furnivall and Mrs. Stark never went to church: they used to read the prayers together, in their quiet gloomy way; they seemed to feel the Sunday very long without their tapestry-work to be busy at. So when I went to Dorothy in the kitchen, to fetch Miss Rosamond and take her up-stairs with me, I did not much wonder when the old woman told me that the ladies had kept the child with them, and that she had never come to the kitchen, as I had bidden her, when she was tired of behaving pretty in the drawing-room. So I took off my things and went to find her, and bring her to her supper in the nursery. But when I went into the best drawing-room, there sat the two old ladies, very still and quiet, dropping out a word now and then, but looking as if nothing so bright and merry as Miss Rosamond had ever been near them. Still I thought she might be hiding from me; it was one of her pretty ways; and that she had persuaded them to look as if they knew nothing about her; so I went softly peeping under this sofa, and behind that chair, making believe I was sadly frightened at not finding her.

"What's the matter, Hester?" said Mrs. Stark sharply. I don't know if Miss Furnivall had seen me, for, as I told you, she was very deaf, and she sat quite still, idly staring into the fire, with her hopeless face. "I'm only looking for my little Rosy-Posy," replied I, still thinking that the child was there, and near me, though I could not see her.

"Miss Rosamond is not here," said Mrs. Stark. "She went away more than an hour ago to find Dorothy." And she too turned and went on looking into the fire.

My heart sank at this, and I began to wish I had never left my darling. I went back to Dorothy and told her. James was gone out for the day, but she and me and Bessy took lights and went up into the nursery first, and then we roamed over the great large house, calling and entreating Miss Rosamond to come out of her hiding place, and not frighten us to death in that way. But there was no answer; no sound.

ELIZABETH GASKELL

"Oh!" said I at last. "Can she have got into the east wing and hidden there?"

But Dorothy said it was not possible, for that she herself had never been in there; that the doors were always locked, and my lord's steward had the keys, she believed; at any rate, neither she, nor James had ever seen them: so, I said I would go back, and see if, after all, she was not hidden in the drawing-room, unknown to the old ladies; and if I found her there, I said, I would whip her well for the fright she had given me; but I never meant to do it. Well, I went back to the west drawing-room, and I told Mrs. Stark we could not find her anywhere, and asked for leave to look all about the furniture there, for I thought now, that she might have fallen asleep in some warm hidden corner; but no! we looked, Miss Furnivall got up and looked, trembling all over, and she was no where there; then we set off again, every one in the house, and looked in all the places we had searched before, but we could not find her. Miss Furnivall shivered and shook so much, that Mrs. Stark took her back into the warm drawing-room; but not before they had made me promise to bring her to them when she was found. Well-a-day! I began to think she never would be found, when I bethought me to look out into the great front court, all covered with snow. I was

50

up-stairs when I looked out; but, it was such clear moonlight, I could see quite plain two little foot-prints, which might be traced from the hall door, and round the corner of the east wing. I don't know how I got down, but I tugged open the great, stiff hall door; and, throwing the skirt of my gown over my head for a cloak, I ran out. I turned the east corner, and there a black shadow fell on the snow; but when I came again into the moonlight, there were the little footmarks going up—up to the Fells. It was bitter cold; so cold that the air almost took the skin off my face as I ran, but I ran on, crying to think how my poor little darling must be perished, and frightened. I was within sight of the holly-trees, when I saw a shepherd coming down the hill, bear-ing something in his arms wrapped in his maud. He shouted to me, and asked me if I had lost a bairn; and, when I could not speak for crying, he bore towards me, and I saw my wee bairnie lying still, and white, and stiff, in his arms, as if she had been dead. He told me he had been up the Fells to gather in his sheep, before the deep cold of night came on, and that under the holly-trees (black marks on the hill-side, where no other bush was for miles around) he had found my little lady—my lamb—my queen—my darling—stiff, and cold, in the terrible sleep which is frost-begotten. Oh! the joy, and the tears of having her in my arms once again! for I would not let him carry her; but took her, maud and all, into my own arms, and held her near my own warm neck, and heart, and felt the life stealing slowly back again into her little gentle limbs. But she was still insensible when we reached the hall, and I had no breath for speech. We went in by the kitchen door.

"Bring the warming-pan," said I; and I carried her up-stairs and began undressing her by the nursery fire, which Bessy had kept up. I called my little lammie all the sweet and playful names I could think of,—even while my eyes were blinded by my tears; and at last, oh! at length she opened her large blue eyes. Then I put her into her warm bed, and sent Dorothy down to tell Miss Furnivall that all was well; and I made up my mind to sit by my darling's bedside the live-long night. She fell away into a soft sleep as soon as her pretty head had touched the pillow, and I watched by her till morning light; when she wakened up bright and clear—or so I thought at first—and, my dears, so I think now.

She said, that she had fancied that she should like to go to Dorothy, for that both the old ladies were asleep, and it was very dull in the drawing-room; and that, as she was going through the west lobby, she saw the snow through the high window falling— falling—soft and steady; but she wanted to see it lying pretty and white on the ground; so she made her way into the great hall; and then, going to the window, she saw it bright and soft upon the drive; but while she stood there, she saw a little girl, not so old as she was, "but so pretty," said my darling, "and this little girl beckoned to me to come out; and oh, she was so pretty and so sweet, I could not choose but go." And then this other little girl had taken her by the hand, and side by side the two had gone round the east corner.

"Now you are a naughty little girl, and telling stories," said I. "What would your good mamma, that is in heaven, and never told a story in her life, say to her little Rosamond, if she heard her—and I dare say she does—telling stories!"

"Indeed, Hester," sobbed out my child, "I'm telling you true. Indeed I am."

"Don't tell me!" said I, very stern. "I tracked you by your foot-marks through the snow; there were only yours to be seen: and if you had had a little girl to go hand-in-hand with you up the hill, don't you think the foot-prints would have gone along with yours?"

"I can't help it, dear, dear Hester," said she, crying, "if they did not; I never looked at her feet, but she held my hand fast and tight in her little one, and it was very, very cold. She took me up the Fell-path, up to the holly trees; and there I saw a lady weeping and crying; but when she saw me, she hushed her weeping, and smiled very proud and grand, and took me on her knee, and began to lull me to sleep; and that's all, Hester—but that is true; and my dear mamma knows it is," said she, crying. So I thought the child was in a fever, and pretended to believe her, as she went over her story—over and over again, and always the same. At last Dorothy knocked at the door with Miss Rosamond's breakfast; and she told me the old ladies were down in the eating parlour, and that they wanted to speak to me. They had both been into the night-nursery the evening before, but it was after Miss Rosamond was asleep; so they had only looked at her—not asked me any questions.

"I shall catch it," thought I to myself, as I went along the north gallery. "And yet," I thought, taking courage, "it was in their charge I left her; and it's they that's to blame for letting her steal away unknown and unwatched." So I went in boldly, and told my story. I told it all to Miss Furnivall, shouting it close to her ear; but when I came to the mention of the other little girl out in the snow, coaxing and tempting her out, and wiling her up to the grand and beautiful lady by the holly-tree, she threw her arms up—her old and withered arms—and cried aloud, "Oh! Heaven, forgive! Have mercy!"

Mrs. Stark took hold of her; roughly enough, I thought; but she was past Mrs. Stark's management, and spoke to me, in a kind of wild warning and authority.

"Hester! keep her from that child! It will lure her to her death! That evil child! Tell her it is a wicked, naughty child." Then, Mrs. Stark hurried me out of the room; where, indeed, I was glad enough to go; but Miss Furnivall kept shrieking out, "Oh! have mercy! Wilt Thou never forgive! It is many a long year ago—"

I was very uneasy in my mind after that. I durst never leave Miss Rosamond, night or day, for fear lest she might slip off again, after some fancy or other; and all the more, because I thought I could make out that Miss Furnivall was crazy, from their odd ways about her; and I was afraid lest something of the same kind (which might be in the family, you know) hung over my darling. And the great frost never ceased all this time; and, whenever it was a more stormy night than usual, between the gusts, and through the wind, we heard the old lord playing on the great organ. But, old lord, or not, wherever Miss Rosamond went, there I followed; for my love for her, pretty helpless orphan, was stronger than my fear for the grand and terrible sound. Besides, it rested with me to keep her cheerful and merry, as beseemed her age. So we played together, and wandered together, here and there, and everywhere; for I never dared to lose sight of her again in that large and rambling house. And so it happened, that one afternoon, not long before Christmas day, we were playing together on the billiard-table in the great hall (not that we knew the right way of playing, but she liked to roll the smooth ivory balls with her pretty hands, and I liked to do whatever she did); and, by-and-by, without our noticing it, it grew dusk indoors, though it was still light in the open air, and I was thinking of taking her back into the nursery, when, all of a sudden, she cried out:

"Look, Hester! look! there is my poor little girl out in the snow!"

I turned towards the long narrow windows, and there, sure enough, I saw a little girl, less than my Miss Rosamond—dressed all unfit to be out-of-doors such a bitter night—crying, and beating against the window-panes, as if she wanted to be let in. She seemed to sob and wail, till Miss Rosamond could bear it no longer, and was flying to the door to open it, when, all of a sudden, and close upon us, the great organ pealed out so loud and thundering, it fairly made me tremble; and all the more, when I remembered me that, even in the stillness of that dead-cold weather, I had heard no sound of little battering hands upon the window-glass, although the Phantom Child had seemed to put forth all its force; and, although I had seen it wail and cry, no faintest touch of sound had fallen upon my ears. Whether I remembered all this at the very moment, I do not know; the great organ sound had so stunned me into terror; but this I know, I caught up Miss Rosamond before she got the hall door opened, and clutched her, and carried her away, kicking and screaming, into the large bright kitchen, where Dorothy and Agnes were busy with their mince-pies.

"What is the matter with my sweet one?" cried Dorothy, as I bore in Miss Rosamond, who was sobbing as if her heart would break.

"She won't let me open the door for my little girl to come in; and she'll die if she is out on the Fells all night. Cruel, naughty Hester," she said, slapping me; but she might have struck harder, for I had seen a look of ghastly terror on Dorothy's face, which made my very blood run cold.

"Shut the back kitchen door fast, and bolt it well," said she to Agnes. She said no more; she gave me raisins and almonds to quiet Miss Rosamond: but she sobbed about the little girl in the snow, and would not touch any of the good things. I was thankful when she cried herself to sleep in bed. Then I

stole down to the kitchen, and told Dorothy I had
made up my mind. I would carry my darling back to
my father's house in Applethwaite; where, if we lived
humbly, we lived at peace. I said I had been frightened enough with the old lord's organ-playing; but
now, that I had seen for myself this little moaning
child, all decked out as no child in the neighbour-
hood could be, beating and battering to get in yet
always without any sound or noise—with the dark
wound on its right shoulder; and that Miss Rosamond had known it again for the phantom that had
nearly lured her to her death (which Dorothy knew
was true); I would stand it no longer.

I saw Dorothy change colour once or twice. When
I had done, she told me she did not think I could take
Miss Rosamond with me, for that she was my lord's
ward, and I had no right over her; and she asked me,
would I leave the child that I was so fond of, just for
sounds and sights that could do me no harm; and
that they had all had to get used to in their turns? I
was all in a hot, trembling passion; and I said it was
very well for her to talk, that knew what these sights
and noises betokened, and that had, perhaps, had
something to do with the spectre child while it was
alive. And I taunted her so, that she told me all she
knew, at last; and then I wished I had never been
told, for it only made me more afraid than ever.

She said she had heard the tale from old neighbours, that were alive when she was first married; when folks used to come to the hall sometimes, before it had got such a bad name on the country side: it might not be true, or it might, what she had been told.

The old lord was Miss Furnivall's father—Miss Grace, as Dorothy called her, for Miss Maude was the elder, and Miss Furnivall by rights. The old lord was eaten up with pride. Such a proud man was never seen or heard of; and his daughters were like him. No one was good enough to wed them, although they had choice enough; for they were the great beauties of their day, as I had seen by their portraits, where they hung in the state drawing-room. But, as the old saying is, "Pride will have a fall;" and these two haughty beauties fell in love with the same man, and he no better than a foreign musician, whom their father had down from London to play music with him at the Manor House. For, above all things, next to his pride, the old lord loved music. He could play on nearly every instrument that ever was heard of: and it was a strange thing it did not soften him; but he was a fierce dour old man, and had broken his poor wife's heart with his cruelty, they said. He was mad after music, and would pay any money for it. So he got this foreigner

59

to come; who made such beautiful music, that they said the very birds on the trees stopped their singing to listen. And, by degrees, this foreign gentleman got such a hold over the old lord, that nothing would serve him but that he must come every year; and it was he that had the great organ brought from Holland, and built up in the hall, where it stood now. He taught the old lord to play on it; but many and many a time, when Lord Furnivall was thinking of nothing but his fine organ, and his finer music, the dark foreigner was walking abroad in the woods with one of the young ladies; now Miss Maude, and then Miss Grace.

Miss Maude won the day and carried off the prize, such as it was; and he and she were married, all unknown to any one; and before he made his next yearly visit, she had been confined of a little girl at a farm-house on the Moors, while her father and Miss Grace thought she was away at Doncaster Races. But though she was a wife and a mother, she was not a bit softened, but as haughty and as passionate as ever; and perhaps more so, for she was jealous of Miss Grace, to whom her foreign husband paid a deal of court—by way of blinding her—as he told his wife. But Miss Grace triumphed over Miss Maude, and Miss Maude grew fiercer and fiercer, both with her husband and with her sister; and the former—who could easily shake off what was disagreeable, and hide himself in foreign countries— went away a month before his usual time that summer, and half-threatened that he would never come back again. Meanwhile, the little girl was left at the farm-house, and her mother used to have her horse saddled and gallop wildly over the hills to see her once every week, at the very least—for where she loved, she loved; and where she hated, she hated. And the old lord went on playing—playing on his organ; and the servants thought the sweet music he made had soothed down his awful temper, of which (Dorothy said) some terrible tales could be told. He grew infirm too, and had to walk with a crutch; and his son—that was the present Lord Furnivall's father—was with the army in America, and the other son at sea; so Miss Maude had it pretty much her own way, and she and Miss Grace grew colder and bitterer to each other every day; till at last they hardly ever spoke, except when the old lord was by. The foreign musician came again the next summer, but it was for the last time; for they led him such a life with their jealousy and their passions, that he grew weary, and went away, and never was heard of again. And Miss Maude, who had always meant to have her marriage acknowledged when her father should be dead, was left now a deserted

wife—whom nobody knew to have been married—
with a child that she dared not own, although she
loved it to distraction; living with a father whom she
feared, and a sister whom she hated. When the next
summer passed over and the dark foreigner never
came, both Miss Maude and Miss Grace grew
gloomy and sad; they had a haggard look about
them, though they looked handsome as ever. But
by-and-by Miss Maude brightened; for her father
grew more and more infirm, and more than ever
carried away by his music; and she and Miss Grace
lived almost entirely apart, having separate rooms,
the one on the west side, Miss Maude on the east—
those very rooms which were now shut up. So she
thought she might have her little girl with her, and
no one need ever know except those who dared not
speak about it, and were bound to believe that it
was, as she said, a cottager's child she had taken a
fancy to. All this, Dorothy said, was pretty well
known; but what came afterwards no one knew,
except Miss Grace, and Mrs. Stark, who was even
then her maid, and much more of a friend to her
than ever her sister had been. But the servants supposed, from words that were dropped, that Miss
Maude had triumphed over Miss Grace, and told
her that all the time the dark foreigner had been
mocking her with pretended love—he was her own

husband; the colour left Miss Grace's cheek and lips that very day for ever, and she was heard to say many a time that sooner or later she would have her revenge; and Mrs. Stark was for ever spying about the east rooms.

One fearful night, just after the New Year had come in, when the snow was lying thick and deep, and the flakes were still falling—fast enough to blind any one who might be out and abroad—there was a great and violent noise heard, and the old lord's voice above all, cursing and swearing awfully,—and the cries of a little child,—and the proud defiance of a fierce woman,—and the sound of a blow,—and a dead stillness,—and moans and wailings dying away on the hill-side! Then the old lord summoned all his servants, and told them, with terrible oaths, and words more terrible, that his daughter had disgraced herself, and that he had turned her out of doors,— her, and her child,—and that if ever they gave her help,—or food—or shelter,—he prayed that they might never enter Heaven. And, all the while, Miss Grace stood by him, white and still as any stone; and when he had ended she heaved a great sigh, as much as to say her work was done, and her end was accomplished. But the old lord never touched his organ again, and died within the year; and no wonder! for, on the morrow of that wild and fearful night, the shepherds, coming down the Fell side, found Miss Maude sitting, all crazy and smiling, under the holly-trees, nursing a dead child,—with a terrible mark on its right shoulder. "But that was not what killed it," said Dorothy; "it was the frost and the cold;—every wild creature was in its hole, and every beast in its fold,—while the child and its mother were turned out to wander on the Fells! And now you know all! and I wonder if you are less frightened now?"

I was more frightened than ever; but I said I was not. I wished Miss Rosamond and myself well out of that dreadful house forever; but I would not leave her, and I dared not take her away. But oh! how I watched her, and guarded her! We bolted the doors, and shut the window-shutters fast, an hour or more before dark, rather than leave them open five minutes too late. But my little lady still heard the weird child crying and mourning; and not all we could do or say, could keep her from wanting to go to her, and let her in from the cruel wind and the snow. All this time, I kept away from Miss Furnivall and Mrs. Stark, as much as ever I could; for I feared them—I knew no good could be about them, with their grey hard faces, and their dreamy eyes, looking back into the ghastly years that were gone. But, even in my fear, I had a kind of pity—for Miss Furnivall, at least. Those gone down to the pit can hardly have a more hopeless look than that which was ever on her face. At last I even got so sorry for her—who never said a word but what was quite forced from her—that I prayed for her; and I taught Miss Rosamond to pray for one who had done a deadly sin; but often when she came to those words, she would listen, and start up from her knees, and say, "I hear my little girl plaining and crying very sad—Oh! let her in, or she will die!"

One night—just after New Year's Day had come at last, and the long winter had taken a turn, as I hoped—I heard the west drawing-room bell ring three times, which was the signal for me. I would not leave Miss Rosamond alone, for all she was asleep—for the old lord had been playing wilder than ever—and I feared lest my darling should waken to hear the spectre child; see her I knew she could not. I had fastened the windows too well for that. So, I took her out of her bed and wrapped her up in such outer clothes as were most handy, and carried her down to the drawing-room, where the old ladies sat at their tapestry work as usual. They looked up when I came in, and Mrs. Stark asked, quite astounded, "Why did I bring Miss Rosamond there, out of her warm bed?" I had begun to whisper, "Because I was afraid of her being tempted out while I was away, by the wild child in the snow," when she stopped me short (with a glance at Miss Furnivall), and said Miss Furnivall wanted me to undo some work she had done wrong, and which neither of them could see to unpick. So, I laid my pretty dear on the sofa, and sat down on a stool by them, and hardened my heart against them, as I heard the wind rising and howling.

Miss Rosamond slept on sound, for all the wind blew so; and Miss Furnivall said never a word, nor looked round when the gusts shook the windows. All at once she started up to her full height, and put up one hand, as if to bid us listen.

"I hear voices!" said she. "I hear terrible screams—I hear my father's voice!"

Just at that moment, my darling wakened with a sudden start: "My little girl is crying, oh, how she is crying!" and she tried to get up and go to her, but she got her feet entangled in the blanket, and I caught her up; for my flesh had begun to creep at these noises, which they heard while we could catch no sound. In a minute or two the noises came, and gathered fast, and filled our ears; we, too, heard voices and screams, and no longer heard the winter's wind that raged abroad. Mrs. Stark looked at me, and I at her, but we dared not speak. Suddenly Miss Furnivall went towards the door, out into the ante-room, through the west lobby, and opened the door into the great hall. Mrs. Stark followed, and I durst not be left, though my heart almost stopped beating for fear. I wrapped my darling tight in my arms, and went out with them. In the hall the screams were louder than ever; they sounded to come from the east wing—nearer and nearer—close on the other side of the locked-up doors—close behind them. Then I noticed that the great bronze chandelier seemed all alight, though the hall was dim, and that a fire was blazing in the vast hearth-place, though it gave no heat; and I shuddered up with terror, and folded my darling closer to me. But as I did so, the east door shook, and she, suddenly struggling to get free from me, cried, "Hester! I must go! My little girl is there; I hear her; she is coming! Hester! I must go!"

I held her tight with all my strength; with a set will, I held her. If I had died, my hands would have grasped her still, I was so resolved in my mind. Miss Furnivall stood listening, and paid no regard to my darling, who had got down to the ground, and whom I, upon my knees now, was holding with both my arms clasped round her neck; she still striving and crying to get free.

All at once, the east door gave way with a thundering crash, as if torn open in a violent passion, and there came into that broad and mysterious light, the figure of a tall old man, with grey hair and gleaming eyes. He drove before him, with many a relentless gesture of abhorrence, a stern and beautiful woman, with a little child clinging to her dress.

"Oh Hester! Hester!" cried Miss Rosamond. "It's the lady! the lady below the holly-trees; and my little girl is with her. Hester! Hester! let me go to her; they are drawing me to them. I feel them—I feel them. I must go!"

Again she was almost convulsed by her efforts to get away; but I held her tighter and tighter, till I feared I should do her a hurt; but rather that than let her go towards those terrible phantoms. They passed along towards the great hall door, where the winds howled and ravened for their prey; but before they reached that, the lady turned; and I could see that she defied the old man with a fierce and proud defiance; but then she quailed—and then she threw up her arms wildly and piteously to save her child— her little child—from a blow from his uplifted crutch.

And Miss Rosamond was torn as by a power stronger than mine, and writhed in my arms, and sobbed (for by this time the poor darling was grow- ing faint).

"They want me to go with them on to the

Fells—they are drawing me to them. Oh, my little girl! I would come, but cruel, wicked Hester holds me very tight." But when she saw the uplifted crutch she swooned away, and I thanked God for it. Just at this moment—when the tall old man, his hair streaming as in the blast of a furnace, was going to strike the little shrinking child—Miss Furnivall, the old woman by my side, cried out, "Oh, father! father! spare the little innocent child!" But just then I saw—we all saw—another phantom shape itself, and grow clear out of the blue and misty light that filled the hall; we had not seen her till now, for it was another lady who stood by the old man, with a look of relentless hate and triumphant scorn. That figure was very beautiful to look upon, with a soft white hat drawn down over the proud brows, and a red and curling lip. It was dressed in an open robe of blue satin. I had seen that figure before. It was the likeness of Miss Furnivall in her youth; and the ter-rible phantoms moved on, regardless of old Miss Furnivall's wild entreaty,—and the uplifted crutch fell on the right shoulder of the little child, and the younger sister looked on, stony and deadly serene. But at that moment, the dim lights, and the fire that gave no heat, went out of themselves, and Miss Furnivall lay at our feet stricken down by the palsy—death-stricken.

Yes! she was carried to her bed that night never to rise again. She lay with her face to the wall, muttering low but muttering alway: "Alas! alas! what is done in youth can never be undone in age! What is done in youth can never be undone in age!"

CHRISTINA ROSSETTI

Christina Rossetti (1830–1894) was of Italian origin, but born and raised in London. The sister of Dante Gabriel Rossetti and niece of John Polidori, she was an artist in her own right, much admired by her brother. Recent studies place her closer to the Pre-Raphaelite Brotherhood than had been previously understood. Rossetti was deeply religious and committed to her Anglican faith, and much of her work reflects this. The Christmas song 'In the Bleak Midwinter' is very popular but few people realize it is hers. Rossetti wrote several fairy stories influenced by Hans Christian Andersen as part of the fairy tale movement that most mid-nineteenth-century social writers took part in. She also wrote *Speaking Likenesses* which, like George MacDonald's *The Princess and Curdie*, imagined what it would be like if people looked like their true personalities, an idea that the modern author Philip Pullman transmuted into his daemons.

Goblin Market

Morning and evening
Maids heard the goblins cry:
"Come buy our orchard fruits,
Come buy, come buy:
Apples and quinces,
Lemons and oranges,
Plump unpecked cherries,
Melons and raspberries,
Bloom-down-cheeked peaches,
Swart-headed mulberries,
Wild free-born cranberries,
Crab-apples, dewberries,
Pine-apples, blackberries,
Apricots, strawberries;—
All ripe together
In summer weather,—
Morns that pass by,
Fair eves that fly;
Come buy, come buy:
Our grapes fresh from the vine,
Pomegranates full and fine,
Dates and sharp bullaces,
Rare pears and greengages,
Damsons and bilberries,
Taste them and try:

Currants and gooseberries,
Bright-fire-like barberries,
Figs to fill your mouth,
Citrons from the South,
Sweet to tongue and sound to eye;
Come buy, come buy."

Evening by evening
Among the brookside rushes,
Laura bowed her head to hear,
Lizzie veiled her blushes:
Crouching close together
In the cooling weather,
With clasping arms and cautioning lips,
With tingling cheeks and finger tips.
"Lie close," Laura said,
Pricking up her golden head:
"We must not look at goblin men,
We must not buy their fruits:
Who knows upon what soil they fed
Their hungry thirsty roots?"
"Come buy," call the goblins
Hobbling down the glen.
"Oh," cried Lizzie, "Laura, Laura,
You should not peep at goblin men."
Lizzie covered up her eyes,
Covered close lest they should look;

Laura reared her glossy head,
And whispered like the restless brook:
"Look, Lizzie, look, Lizzie,
Down the glen tramp little men.
One hauls a basket,
One bears a plate,
One lugs a golden dish
Of many pounds weight.
How fair the vine must grow
Whose grapes are so luscious;
How warm the wind must blow
Through those fruit bushes."
"No," said Lizzie: "No, no, no;
Their offers should not charm us,
Their evil gifts would harm us."
She thrust a dimpled finger
In each ear, shut eyes and ran:
Curious Laura chose to linger
Wondering at each merchant man.
One had a cat's face,
One whisked a tail,
One tramped at a rat's pace,
One crawled like a snail,
One like a wombat prowled obtuse and
furry,
One like a ratel tumbled hurry skurry.
She heard a voice like voice of doves

Cooing all together:
They sounded kind and full of loves
In the pleasant weather.
Laura stretched her gleaming neck
Like a rush-imbedded swan,
Like a lily from the beck,
Like a moonlit poplar branch,
Like a vessel at the launch
When its last restraint is gone.

Backwards up the mossy glen
Turned and trooped the goblin men,
With their shrill repeated cry,
"Come buy, come buy."
When they reached where Laura was
They stood stock still upon the moss,
Leering at each other,
Brother with queer brother;
Signalling each other,
Brother with sly brother.
One set his basket down,
One reared his plate;
One began to weave a crown
Of tendrils, leaves, and rough nuts brown
(Men sell not such in any town);
One heaved the golden weight
Of dish and fruit to offer her:

"Come buy, come buy," was still their cry.
Laura stared but did not stir,
Longed but had no money:
The whisk-tailed merchant bade her taste
In tones as smooth as honey,
The cat-faced purr'd,
The rat-paced spoke a word
Of welcome, and the snail-paced even was heard;
One parrot-voiced and jolly
Cried "Pretty Goblin" still for "Pretty Polly;"—
One whistled like a bird.

But sweet-tooth Laura spoke in haste:
"Good Folk, I have no coin;
To take were to purloin:
I have no copper in my purse,
I have no silver either,
And all my gold is on the furze
That shakes in windy weather
Above the rusty heather."
"You have much gold upon your head,"
They answered all together:
"Buy from us with a golden curl."
She clipped a precious golden lock,
She dropped a tear more rare than pearl,
Then sucked their fruit globes fair or red:
Sweeter than honey from the rock,

Stronger than man-rejoicing wine,
Clearer than water flowed that juice;
She never tasted such before,
How should it cloy with length of use?
She sucked and sucked and sucked the more
Fruits which that unknown orchard bore;
She sucked until her lips were sore;
Then flung the emptied rinds away
But gathered up one kernel stone,
And knew not was it night or day
As she turned home alone.

Lizzie met her at the gate
Full of wise upbraidings:
"Dear, you should not stay so late,
Twilight is not good for maidens;
Should not loiter in the glen
In the haunts of goblin men.
Do you not remember Jeanie,
How she met them in the moonlight,
Took their gifts both choice and many,
Ate their fruits and wore their flowers
Plucked from bowers
Where summer ripens at all hours?
But ever in the noonlight
She pined and pined away;
Sought them by night and day,

Found them no more, but dwindled and grew
grey;
Then fell with the first snow,
While to this day no grass will grow
Where she lies low:
I planted daisies there a year ago
That never blow.
You should not loiter so."
"Nay, hush," said Laura:
"Nay, hush, my sister:
I ate and ate my fill,
Yet my mouth waters still;
To-morrow night I will
Buy more;" and kissed her:
"Have done with sorrow;
I'll bring you plums to-morrow
Fresh on their mother twigs,
Cherries worth getting;
You cannot think what figs
My teeth have met in,
What melons icy-cold
Piled on a dish of gold
Too huge for me to hold,
What peaches with a velvet nap,
Pellucid grapes without one seed:
Odorous indeed must be the mead

Whereon they grow, and pure the wave they
drink
With lilies at the brink,
And sugar-sweet their sap."

Golden head by golden head,
Like two pigeons in one nest
Folded in each other's wings,
They lay down in their curtained bed:
Like two blossoms on one stem,
Like two flakes of new-fall'n snow,
Like two wands of ivory
Tipped with gold for awful kings.
Moon and stars gazed in at them,
Wind sang to them lullaby,
Lumbering owls forebore to fly,
Not a bat flapped to and fro
Round their rest:
Cheek to cheek and breast to breast
Locked together in one nest.

Early in the morning
When the first cock crowed his warning,
Neat like bees, as sweet and busy,
Laura rose with Lizzie:
Fetched in honey, milked the cows,
Aired and set to rights the house,

Kneaded cakes of whitest wheat,
Cakes for dainty mouths to eat,
Next churned butter, whipped up cream,
Fed their poultry, sat and sewed;
Talked as modest maidens should:
Lizzie with an open heart,
Laura in an absent dream,
One content, one sick in part;
One warbling for the mere bright day's delight,
One longing for the night.

At length slow evening came:
They went with pitchers to the reedy brook;
Lizzie most placid in her look,
Laura most like a leaping flame.
They drew the gurgling water from its deep;
Lizzie plucked purple and rich golden flags,
Then turning homeward said: "The sunset
flushes
Those furthest loftiest crags;
Come, Laura, not another maiden lags.
No wilful squirrel wags,
The beasts and birds are fast asleep."
But Laura loitered still among the rushes
And said the bank was steep.

And said the hour was early still,

The dew not fall'n, the wind not chill;
Listening ever, but not catching
The customary cry,
"Come buy, come buy,"
With its iterated jingle
Of sugar-baited words:
Not for all her watching
Once discerning even one goblin
Racing, whisking, tumbling, hobbling;
Let alone the herds
That used to tramp along the glen,
In groups or single,
Of brisk fruit-merchant men.

Till Lizzie urged, "O Laura, come;
I hear the fruit-call, but I dare not look:
You should not loiter longer at this brook:
Come with me home.
The stars rise, the moon bends her arc,
Each glowworm winks her spark,
Let us get home before the night grows dark:
For clouds may gather
Though this is summer weather,
Put out the lights and drench us through;
Then if we lost our way what should we do?"

Laura turned cold as stone

To find her sister heard that cry alone,
That goblin cry,
"Come buy our fruits, come buy."
Must she then buy no more such dainty fruit?
Must she no more such succous pasture find,
Gone deaf and blind?
Her tree of life drooped from the root:
She said not one word in her heart's sore ache;
But peering thro' the dimness, nought discerning,
Trudged home, her pitcher dripping all the way;
So crept to bed, and lay
Silent till Lizzie slept;
Then sat up in a passionate yearning,
And gnashed her teeth for baulked desire, and
wept
As if her heart would break.

Day after day, night after night,
Laura kept watch in vain
In sullen silence of exceeding pain.
She never caught again the goblin cry:
"Come buy, come buy;"—
She never spied the goblin men
Hawking their fruits along the glen:
But when the noon waxed bright
Her hair grew thin and grey;
She dwindled, as the fair full moon doth turn

To swift decay and burn
Her fire away.

One day remembering her kernel-stone
She set it by a wall that faced the south;
Dewed it with tears, hoped for a root,
Watched for a waxing shoot,
But there came none;
It never saw the sun,
It never felt the trickling moisture run:
While with sunk eyes and faded mouth
She dreamed of melons, as a traveller sees
False waves in desert drouth
With shade of leaf-crowned trees,
And burns the thirstier in the sandful breeze.

She no more swept the house,
Tended the fowls or cows,
Fetched honey, kneaded cakes of wheat,
Brought water from the brook:
But sat down listless in the chimney-nook
And would not eat.

Tender Lizzie could not bear
To watch her sister's cankerous care
Yet not to share.
She night and morning

Caught the goblins' cry:
"Come buy our orchard fruits,
Come buy, come buy:"—
Beside the brook, along the glen,
She heard the tramp of goblin men,
The voice and stir
Poor Laura could not hear;
Longed to buy fruit to comfort her,
But feared to pay too dear.
She thought of Jeanie in her grave,
Who should have been a bride;
But who for joys brides hope to have
Fell sick and died
In her gay prime,
In earliest Winter time,
With the first glazing rime,
With the first snow-fall of crisp Winter time.

Till Laura dwindling
Seemed knocking at Death's door:
Then Lizzie weighed no more
Better and worse;
But put a silver penny in her purse,
Kissed Laura, crossed the heath with clumps of
furze
At twilight, halted by the brook:
And for the first time in her life

Began to listen and look.

Laughed every goblin
When they spied her peeping:
Came towards her hobbling,
Flying, running, leaping,
Puffing and blowing,
Chuckling, clapping, crowing,
Clucking and gobbling,
Mopping and mowing,
Full of airs and graces,
Pulling wry faces,
Demure grimaces,
Cat-like and rat-like,
Ratel- and wombat-like,
Snail-paced in a hurry,
Parrot-voiced and whistler,
Helter skelter, hurry skurry,
Chattering like magpies,
Fluttering like pigeons,
Gliding like fishes,—
Hugged her and kissed her:
Squeezed and caressed her:
Stretched up their dishes,
Panniers, and plates:
"Look at our apples
Russet and dun,

Bob at our cherries,
Bite at our peaches,
Citrons and dates,
Grapes for the asking,
Pears red with basking
Out in the sun,
Plums on their twigs;
Pluck them and suck them,
Pomegranates, figs."—

"Good folk," said Lizzie,
Mindful of Jeanie:
"Give me much and many:"—

Held out her apron,
Tossed them her penny.
"Nay, take a seat with us,
Honour and eat with us,"
They answered grinning:
"Our feast is but beginning.
Night yet is early,
Warm and dew pearly,
Wakeful and starry:
Such fruits as these
No man can carry;
Half their bloom would fly,
Half their dew would dry,

Half their flavour would pass by.
Sit down and feast with us,
Be welcome guest with us,
Cheer you and rest with us."—
"Thank you," said Lizzie: "But one waits
At home alone for me:
So without further parleying,
If you will not sell me any
Of your fruits though much and many,
Give me back my silver penny
I tossed you for a fee."—
They began to scratch their pates,
No longer wagging, purring,
But visibly demurring,
Grunting and snarling.
One called her proud,
Cross-grained, uncivil;
Their tones waxed loud,
Their looks were evil
Lashing their tails
They trod and hustled her,
Elbowed and jostled her,
Clawed with their nails,
Barking, mewing, hissing, mocking,
Tore her gown and soiled her stocking,
Twitched her hair out by the roots,
Stamped upon her tender feet,

Held her hands and squeezed their fruits
Against her mouth to make her eat.

White and golden Lizzie stood,
Like a lily in a flood,—
Like a rock of blue-veined stone
Lashed by tides obstreperously,—
Like a beacon left alone
In a hoary roaring sea,
Sending up a golden fire,—
Like a fruit-crowned orange-tree
White with blossoms honey-sweet
Sore beset by wasp and bee,—
Like a royal virgin town
Topped with gilded dome and spire
Close beleaguered by a fleet
Mad to tug her standard down.

One may lead a horse to water,
Twenty cannot make him drink.
Though the goblins cuffed and caught her,
Coaxed and fought her,
Bullied and besought her,
Scratched her, pinched her black as ink,
Kicked and knocked her,
Mauled and mocked her,
Lizzie uttered not a word;

Would not open lip from lip
Lest they should cram a mouthful in:
But laughed in heart to feel the drip
Of juice that syrupped all her face,
And lodged in dimples of her chin,
And streaked her neck which quaked like curd.
At last the evil people,
Worn out by her resistance,
Flung back her penny, kicked their fruit
Along whichever road they took,
Not leaving root or stone or shoot;
Some writhed into the ground,
Some dived into the brook
With ring and ripple,
Some scudded on the gale without a sound,
Some vanished in the distance.

In a smart, ache, tingle,
Lizzie went her way;
Knew not was it night or day;
Sprang up the bank, tore thro' the furze,
Threaded copse and dingle,
And heard her penny jingle
Bouncing in her purse,—
Its bounce was music to her ear.
She ran and ran
As if she feared some goblin man

Dogged her with gibe or curse
Or something worse:
But not one goblin skurried after,
Nor was she pricked by fear;
The kind heart made her windy-paced
That urged her home quite out of breath with
haste
And inward laughter.

She cried, "Laura," up the garden,
"Did you miss me?
Come and kiss me.
Never mind my bruises,
Hug me, kiss me, suck my juices
Squeezed from goblin fruits for you,
Goblin pulp and goblin dew.
Eat me, drink me, love me;
Laura, make much of me;
For your sake I have braved the glen
And had to do with goblin merchant men."

Laura started from her chair,
Flung her arms up in the air,
Clutched her hair:
"Lizzie, Lizzie, have you tasted
For my sake the fruit forbidden?
Must your light like mine be hidden,

Your young life like mine be wasted,
Undone in mine undoing,
And ruined in my ruin,
Thirsty, cankered, goblin-ridden?"—
She clung about her sister,
Kissed and kissed and kissed her:
Tears once again
Refreshed her shrunken eyes,
Dropping like rain
After long sultry drouth;
Shaking with aguish fear, and pain,
She kissed and kissed her with a hungry mouth.

Her lips began to scorch,
That juice was wormwood to her tongue,
She loathed the feast:
Writhing as one possessed she leaped and sung,
Rent all her robe, and wrung
Her hands in lamentable haste,
And beat her breast
Her locks streamed like the torch
Borne by a racer at full speed,
Or like the mane of horses in their flight,
Or like an eagle when she stems the light
Straight toward the sun,
Or like a caged thing freed,
Or like a flying flag when armies run.

Swift fire spread through her veins, knocked at her
heart,
Met the fire smouldering there
And overbore its lesser flame;
She gorged on bitterness without a name:
Ah! fool, to choose such part
Of soul-consuming care!
Sense failed in the mortal strife:
Like the watch-tower of a town
Which an earthquake shatters down,
Like a lightning-stricken mast,
Like a wind-uprooted tree
Spun about,
Like a foam-topped waterspout
Cast down headlong in the sea,
She fell at last;
Pleasure past and anguish past,
Is it death or is it life?

Life out of death.
That night long Lizzie watched by her,
Counted her pulse's flagging stir,
Felt for her breath,
Held water to her lips, and cooled her face
With tears and fanning leaves:
But when the first birds chirped about their eaves,
And early reapers plodded to the place

Of golden sheaves,
And dew-wet grass
Bowed in the morning winds so brisk to pass,
And new buds with new day
Opened of cup-like lilies on the stream,
Laura awoke as from a dream.
Laughed in the innocent old way,
Hugged Lizzie but not twice or thrice;
Her gleaming locks showed not one thread of
grey,
Her breath was sweet as May
And light danced in her eyes.

Days, weeks, months, years
Afterwards, when both were wives
With children of their own;
Their mother-hearts beset with fears,
Their lives bound up in tender lives;
Laura would call the little ones
And tell them of her early prime,
Those pleasant days long gone
Of not-returning time:
Would talk about the haunted glen,
The wicked, quaint fruit-merchant men,
Their fruits like honey to the throat
But poison in the blood;
(Men sell not such in any town):

Would tell them how her sister stood
In deadly peril to do her good,
And win the fiery antidote:
Then joining hands to little hands
Would bid them cling together,
"For there is no friend like a sister
In calm or stormy weather;
To cheer one on the tedious way,
To fetch one if one goes astray,
To lift one if one totters down,
To strengthen whilst one stands."

CHARLES DICKENS

Charles Dickens (1812–1870) is a household name known largely for his social realist work. But Dickens's work was extensive and varied: he was, after all, a newspaperman, a columnist, a sketch writer and a short story writer, as well as a novelist. Like many of his liberal and radical contemporaries, he found in fantasy a way to deliver excoriating social critique. 'A Christmas Carol' is his most famous foray into the fantastic, although it has often been divorced from its publishing context as part of the then-traditional Christmas ghost stories. Of his other ghost stories, 'The Signal-Man' (1866) is the best known and has inspired adaptations for stage and screen. But he was also interested in fairy stories, as were many in England after Edgar Taylor's first translation of some of the Grimm Brothers' stories in 1823. 'The Magic Fishbone', which Dickens pretends to have been written by a seven-year-old, is his sardonic commentary on the genre.

The Magic Fishbone

ROMANCE. FROM THE PEN OF MISS
ALICE RAINBIRD[1]

There was once a king, and he had a queen; and he was the manliest of his sex, and she was the loveliest of hers. The king was, in his private profession, under government. The queen's father had been a medical man out of town.

They had nineteen children, and were always having more. Seventeen of these children took care of the baby; and Alicia, the eldest, took care of them all. Their ages varied from seven years to seven months.

Let us now resume our story.

One day the king was going to the office, when he stopped at the fishmonger's to buy a pound and a half of salmon not too near the tail, which the queen (who was a careful housekeeper) had requested him to send home. Mr. Pickles, the fishmonger, said, "Certainly, sir, is there any other article? good-morning."

The king went on towards the office in a melancholy mood; for quarter-day was such a long way off, and several of the dear children were growing

[1] Aged seven.

out of their clothes. He had not proceeded far, when Mr. Pickles's errand-boy came running after him, and said, "Sir, you didn't notice the old lady in our shop."

"What old lady?" inquired the king. "I saw none."

Now, the king had not seen any old lady, because this old lady had been invisible to him, though visible to Mr. Pickles's boy. Probably because he messed and splashed the water about to that degree, and flopped the pairs of soles down in that violent manner, that, if she had not been visible to him, he would have spoilt her clothes.

Just then the old lady came trotting up. She was dressed in shot-silk of the richest quality, smelling of dried lavender.

"King Watkins the First, I believe?" said the old lady.

"Watkins," replied the king, "is my name."

"Papa, if I am not mistaken, of the beautiful Princess Alicia?" said the old lady.

"And of eighteen other darlings," replied the king.

"Listen. You are going to the office," said the old lady.

It instantly flashed upon the king that she must be a fairy, or how could she know that?

"You are right," said the old lady, answering his thoughts. "I am the good Fairy Grandmarina.

Attend! When you return home to dinner, politely invite the Princess Alicia to have some of the salmon you bought just now."

"It may disagree with her," said the king.

The old lady became so very angry at this absurd idea, that the king was quite alarmed, and humbly begged her pardon.

"We hear a great deal too much about this thing disagreeing, and that thing disagreeing," said the old lady, with the greatest contempt it was possible to express. "Don't be greedy. I think you want it all yourself."

The king hung his head under this reproof, and said he wouldn't talk about things disagreeing any more.

"Be good, then," said the Fairy Grandmarina, "and don't! When the beautiful Princess Alicia consents to partake of the salmon,—as I think she will,—you will find she will leave a fish-bone on her plate. Tell her to dry it and to rub it, and to polish it till it shines like mother-of-pearl, and to take care of it as a present from me."

"Is that all?" asked the king.

"Don't be impatient, sir," returned the Fairy Grandmarina, scolding him severely. "Don't catch people short, before they have done speaking. Just the way with you grown-up persons. You are always doing it."

The king again hung his head, and said he wouldn't do so any more.

"Be good, then," said the Fairy Grandmarina, "and don't! Tell the Princess Alicia, with my love, that the fish-bone is a magic present which can only be used once; but that it will bring her, that once, whatever she wishes for, PROVIDED SHE WISHES FOR IT AT THE RIGHT TIME. That is the message. Take care of it."

The king was beginning, "Might I ask the reason?" when the fairy became absolutely furious.

"*Will* you be good, sir?" she exclaimed, stamping her foot on the ground. "The reason for this, and the reason for that, indeed! You are always wanting the reason. No reason. There! Hoity toity me! I am sick of your grown-up reasons."

The king was extremely frightened by the old lady's flying into such a passion, and said he was very sorry to have offended her, and he wouldn't ask for reasons any more.

"Be good, then," said the old lady, "and don't!"

With those words, Grandmarina vanished, and the king went on and on and on, till he came to the office. There he wrote and wrote and wrote, till it was time to go home again. Then he politely invited the Princess Alicia, as the fairy had directed him, to partake of the salmon. And when she had enjoyed it very much, he saw the fish-bone on her plate, as the fairy had told him he would, and he delivered the fairy's message, and the Princess Alicia took care to dry the bone, and to rub it, and to polish it till it shone like mother-of-pearl.

And so, when the queen was going to get up in the morning, she said, "Oh, dear me, dear me; my head, my head!" and then she fainted away.

The Princess Alicia, who happened to be looking in at the chamber door, asking about breakfast, was very much alarmed when she saw her royal mamma in this state, and she rang the bell for Peggy, which was the name of the lord chamberlain. But remembering where the smelling-bottle was, she climbed on a chair and got it; and after that she climbed on another chair by the bedside, and held the smelling-bottle to the queen's nose; and after that she jumped down and got some water; and after that she jumped up again and wetted the queen's forehead; and, in short, when the lord chamberlain came in, that dear old woman said to the little princess, "What a trot you are! I couldn't have done it better myself!"

But that was not the worst of the good queen's illness. Oh, no! She was very ill indeed, for a long time. The Princess Alicia kept the seventeen young princes and princesses quiet, and dressed and undressed and danced the baby, and made the kettle boil, and heated the soup, and swept the hearth, and poured out the medicine, and nursed the queen, and did all that ever she could, and was as busy, busy, busy as busy could be; for there were not many servants at that palace for three reasons: because the king was short of money, because a rise in his office never seemed to come, and because quarter-day was so far off that it looked almost as far off and as little as one of the stars.

But on the morning when the queen fainted away, where was the magic fish-bone? Why, there it was in the Princess Alicia's pocket! She had almost taken it out to bring the queen to life again, when she put it back, and looked for the smelling-bottle.

After the queen had come out of her swoon that morning, and was dozing, the Princess Alicia hurried upstairs to tell a most particular secret to a most particularly confidential friend of hers, who was a duchess. People did suppose her to be a doll; but she was really a duchess, though nobody knew it except the princess.

This most particular secret was the secret about the magic fish-bone, the history of which was well known to the duchess, because the princess told her everything. The princess kneeled down by the bed on which the duchess was lying, full-dressed and wide-awake, and whispered the secret to her. The duchess smiled and nodded. People might have supposed that she never smiled and nodded; but she often did, though nobody knew it except the princess.

Then the Princess Alicia hurried downstairs again, to keep watch in the queen's room. She often kept watch by herself in the queen's room; but every evening, while the illness lasted, she sat there watching with the king. And every evening the king sat looking at her with a cross look, wondering why she never brought out the magic fish-bone. As often as she noticed this, she ran upstairs, whispered the secret to the duchess over again, and said to the duchess besides, "They think we children never have a reason or a meaning!" And the duchess, though the most fashionable duchess that ever was heard of, winked her eye.

"Alicia," said the king, one evening, when she wished him good night.

"Yes, papa."

"What is become of the magic fish-bone?"

"In my pocket, papa!"

"I thought you had lost it?"

"Oh, no, papa!"

"Or forgotten it?"

"No, indeed, papa."

And so another time the dreadful little snapping pug-dog, next door, made a rush at one of the young princes as he stood on the steps coming home from school, and terrified him out of his wits; and he put his hand through a pane of glass, and bled, bled, bled. When the seventeen other young princes and princesses saw him bleed, bleed, bleed, they were terrified out of their wits too, and screamed themselves black in their seventeen faces all at once. But the Princess Alicia put her hands over all their seventeen mouths, one after another, and persuaded them to be quiet because of the sick queen. And then she put the wounded prince's hand in a basin of fresh cold water, while they stared with their twice seventeen are thirty-four, put down four and carry three, eyes, and then she looked in the hand for bits of glass, and there were fortunately no bits of glass there. And then she said to two chubby-legged princes, who were sturdy though small, "Bring me in the royal rag-bag; I must snip, and stitch, and cut, and contrive." So these two young princes tugged at the royal rag-bag, and lugged it in; and the Princess Alicia sat down on the floor, with a large pair of scissors and a needle and thread, and snipped, and stitched, and cut, and contrived, and made a bandage, and put it on, and it fitted beautifully; and so when it was all done, she saw the king her papa looking on by the door.

"Alicia."

"Yes, papa."

"What have you been doing?"

"Snipping, stitching, cutting, and contriving, papa."

"Where is the magic fish-bone?"

"In my pocket, papa."

"I thought you had lost it?"

"Oh, no, papa!"

"Or forgotten it?"

"No, indeed, papa."

After that, she ran upstairs to the duchess, and told her what had passed, and told her the secret over again; and the duchess shook her flaxen curls, and laughed with her rosy lips.

Well! and so another time the baby fell under the grate. The seventeen young princes and princesses were used to it; for they were almost always falling under the grate or down the stairs; but the baby was not used to it yet, and it gave him a swelled face and a black eye. The way the poor little darling came to tumble was, that he was out of the Princess Alicia's lap just as she was sitting, in a great coarse apron that quite smothered her, in front of the kitchen fire, beginning to peel the turnips for the broth for dinner; and the way she came to be doing that was, that the king's cook had run away that morning with her own true love, who was a very tall but very tipsy soldier. Then the seventeen young princes and princesses, who cried at everything that happened, cried and roared. But the Princess Alicia (who couldn't help crying a little herself) quietly called to them to be still, on account of not throwing back the queen upstairs, who was fast getting well, and said, "Hold your tongues, you wicked little monkeys, every one of you, while I examine baby!" Then she examined baby, and found that he hadn't broken anything; and she held cold iron to his poor dear eye, and smoothed his poor dear face, and he presently fell asleep in her arms. Then she said to the seventeen princes and princesses, "I am afraid to let him down yet, lest he should wake and feel pain; be good, and you shall all be cooks." They jumped for joy when they heard that, and began making themselves cooks' caps out of old newspapers. So to one she gave the salt-box, and to one she gave the barley, and to one she gave the herbs, and to one she gave the turnips, and to one she gave the carrots, and to one she gave the onions, and to one she gave the spice-box, till they were all cooks, and all running about at work, she sitting in the middle, smothered in the great coarse apron, nursing baby. By and by the broth was done; and the baby woke up, smiling like an angel, and was trusted to the sedatest princess to hold, while the other princes and princesses were squeezed into a far-off corner to look at the Princess Alicia turning out the saucepanful of broth, for fear (as they were always getting into trouble) they should get splashed and scalded. When the broth came tumbling out, steaming beautifully, and smelling like a nosegay good to eat, they clapped their hands. That made the baby clap his hands; and that, and his looking as if he had a comic toothache, made all the princes and princesses laugh. So the Princess Alicia said, "Laugh and be good; and after dinner we will make him a nest on the floor in a corner, and he shall sit in his nest and see a dance of eighteen cooks." That delighted the young princes and princesses, and they ate up all the broth, and washed up all the plates and dishes, and cleared away, and pushed the table into a corner; and then they in their cooks' caps, and the Princess Alicia in the smothering coarse apron that belonged to the cook that had run away with her own true love that was the very tall but very tipsy soldier, danced a dance of eighteen cooks before the angelic baby, who forgot his swelled face and his black eye, and crowed with joy.

And so then, once more the Princess Alicia saw

King Watkins the First, her father, standing in the doorway looking on, and he said, "What have you been doing, Alicia?"

"Cooking and contriving, papa."

"What else have you been doing, Alicia?"

"Keeping the children light-hearted, papa."

"Where is the magic fish-bone, Alicia?"

"In my pocket, papa."

"I thought you had lost it?"

"Oh, no, papa!"

"Or forgotten it?"

"No, indeed, papa."

The king then sighed so heavily, and seemed so low-spirited, and sat down so miserably, leaning his head upon his hand, and his elbow upon the kitchen table pushed away in the corner, that the seventeen princes and princesses crept softly out of the kitchen, and left him alone with the Princess Alicia and the angelic baby.

"What is the matter, papa?"

"I am dreadfully poor, my child."

"Have you no money at all, papa?"

"None, my child."

"Is there no way of getting any, papa?"

"No way," said the king. "I have tried very hard, and I have tried all ways."

When she heard those last words, the Princess

Alicia began to put her hand into the pocket where she kept the magic fish-bone.

"Papa," said she, "when we have tried very hard, and tried all ways, we must have done our very, very best?"

"No doubt, Alicia."

"When we have done our very, very best, papa, and that is not enough, then I think the right time must have come for asking help of others." This was the very secret connected with the magic fish-bone, which she had found out for herself from the good Fairy Grandmarina's words, and which she had so often whispered to her beautiful and fashionable friend, the duchess.

So she took out of her pocket the magic fish-bone that had been dried and rubbed and polished till it shone like mother-of-pearl; and she gave it one little kiss, and wished it was quarter-day. And immediately it *was* quarter-day; and the king's quarter's salary came rattling down the chimney, and bounced into the middle of the floor.

But this was not half of what happened,—no, not a quarter; for immediately afterwards the good Fairy Grandmarina came riding in, in a carriage and four (peacocks), with Mr. Pickles's boy up behind, dressed in silver and gold, with a cocked hat, powdered hair, pink silk stockings, a jewelled cane, and a nosegay. Down jumped Mr. Pickles's boy, with his cocked hat in his hand, and wonderfully polite (being entirely changed by enchantment), and handed Grandmarina out; and there she stood, in her rich shot-silk smelling of dried lavender, fanning herself with a sparkling fan.

"Alicia, my dear," said this charming old fairy, "how do you do? I hope I see you pretty well? Give me a kiss."

The Princess Alicia embraced her; and then Grandmarina turned to the king, and said rather sharply, "Are you good?"

The king said he hoped so.

"I suppose you know the reason *now* why my god-daughter, here," kissing the princess again, "did not apply to the fish-bone sooner?" said the fairy.

The king made a shy bow.

"Ah! but you didn't *then*?" said the fairy.

The king made a shyer bow.

"Any more reasons to ask for?" said the fairy.

The king said, No, and he was very sorry.

"Be good, then," said the fairy, "and live happy ever afterwards."

Then Grandmarina waved her fan, and the queen came in most splendidly dressed; and the seventeen young princes and princesses, no longer grown out of their clothes, came in, newly fitted out from top to toe, with tucks in everything to admit of its being let out. After that, the fairy tapped the Princess Alicia with her fan; and the smothering coarse apron flew away, and she appeared exquisitely dressed, like a little bride, with a wreath of orange-flowers and a silver veil. After that, the kitchen dresser changed of itself into a wardrobe, made of beautiful woods and gold and looking-glass, which was full of dresses of all sorts, all for her and all exactly fitting her. After that, the angelic baby came in, running alone, with his face and eye not a bit the worse, but much the better. Then Grandmarina begged to be introduced to the duchess; and when the duchess was brought down, many compliments passed between them.

A little whispering took place between the fairy and the duchess; and then the fairy said out loud, "Yes, I thought she would have told you." Grandmarina then turned to the king and queen, and said, "We are going in search of Prince Certainpersonio. The pleasure of your company is requested at church in half an hour precisely." So she and the Princess Alicia got into the carriage; and Mr. Pickles's boy handed in the duchess, who sat by herself on the opposite seat; and then Mr. Pickles's boy put up the steps and got up behind, and the peacocks flew away with their tails behind.

Prince Certainpersonio was sitting by himself, eating barley-sugar, and waiting to be ninety. When he saw the peacocks, followed by the carriage, coming in at the window, it immediately occurred to him that something uncommon was going to happen.

"Prince," said Grandmarina, "I bring you your bride."

The moment the fairy said those words, Prince Certainpersonio's face left off being sticky, and his jacket and corduroys changed to peach-bloom velvet, and his hair curled, and a cap and feather flew in like a bird and settled on his head. He got into the carriage by the fairy's invitation; and there he renewed his acquaintance with the duchess, whom he had seen before.

In the church were the prince's relations and friends, and the Princess Alicia's relations and friends, and the seventeen princes and princesses, and the baby, and a crowd of the neighbours. The marriage was beautiful beyond expression. The duchess was bridesmaid, and beheld the ceremony from the pulpit, where she was supported by the cushion of the desk.

Grandmarina gave a magnificent wedding-feast afterwards, in which there was everything and more to eat, and everything and more to drink. The wedding-cake was delicately ornamented with white satin ribbons, frosted silver, and white lilies, and was forty-two yards round.

When Grandmarina had drunk her love to the young couple, and Prince Certainpersonio had made a speech, and everybody had cried, Hip, hip, hip, hurrah! Grandmarina announced to the king and queen that in future there would be eight quarter-days in every year, except in leap-year, when there would be ten. She then turned to Certainpersonio and Alicia, and said, "My dears, you will have thirty-five children, and they will all be good and beautiful. Seventeen of your children will be boys, and eighteen will be girls. The hair of the whole of your children will curl naturally. They will never have the measles, and will have recovered from the whooping-cough before being born."

On hearing such good news, everybody cried out "Hip, hip, hip, hurrah!" again.

"It only remains," said Grandmarina in conclusion, "to make an end of the fish-bone."

So she took it from the hand of the Princess Alicia, and it instantly flew down the throat of the dreadful little snapping pug-dog, next door, and choked him, and he expired in convulsions.

FRANK R. STOCKTON

Frank R. Stockton (1834–1902) was a US author and editor who wrote under several pseudonyms. He became assistant editor of *St. Nicholas Magazine* in 1873 and in that capacity wrote and published stories for children. His first collection was *Ting-a-Ling*, and he went on to produce over twenty such collections. Stockton wrote some novels, which are cited in the history of science fiction, and also a fantasy novel, *The Vizier of the Two-Horned Alexander* (1899), which uses the idea of the immortal wandering man who travels through different eras. Stockton's trademark style is a mode of humorous whimsy that came to be a hallmark of the kinds of fantastical short stories published by the more upmarket fantasy magazines, known as the 'slicks'. In this story he also generates the tone that was to become one of the recognizable voices of the fantastic, in which fantasy is just part of the everyday.

The Griffin and the Minor Canon

Over the great door of an old, old church which stood in a quiet town of a far-away land there was carved in stone the figure of a large griffin. The old-time sculptor had done his work with great care, but the image he had made was not a pleasant one to look at. It had a large head, with enormous open mouth and savage teeth; from its back arose great wings, armed with sharp hooks and prongs; it had stout legs in front, with projecting claws; but there were no legs behind,—the body running out into a long and powerful tail, finished off at the end with a barbed point. This tail was coiled up under him, the end sticking up just back of his wings.

The sculptor, or the people who had ordered this stone figure, had evidently been very much pleased with it, for little copies of it, also in stone, had been placed here and there along the sides of the church, not very far from the ground, so that people could easily look at them, and ponder on their curious forms. There were a great many other sculptures on the outside of this church,—saints, martyrs, grotesque heads of men, beasts, and birds, as well as those of other creatures which cannot be named, because nobody knows exactly what they were; but none were so curious and interesting as the great griffin over the door, and the little griffins on the sides of the church.

A long, long distance from the town, in the midst of dreadful wilds scarcely known to man, there dwelt the Griffin whose image had been put up over the church-door. In some way or other, the old-time sculptor had seen him, and afterward, to the best of his memory, had copied his figure in stone. The Griffin had never known this, until, hundreds of years afterward, he heard from a bird, from a wild animal, or in some manner which it is not now easy to find out, that there was a likeness of him on the old church in the distant town. Now, this Griffin had no idea how he looked. He had never seen a mirror, and the streams where he lived were so turbulent and violent that a quiet piece of water, which would reflect the image of any thing looking into it, could not be found. Being, as far as could be ascertained, the very last of his race, he had never seen another griffin. Therefore it was, that, when he heard of this stone image of himself, he became very anxious to know what he looked like, and at last he determined to go to the old church, and see for himself what manner of being he was. So he started off from the dreadful wilds, and flew on and on until he came to the countries inhabited by men, where his appearance in the air created great consternation; but he alighted nowhere, keeping up a steady flight until he reached the suburbs of the town which had his image on its church. Here, late in the afternoon, he alighted in a green meadow by the side of a brook, and stretched himself on the grass to rest. His great wings were tired, for he had not made such a long flight in a century, or more.

The news of his coming spread quickly over the town, and the people, frightened nearly out of their wits by the arrival of so extraordinary a visitor, fled into their houses, and shut themselves up. The Griffin called loudly for some one to come to him, but the more he called, the more afraid the people were to show themselves. At length he saw two laborers hurrying to their homes through the fields, and in a terrible voice he commanded them to stop. Not daring to disobey, the men stood, trembling.

"What is the matter with you all?" cried the Griffin. "Is there not a man in your town who is brave enough to speak to me?"

"I think," said one of the laborers, his voice shaking so that his words could hardly be understood, "that—perhaps—the Minor Canon—would come."

"Go, call him, then!" said the Griffin; "I want to see him."

The Minor Canon, who filled a subordinate position in the old church, had just finished the afternoon services, and was coming out of a side door, with three aged women who had formed the week-day congregation. He was a young man of a kind disposition, and very anxious to do good to the people of the town. Apart from his duties in the church, where he conducted services every week-day, he visited the sick and the poor, counselled and assisted persons who were in trouble, and taught a school composed entirely of the bad children in the town with whom nobody else would have any thing to do. Whenever the people wanted something difficult done for them, they always went to the Minor Canon. Thus it was that the laborer thought of the young priest when he found that some one must come and speak to the Griffin.

The Minor Canon had not heard of the strange event, which was known to the whole town except himself and the three old women, and when he was informed of it, and was told that the Griffin had asked to see him, he was greatly amazed, and frightened.

"Me!" he exclaimed. "He has never heard of me! What should he want with *me*?"

"Oh! you must go instantly!" cried the two men. "He is very angry now because he has been kept waiting so long; and nobody knows what may happen if you don't hurry to him."

The poor Minor Canon would rather have had his hand cut off than go out to meet an angry griffin; but he felt that it was his duty to go, for it would be a woful thing if injury should come to the people of the town because he was not brave enough to obey the summons of the Griffin. So, pale and frightened, he started off.

"Well," said the Griffin, as soon as the young man came near, "I am glad to see that there is some one who has the courage to come to me."

The Minor Canon did not feel very courageous, but he bowed his head.

"Is this the town," said the Griffin, "where there is a church with a likeness of myself over one of the doors?"

The Minor Canon looked at the frightful creature before him and saw that it was, without doubt, exactly like the stone image on the church. "Yes," he said, "you are right."

"Well, then," said the Griffin, "will you take me to it? I wish very much to see it."

The Minor Canon instantly thought that if the Griffin entered the town without the people knowing what he came for, some of them would probably be frightened to death, and so he sought to gain time to prepare their minds.

"It is growing dark, now," he said, very much

afraid, as he spoke, that his words might enrage the Griffin, "and objects on the front of the church can not be seen clearly. It will be better to wait until morning, if you wish to get a good view of the stone image of yourself."

"That will suit me very well," said the Griffin. "I see you are a man of good sense. I am tired, and I will take a nap here on this soft grass, while I cool my tail in the little stream that runs near me. The end of my tail gets red-hot when I am angry or excited, and it is quite warm now. So you may go, but be sure and come early to-morrow morning, and show me the way to the church."

The Minor Canon was glad enough to take his leave, and hurried into the town. In front of the church he found a great many people assembled to hear his report of his interview with the Griffin. When they found that he had not come to spread ruin and devastation, but simply to see his stony likeness on the church, they showed neither relief nor gratification, but began to upbraid the Minor Canon for consenting to conduct the creature into the town.

"What could I do?" cried the young man. "If I should not bring him he would come himself and, perhaps, end by setting fire to the town with his red-hot tail."

Still the people were not satisfied, and a great many plans were proposed to prevent the Griffin from coming into the town. Some elderly persons urged that the young men should go out and kill him; but the young men scoffed at such a ridiculous idea. Then some one said that it would be a good thing to destroy the stone image so that the Griffin would have no excuse for entering the town; and this proposal was received with such favor that many of the people ran for hammers, chisels, and crowbars, with which to tear down and break up the stone griffin. But the Minor Canon resisted this plan with all the strength of his mind and body. He assured the people that this action would enrage the Griffin beyond measure, for it would be impossible to conceal from him that his image had been destroyed during the night. But the people were so determined to break up the stone griffin that the Minor Canon saw that there was nothing for him to do but to stay there and protect it. All night he walked up and down in front of the church-door, keeping away the men who brought ladders, by which they might mount to the great stone griffin, and knock it to pieces with their hammers and crowbars. After many hours the people were obliged to give up their attempts, and went home to sleep; but the Minor Canon remained at his post till early morning, and then he hurried away to the field where he had left the Griffin.

The monster had just awakened, and rising to his fore-legs and shaking himself, he said that he was ready to go into the town. The Minor Canon, there-fore, walked back, the Griffin flying slowly through the air, at a short distance above the head of his guide. Not a person was to be seen in the streets, and they proceeded directly to the front of the church, where the Minor Canon pointed out the stone griffin.

The real Griffin settled down in the little square before the church and gazed earnestly at his sculp-tured likeness. For a long time he looked at it. First he put his head on one side, and then he put it on the other; then he shut his right eye and gazed with his left, after which he shut his left eye and gazed with his right. Then he moved a little to one side and looked at the image, then he moved the other way. After a while he said to the Minor Canon, who had been standing by all this time:

"It is, it must be, an excellent likeness! That breadth between the eyes, that expansive forehead, those massive jaws! I feel that it must resemble me. If there is any fault to find with it, it is that the neck seems a little stiff. But that is nothing. It is an admir-able likeness,—admirable!"

The Griffin sat looking at his image all the morning and all the afternoon. The Minor Canon had been afraid to go away and leave him, and had hoped all through the day that he would soon be satisfied with his inspection and fly away home. But by evening the poor young man was utterly exhausted, and felt that he must eat and sleep. He frankly admitted this fact to the Griffin, and asked him if he would not like something to eat. He said this because he felt obliged in politeness to do so, but as soon as he had spoken the words, he was seized with dread lest the monster should demand half a dozen babies, or some tempting repast of that kind.

"Oh, no," said the Griffin, "I never eat between the equinoxes. At the vernal and at the autumnal equinox I take a good meal, and that lasts me for half a year. I am extremely regular in my habits, and do not think it healthful to eat at odd times. But if you need food, go and get it, and I will return to the soft grass where I slept last night and take another nap."

The next day the Griffin came again to the little square before the church, and remained there until evening, steadfastly regarding the stone griffin over the door. The Minor Canon came once or twice to look at him, and the Griffin seemed very glad to see him; but the young clergyman could not stay as he had done before, for he had many duties to perform. Nobody went to the church, but the people came to the Minor Canon's house, and anxiously asked him how long the Griffin was going to stay.

"I do not know," he answered, "but I think he will soon be satisfied with regarding his stone likeness, and then he will go away."

But the Griffin did not go away. Morning after morning he came to the church, but after a time he did not stay there all day. He seemed to have taken a great fancy to the Minor Canon, and followed him about as he pursued his various avocations. He would wait for him at the side door of the church, for the Minor Canon held services every day, morning and evening, though nobody came now. "If any one should come," he said to himself, "I must be found at my post." When the young man came out, the Griffin would accompany him in his visits to the sick and the poor, and would often look into the windows of the school-house where the Minor Canon was teaching his unruly scholars. All the other schools were closed, but the parents of the Minor Canon's scholars forced them to go to school, because they were so bad they could not endure them all day at home,—griffin or no griffin. But it must be said they generally behaved very well when that great monster sat up on his tail and looked in at the school-room window.

When it was perceived that the Griffin showed no sign of going away, all the people who were able to do so left the town. The canons and the higher officers of the church had fled away during the first day of the Griffin's visit, leaving behind only the Minor Canon and some of the men who opened the doors and swept the church. All the citizens who could afford it shut up their houses and travelled to distant parts, and only the working people and the poor were left behind. After some days these ventured to go about and attend to their business, for if they did not work they would starve. They were getting a little used to seeing the Griffin, and having been told that he did not eat between equinoxes, they did not feel so much afraid of him as before.

Day by day the Griffin became more and more attached to the Minor Canon. He kept near him a great part of the time, and often spent the night in front of the little house where the young clergyman lived alone. This strange companionship was often burdensome to the Minor Canon; but, on the other hand, he could not deny that he derived a great deal of benefit and instruction from it. The Griffin had lived for hundreds of years, and had seen much; and he told the Minor Canon many wonderful things.

"It is like reading an old book," said the young clergyman to himself; "but how many books I would have had to read before I would have found out what the Griffin has told me about the earth, the air, the water, about minerals, and metals, and growing things, and all the wonders of the world!"

Thus the summer went on, and drew toward its close. And now the people of the town began to be very much troubled again.

"It will not be long," they said, "before the autumnal equinox is here, and then that monster will want to eat. He will be dreadfully hungry, for he has taken so much exercise since his last meal. He will devour our children. Without doubt, he will eat them all. What is to be done?"

To this question no one could give an answer, but all agreed that the Griffin must not be allowed to remain until the approaching equinox. After talking over the matter a great deal, a crowd of the people went to the Minor Canon, at a time when the Griffin was not with him.

"It is all your fault," they said, "that that monster is among us. You brought him here, and you ought to see that he goes away. It is only on your account that he stays here at all, for, although he visits his image every day, he is with you the greater part of the time. If you were not here, he would not stay. It is your duty to go away and then he will follow you, and we shall be free from the dreadful danger which hangs over us."

"Go away!" cried the Minor Canon, greatly grieved at being spoken to in such a way. "Where shall I go? If I go to some other town, shall I not take this trouble there? Have I a right to do that?"

"No," said the people, "you must not go to any other town. There is no town far enough away. You must go to the dreadful wilds where the Griffin lives; and then he will follow you and stay there."

They did not say whether or not they expected the Minor Canon to stay there also, and he did not ask them any thing about it. He bowed his head, and went into his house, to think. The more he thought, the more clear it became to his mind that it was his duty to go away, and thus free the town from the presence of the Griffin.

That evening he packed a leathern bag full of bread and meat, and early the next morning he set out on his journey to the dreadful wilds. It was a long, weary, and doleful journey, especially after he had gone beyond the habitations of men, but the Minor Canon kept on bravely, and never faltered. The way was longer than he had expected, and his provisions soon grew so scanty that he was obliged to eat but a little every day, but he kept up his courage, and pressed on, and, after many days of toilsome travel, he reached the dreadful wilds.

When the Griffin found that the Minor Canon had left the town he seemed sorry, but showed no disposition to go and look for him. After a few days had passed, he became much annoyed, and asked some of the people where the Minor Canon had gone. But, although the citizens had been so anxious that the young clergyman should go to the dreadful wilds, thinking that the Griffin would immediately follow him, they were now afraid to mention the Minor Canon's destination, for the monster seemed angry already, and, if he should suspect their trick he would, doubtless, become very much enraged. So every one said he did not know, and the Griffin wandered about disconsolate. One morning he looked into the Minor Canon's school-house, which was always empty now, and thought that it was a shame that every thing should suffer on account of the young man's absence.

"It does not matter so much about the church," he said, "for nobody went there; but it is a pity about the school. I think I will teach it myself until he returns."

It was the hour for opening the school, and the Griffin went inside and pulled the rope which rang the school-bell. Some of the children who heard the bell ran in to see what was the matter, supposing it to be a joke of one of their companions; but when they saw the Griffin they stood astonished, and scared.

"Go tell the other scholars," said the monster, "that school is about to open, and that if they are not all here in ten minutes, I shall come after them."

In seven minutes every scholar was in place.

Never was seen such an orderly school. Not a boy or girl moved, or uttered a whisper. The Griffin climbed into the master's seat, his wide wings spread on each side of him, because he could not lean back in his chair while they stuck out behind, and his great tail coiled around, in front of the desk, the barbed end sticking up, ready to tap any boy or girl who might misbehave. The Griffin now addressed the scholars, telling them that he intended to teach them while their master was away. In speaking he endeavored to imitate, as far as possible, the mild and gentle tones of the Minor Canon, but it must be admitted that in this he was not very successful. He had paid a good deal of attention to the studies of the school, and he determined not to attempt to teach them any thing new, but to review them in what they had been studying; so he called up the various classes, and questioned them upon their previous lessons. The children racked their brains to remember what they had learned. They were so afraid of the Griffin's displeasure that they recited as they had never recited before. One of the boys, far down in his class, answered so well that the Griffin was astonished.

"I should think you would be at the head," said he. "I am sure you have never been in the habit of reciting so well. Why is this?"

"Because I did not choose to take the trouble," said the boy, trembling in his boots. He felt obliged to speak the truth, for all the children thought that the great eyes of the Griffin could see right through them, and that he would know when they told a falsehood.

"You ought to be ashamed of yourself," said the Griffin. "Go down to the very tail of the class, and if you are not at the head in two days, I shall know the reason why."

The next afternoon this boy was number one.

It was astonishing how much these children now learned of what they had been studying. It was as if they had been educated over again. The Griffin used no severity toward them, but there was a look about him which made them unwilling to go to bed until they were sure they knew their lessons for the next day.

The Griffin now thought that he ought to visit

the sick and the poor; and he began to go about the town for this purpose. The effect upon the sick was miraculous. All, except those who were very ill indeed, jumped from their beds when they heard he was coming, and declared themselves quite well. To those who could not get up, he gave herbs and roots, which none of them had ever before thought of as medicines, but which the Griffin had seen used in various parts of the world; and most of them recovered. But, for all that, they afterward said that no matter what happened to them, they hoped that they should never again have such a doctor coming to their bed-sides, feeling their pulses and looking at their tongues.

As for the poor, they seemed to have utterly disappeared. All those who had depended upon charity for their daily bread were now at work in some way or other; many of them offering to do odd jobs for their neighbors just for the sake of their meals,—a thing which before had been seldom heard of in the town. The Griffin could find no one who needed his assistance.

The summer had now passed, and the autumnal equinox was rapidly approaching. The citizens were in a state of great alarm and anxiety. The Griffin showed no signs of going away, but seemed to have settled himself permanently among them. In a short time, the day for his semi-annual meal would arrive, and then what would happen? The monster would certainly be very hungry, and would devour all their children.

Now they greatly regretted and lamented that they had sent away the Minor Canon; he was the only one on whom they could have depended in this trouble, for he could talk freely with the Griffin, and so find out what could be done. But it would not do to be inactive. Some step must be taken immediately. A meeting of the citizens was called, and two old men were appointed to go and talk to the Griffin. They were instructed to offer to prepare a splendid dinner for him on equinox day,—one which would entirely satisfy his hunger. They would offer him the fattest mutton, the most tender beef, fish, and game of various sorts, and any thing of the kind that he might fancy. If none of these suited, they were to mention that there was an orphan asylum in the next town.

"Anything would be better," said the citizens, "than to have our dear children devoured."

The old men went to the Griffin, but their propositions were not received with favor.

"From what I have seen of the people of this town," said the monster, "I do not think I could relish any thing which was prepared by them. They appear to be all cowards, and, therefore, mean and selfish. As for eating one of them, old or young, I could not think of it for a moment. In fact, there was only one creature in the whole place for whom I could have had any appetite, and that is the Minor Canon, who has gone away. He was brave, and good, and honest, and I think I should have relished him."

"Ah!" said one of the old men very politely, "in that case I wish we had not sent him to the dreadful wilds!"

"What!" cried the Griffin. "What do you mean? Explain instantly what you are talking about!"

The old man, terribly frightened at what he had said, was obliged to tell how the Minor Canon had been sent away by the people, in the hope that the Griffin might be induced to follow him.

When the monster heard this, he became furiously angry. He dashed away from the old men and, spreading his wings, flew backward and forward over the town. He was so much excited that his tail became red-hot, and glowed like a meteor against the evening sky. When at last he settled down in the little field where he usually rested, and thrust his tail into the brook, the steam arose like a cloud, and the water of the stream ran hot through the town. The citizens were greatly frightened, and bitterly blamed the old man for telling about the Minor Canon.

"It is plain," they said, "that the Griffin intended at last to go and look for him, and we should have been saved. Now who can tell what misery you have brought upon us."

The Griffin did not remain long in the little field. As soon as his tail was cool he flew to the town-hall and rang the bell. The citizens knew that they were expected to come there, and although they were afraid to go, they were still more afraid to stay away; and they crowded into the hall. The Griffin was on the platform at one end, flapping his wings and walking up and down, and the end of his tail was still so warm that it slightly scorched the boards as he dragged it after him.

When everybody who was able to come was there, the Griffin stood still and addressed the meeting.

"I have had a contemptible opinion of you," he said, "ever since I discovered what cowards you are, but I had no idea that you were so ungrateful, self-ish, and cruel, as I now find you to be. Here was your Minor Canon, who labored day and night for your good, and thought of nothing else but how he might benefit you and make you happy; and as soon as you imagine yourselves threatened with a danger,—for well I know you are dreadfully afraid of me,—you send him off, caring not whether he

returns or perishes, hoping thereby to save yourselves. Now, I had conceived a great liking for that
young man. and had intended, in a day or two, to go
and look him up. But I have changed my mind
about him. I shall go and find him, but I shall send
him back here to live among you, and I intend that
he shall enjoy the reward of his labor and his sacrifices. Go, some of you, to the officers of the church,
who so cowardly ran away when I first came here,
and tell them never to return to this town under
penalty of death. And if, when your Minor Canon
comes back to you, you do not bow yourselves
before him, put him in the highest place among you,
and serve and honor him all his life, beware of my
terrible vengeance! There were only two good things
in this town: the Minor Canon and the stone image
of myself over your church-door. One of these you
have sent away, and the other I shall carry away
myself."

With these words he dismissed the meeting, and
it was time, for the end of his tail had become so
hot that there was danger of its setting fire to the
building.

The next morning, the Griffin came to the
church, and tearing the stone image of himself from
its fastenings over the great door, he grasped it with
his powerful fore-legs and flew up into the air. Then,

after hovering over the town for a moment, he gave his tail an angry shake and took up his flight to the dreadful wilds. When he reached this desolate region, he set the stone Griffin upon a ledge of a rock which rose in front of the dismal cave he called his home. There the image occupied a position somewhat similar to that it had had over the church-door; and the Griffin, panting with the exertion of carrying such an enormous load to so great a distance, lay down upon the ground, and regarded it with much satisfaction. When he felt somewhat rested he went to look for the Minor Canon. He found the young man, weak and half starved, lying under the shadow of a rock. After picking him up and carrying him to his cave, the Griffin flew away to a distant marsh, where he procured some roots and herbs which he well knew were strengthening and beneficial to man, though he had never tasted them himself. After eating these the Minor Canon was greatly revived, and sat up and listened while the Griffin told him what had happened in the town.

"Do you know," said the monster, when he had finished, "that I have had, and still have, a great liking for you?"

"I am very glad to hear it," said the Minor Canon, with his usual politeness.

"I am not at all sure that you would be," said the

Griffin, "if you thoroughly understood the state of the case, but we will not consider that now. If some things were different, other things would be otherwise. I have been so enraged by discovering the manner in which you have been treated that I have determined that you shall at last enjoy the rewards and honors to which you are entitled. Lie down and have a good sleep, and then I will take you back to the town."

As he heard these words, a look of trouble came over the young man's face.

"You need not give yourself any anxiety," said the Griffin, "about my return to the town. I shall not remain there. Now that I have that admirable likeness of myself in front of my cave, where I can sit at my leisure, and gaze upon its noble features and magnificent proportions, I have no wish to see that abode of cowardly and selfish people."

The Minor Canon, relieved from his fears, lay back, and dropped into a doze; and when he was sound asleep the Griffin took him up, and carried him back to the town. He arrived just before daybreak, and putting the young man gently on the grass in the little field where he himself used to rest, the monster, without having been seen by any of the people, flew back to his home.

When the Minor Canon made his appearance in

the morning among the citizens, the enthusiasm and cordiality with which he was received were truly wonderful. He was taken to a house which had been occupied by one of the banished high officers of the place, and every one was anxious to do all that could be done for his health and comfort. The people crowded into the church when he held services, so that the three old women who used to be his week-day congregation could not get to the best seats, which they had always been in the habit of taking; and the parents of the bad children determined to reform them at home, in order that he might be spared the trouble of keeping up his former school. The Minor Canon was appointed to the highest office of the old church, and before he died, he became a bishop.

During the first years after his return from the dreadful wilds, the people of the town looked up to him as a man to whom they were bound to do honor and reverence; but they often, also, looked up to the sky to see if there were any signs of the Griffin coming back. However, in the course of time, they learned to honor and reverence their former Minor Canon without the fear of being punished if they did not do so.

But they need never have been afraid of the Griffin. The autumnal equinox day came round, and the monster ate nothing. If he could not have the Minor Canon, he did not care for any thing. So, lying down, with his eyes fixed upon the great stone griffin, he gradually declined, and died. It was a good thing for some of the people of the town that they did not know this.

If you should ever visit the old town, you would still see the little griffins on the sides of the church; but the great stone griffin that was over the door is gone.

SARAH ORNE JEWETT

Sarah Orne Jewett (1849–1909) was an American writer descended from a long line of New Englanders and steeped in the tradition of north-eastern nature writing. Her work reflects a sensitivity to landscape and yet also a fear of the deep woodlands and isolated valleys that is often found in American fiction and is reflected today in modern American horror fiction. Although, like many writers of her era, Jewett wrote in a number of modes including novels and stories for children, her reputation is built on her contribution to the genre of country life writing, in the style of vignettes rather than full stories, some of which are clearly fantastical tales. Jewett was interested in the teaching of Emanuel Swedenborg, an eighteenth-century Swedish scientist and theologian, who believed that the divine was always present in everything around us, a concept which is reflected in the story below.

High on the southern slope of Agamenticus there may still be seen the remnant of an old farm. Frost-shaken stone walls surround a fast-narrowing expanse of smooth turf which the forest is overgrowing on every side. The cellar is nearly filled up, never having been either wide or deep, and the fruit of a few mossy apple-trees drops ungathered to the ground. Along one side of the forsaken garden is a thicket of seedling cherry-trees to which the shouting robins come year after year in busy flights; the caterpillars' nests are unassailed and populous in this untended hedge. At night, perhaps, when summer twilights are late in drawing their brown curtain of dusk over the great rural scene,—at night an owl may sit in the hemlocks near by and hoot and shriek until the far echoes answer back again. As for the few men and women who pass this deserted spot, most will be repulsed by such loneliness, will even grow impatient with those mistaken fellow-beings who choose to live in solitude, away from neighbors and from schools,—yes, even from gossip and petty care of self or knowledge of the trivial fashions of a narrow life.

Now and then one looks out from this eyrie, across the wide-spread country, who turns to look at the sea or toward the shining foreheads of the mountains that guard the inland horizon, who will remember the place long afterward. A peaceful vision will come, full of rest and benediction into busy and troubled hours, to those who understand why some one came to live in this place so near the sky, so silent, so full of sweet air and woodland fragrance; so beaten and buffeted by winter storms and garlanded with summer greenery; where the birds are nearest neighbors and a clear spring the only wine-cellar, and trees of the forest a choir of singers who rejoice and sing aloud by day and night as the winds sweep over. Under the cherry thicket or at the edge of the woods you may find a stray-away blossom, some half-savage, slender grandchild of the old flower-plots, that you gather gladly to take away, and every year in June a red rose blooms toward which the wild pink roses and the pale sweet briars turn wondering faces as if a queen had shown her noble face suddenly at a peasant's festival.

There is everywhere a token of remembrance, of silence and secrecy. Some stronger nature once ruled these neglected trees and this fallow ground. They will wait the return of their master as long as roots can creep through mould, and the mould make way for them. The stories of strange lives have been whispered to the earth, their thoughts have burned themselves into the cold rocks. As one looks from the lower country toward the long slope of the great hillside, this old abiding-place marks the dark covering of trees like a scar. There is nothing to hide either the sunrise or the sunset. The low lands reach out of sight into the west and the sea fills all the east.

The first owner of the farm was a seafaring man who had through freak or fancy come ashore and cast himself upon the bounty of nature for support in his later years, though tradition keeps a suspicion of buried treasure and of a dark history. He cleared his land and built his house, but save the fact that he was a Scotsman no one knew to whom he belonged, and when he died the state inherited the unclaimed property. The only piece of woodland that was worth anything was sold and added to another farm, and the dwelling-place was left to the sunshine and the rain, to the birds that built their nests in the chimney or under the eaves. Sometimes a strolling company of country boys would find themselves near the house on a holiday afternoon, but the more dilapidated the small structure became, the more they believed that some uncanny existence possessed the lonely place, and the path that led toward the clearing at last became almost impassable.

Once a number of officers and men in the employ of the Coast Survey were encamped at the top of the mountain, and they smoothed the rough track that led down to the spring that bubbled from under a sheltering edge. One day a laughing fellow, not content with peering in at the small windows of the house, put his shoulder against the rain-blackened door and broke the simple fastening. He hardly knew that he was afraid as he first stood within the single spacious room, so complete a curiosity took possession of him. The place was clean and bare, the empty cupboard doors stood open, and yet the sound of his companions' voices outside seemed far away, and an awful sense that some unseen inhabitant followed his footsteps made him hurry out again pale and breathless to the fresh air and sunshine. Was this really a dwelling-place of spirits, as had been already hinted? The story grew more fearful, and spread quickly like a mist of terror among the lowland farms. For years the tale of the coast-surveyor's adventure in the haunted house was slowly magnified and told to strangers or to wide-eyed children by the dim firelight. The former owner was supposed to linger still about his old home, and was held accountable for deep offense in choosing for the scene of his unsuccessful husbandry a place that escaped the proprieties and restraints of life upon lower levels. His grave was concealed by the new growth of oaks and beeches, and many a lad and full-grown man beside has taken to his heels at the flicker of light from across a swamp or under a decaying tree in that neighborhood. As the world in some respects grew wiser, the good people near the mountain understood less and less the causes of these simple effects, and as they became familiar with the visible world, grew more shy of the unseen and more sensitive to unexplained foreboding.

One day a stranger was noticed in the town, as a stranger is sure to be who goes his way with quick, furtive steps straight through a small village or along a country road. This man was tall and had just passed middle age. He was well made and vigorous, but there was an unusual pallor in his face, a grayish look, as if he had been startled by bad news. His clothes were somewhat peculiar, as if they had been made in another country, yet they suited the chilly weather, being homespun of undyed wools, just the color of his hair, and only a little darker than his face or hands. Some one observed in one brief glance as he and this gray man met and passed each other, that his eyes had a strange faded look; they might, however, flash and be coal-black in a moment of rage. Two or three persons stepped forward to watch the wayfarer as he went along the road with long, even strides, like one taking a journey on foot, but he quickly reached a turn of the way and was out of sight. They wondered who he was; one recalled some recent advertisement of an escaped criminal, and another the appearance of a native of the town who was supposed to be long ago lost at sea, but one surmiser knew as little as the next. If they had followed fast enough they might have tracked the mysterious man straight across the country, threading the by-ways, the shorter paths that led across the fields where the road was roundabout and hindering. At last he disappeared in the leafless, trackless woods that skirted the mountain.

That night there was for the first time in many years a twinkling light in the window of the haunted house, high on the hill's great shoulder; one farmer's wife and another looked up curiously, while they wondered what daring human being had chosen that awesome spot of all others for his home or for even a transient shelter. The sky was already heavy with snow; he might be a fugitive from justice, and the startled people looked to the fastening of their doors unwontedly that night, and waked often from a troubled sleep.

An instinctive curiosity and alarm possessed the country men and women for a while, but soon faded out and disappeared. The newcomer was by no means a hermit; he tried to be friendly, and inclined toward a certain kindliness and familiarity. He

bought a comfortable store of winter provisions from
his new acquaintances, giving every one his price,
and spoke more at length, as time went on, of current events, of politics and the weather, and the
town's own news and concerns. There was a sober
cheerfulness about the man, as if he had known
trouble and perplexity, and was fulfilling some mission that gave him pain; yet he saw some gain and
reward beyond; therefore he could be contented
with his life and such strange surroundings. He was
more and more eager to form brotherly relations
with the farmers near his home. There was almost a
pleading look in his kind face at times, as if he feared
the later prejudice of his associates. Surely this was
no common or uneducated person, for in every way
he left the stamp of his character and influence upon
men and things. His reasonable words of advice and
warning are current as sterling coins in that region
yet; to one man he taught a new rotation of crops,
to another he gave some priceless cures for devastat-
ing diseases of cattle. The lonely women of those
remote country homes learned of him how to
achieve their household toil with less labor and
drudgery, and here and there he singled out prom-
ising children and kept watch of their growth, giving
freely a most affectionate companionship, and a fair
start in the journey of life. He taught those who were

guardians of such children to recognize and further the true directions and purposes of existence; and the easily warped natures grew strong and well-established under his thoughtful care. No wonder that some people were filled with amazement, and thought his wisdom supernatural, from so many proofs that his horizon was wider than their own.

Perhaps some envious soul, or one aggrieved by being caught in treachery or deception, was the first to find fault with the stranger. The prejudice against his dwelling-place, and the superstition which had become linked to him in consequence, may have led back to the first suspicious attitude of the community. The whisper of distrust soon started on an evil way. If he were not a criminal, his past was surely a hidden one, and shocking to his remembrance, but the true foundation of all dislike was the fact that the gray man who went to and fro, living his simple, harmless life among them, *never was seen to smile.* Persons who remember him speak of this with a shudder, for nothing is more evident than that his peculiarity became at length intolerable to those whose minds lent themselves readily to suspicion. At first, blinded by the gentle good fellowship of the stranger, the changeless expression of his face was scarcely observed, but as the winter wore away he was watched with renewed disbelief and dismay.

After the first few attempts at gayety nobody tried to tell a merry story in his presence. The most conspicuous of a joker's audience does a deep-rankling injustice if he sits with unconscious, unamused face at the receipt of raillery. What a chilling moment when the gray man softly opened the door of a farmhouse kitchen, and seated himself like a skeleton at the feast of walnuts and roasted apples beside the glowing fire! The children whom he treated so lovingly, to whom he ever gave his best, though they were won at first by his gentleness, when they began to prattle and play with him would raise their innocent eyes to his face and hush their voices and creep away out of his sight. Once only he was bidden to a wedding, but never afterward, for a gloom was quickly spread through the boisterous company; the man who never smiled had no place at such a festival. The wedding guests looked over their shoulders again and again in strange foreboding, while he was in the house, and were burdened with a sense of coming woe for the newly-married pair. As one caught sight of his, among the faces of the rural folk, the gray man was like a sombre mask, and at last the bridegroom flung open the door with a meaning gesture, and the stranger went out like a hunted creature, into the bitter coldness and silence of the winter night.

Through the long days of the next summer the
outcast of the wedding, forbidden, at length, all the
once-proffered hospitality, was hardly seen from one
week's end to another's. He cultivated his poor
estate with patient care, and the successive crops of
his small garden, the fruits and berries of the wilderness, were food enough. He seemed unchangeable,
and was always ready when he even guessed at a
chance to be of use. If he were repulsed, he only
turned away and went back to his solitary home.
Those persons who by chance visited him there tell
wonderful tales of the wild birds which had been
tamed to come at his call and cluster about him, of
the orderliness and delicacy of his simple life. The
once-neglected house was covered with vines that he
had brought from the woods, and planted about the
splintering, decaying walls. There were three or four
books in worn bindings on a shelf above the fire-
place; one longs to know what volumes this
mysterious exile had chosen to keep him company!

There may have been a deeper reason for the
withdrawal of friendliness; there are vague rumors of
the gray man's possession of strange powers. Some
say that he was gifted with amazing strength, and
once when some belated hunters found shelter at his
fireside, they told eager listeners afterward that he
did not sleep but sat by the fire reading gravely while

they slumbered uneasily on his own bed of boughs. And in the dead of night an empty chair glided silently toward him across the floor as he softly turned his pages in the flickering light.

But such stories are too vague, and in that neighborhood too common to weigh against the true dignity and bravery of the man. At the beginning of the war of the rebellion he seemed strangely troubled and disturbed, and presently disappeared, leaving his house key with a neighbor as if for a few days' absence. He was last seen striding rapidly through the village a few miles away, going back along the road by which he had come a year or two before. No, not last seen either; for in one of the first battles of the war, as the smoke suddenly lifted, a farmer's boy, reared in the shadow of the mountain, opened his languid pain-dulled eyes as he lay among the wounded, and saw the gray man riding by on a tall horse. At that moment the poor lad thought in his faintness and fear that Death himself rode by in the gray man's likeness; unsmiling Death who tries to teach and serve mankind so that he may at the last win welcome as a faithful friend!

OSCAR WILDE

Oscar Wilde (1854–1900) is best known for his plays and also for the sexual scandal that enveloped his later life. For readers of fantasy, however, he is also the author of *The Picture of Dorian Gray* (1890) to which everyone refers when they accuse someone of having a portrait in their attic. Wilde also wrote a number of short fantasies including 'The Canterville Ghost' as well as fairy stories for adults, at a time when adult fairy stories had become a vehicle for Victorian moralizing. This is a term that is frequently misappropriated to imply dour disapproval but the Victorians came in many political persuasions, and Wilde, like William Morris and Charles Kingsley (author of *The Water Babies*), used the fairy tale to argue for a kinder, more compassionate world.

The Happy Prince

High above the city, on a tall column, stood the statue of the Happy Prince.

He was gilded all over with thin leaves of fine gold, for eyes he had two bright sapphires, and a large red ruby glowed on his sword-hilt.

He was very much admired indeed. "He is as beautiful as a weathercock," remarked one of the Town Councillors who wished to gain a reputation for having artistic tastes; "only not quite so useful," he added, fearing lest people should think him unpractical, which he really was not.

"Why can't you be like the Happy Prince?" asked a sensible mother of her little boy who was crying for the moon. "The Happy Prince never dreams of crying for anything."

"I am glad there is some one in the world who is quite happy," muttered a disappointed man as he gazed at the wonderful statue.

"He looks just like an angel," said the Charity Children as they came out of the cathedral in their bright scarlet cloaks, and their clean white pinafores.

"How do you know?" said the Mathematical Master, "you have never seen one."

"Ah! but we have, in our dreams," answered the children; and the Mathematical Master frowned and looked very severe, for he did not approve of children dreaming.

One night there flew over the city a little Swallow. His friends had gone away to Egypt six weeks before, but he had stayed behind, for he was in love with the most beautiful Reed. He had met her early in the spring as he was flying down the river after a big yellow moth, and had been so attracted by her slender waist that he had stopped to talk to her.

"Shall I love you?" said the Swallow, who liked to come to the point at once, and the Reed made him a low bow. So he flew round and round her, touching the water with his wings, and making silver ripples. This was his courtship, and it lasted all through the summer.

"It is a ridiculous attachment," twittered the other Swallows, "she has no money, and far too many relations;" and indeed the river was quite full of Reeds. Then, when the autumn came, they all flew away.

After they had gone he felt lonely, and began to tire of his lady-love. "She has no conversation," he said, "and I am afraid that she is a coquette, for she is always flirting with the wind." And certainly, whenever the wind blew, the Reed made the most graceful curtsies. "I admit that she is domestic," he continued, "but I love travelling, and my wife, consequently, should love travelling also."

"Will you come away with me?" he said finally to her; but the Reed shook her head, she was so attached to her home.

"You have been trifling with me," he cried, "I am off to the Pyramids. Good-bye!" and he flew away.

All day long he flew, and at night-time he arrived at the city. "Where shall I put up?" he said; "I hope the town has made preparations."

Then he saw the statue on the tall column. "I will put up there," he cried; "it is a fine position with plenty of fresh air." So he alighted just between the feet of the Happy Prince.

"I have a golden bedroom," he said softly to himself as he looked round, and he prepared to go to sleep; but just as he was putting his head under his wing a large drop of water fell on him. "What a curious thing!" he cried, "there is not a single cloud in the sky, the stars arc quite clear and bright, and yet it is raining. The climate in the north of Europe is really dreadful. The Reed used to like the rain, but that was merely her selfishness."

Then another drop fell.

"What is the use of a statue if it cannot keep the rain off?" he said; "I must look for a good chimney-pot," and he determined to fly away.

But before he had opened his wings, a third drop fell, and he looked up, and saw— Ah! what did he see?

The eyes of the Happy Prince were filled with tears, and tears were running down his golden cheeks. His face was so beautiful in the moonlight that the little Swallow was filled with pity.

"Who are you?" he said.

"I am the Happy Prince."

"Why are you weeping then?" asked the Swallow; "you have quite drenched me."

"When I was alive and had a human heart," answered the statue, "I did not know what tears were, for I lived in the Palace of Sans-Souci, where sorrow is not allowed to enter. In the daytime I played with my companions in the garden, and in the evening I led the dance in the Great Hall. Round the garden ran a very lofty wall, but I never cared to ask what lay beyond it, everything about me was so beautiful. My courtiers called me the Happy Prince, and happy indeed I was, if pleasure be happiness. So I lived, and so I died. And now that I am dead they have set me up here so high that I can see all the ugliness and all the misery of my city, and though my heart is made of lead yet I cannot choose but weep."

"What, is he not solid gold?" said the Swallow to

himself. He was too polite to make any personal remarks out loud.

"Far away," continued the statue in a low musical voice, "far away in a little street there is a poor house. One of the windows is open, and through it I can see a woman seated at a table. Her face is thin and worn, and she has coarse, red hands, all pricked by the needle, for she is a seamstress. She is embroidering passion-flowers on a satin gown for the loveliest of the Queen's maids-of-honour to wear at the next Court-ball. In a bed in the corner of the room her little boy is lying ill. He has a fever, and is asking for oranges. His mother has nothing to give him but river water, so he is crying. Swallow, Swallow, little Swallow, will you not bring her the ruby out of my sword-hilt? My feet are fastened to this pedestal and I cannot move."

"I am waited for in Egypt," said the Swallow. "My friends are flying up and down the Nile, and talking to the large lotus-flowers. Soon they will go to sleep in the tomb of the great King. The King is there himself in his painted coffin. He is wrapped in yellow linen, and embalmed with spices. Round his neck is a chain of pale green jade, and his hands are like withered leaves."

"Swallow, Swallow, little Swallow," said the Prince, "will you not stay with me for one night, and be my messenger? The boy is so thirsty, and the mother so sad."

"I don't think I like boys," answered the Swallow. "Last summer, when I was staying on the river, there were two rude boys, the miller's sons, who were always throwing stones at me. They never hit me, of course; we swallows fly far too well for that, and besides, I come of a family famous for its agility; but still, it was a mark of disrespect."

But the Happy Prince looked so sad that the little Swallow was sorry. "It is very cold here," he said; "but I will stay with you for one night, and be your messenger."

"Thank you, little Swallow," said the Prince.

So the Swallow picked out the great ruby from the Prince's sword, and flew away with it in his beak over the roofs of the town.

He passed by the cathedral tower, where the white marble angels were sculptured. He passed by the palace and heard the sound of dancing. A beautiful girl came out on the balcony with her lover. "How wonderful the stars are," he said to her, "and how wonderful is the power of love!" "I hope my dress will be ready in time for the State-ball," she answered; "I have ordered passion-flowers to be embroidered on it; but the seamstresses are so lazy."

He passed over the river, and saw the lanterns

hanging to the masts of the ships. He passed over the Ghetto, and saw the old Jews bargaining with each other, and weighing out money in copper scales. At last he came to the poor house and looked in. The boy was tossing feverishly on his bed, and the mother had fallen asleep, she was so tired. In he hopped, and laid the great ruby on the table beside the woman's thimble. Then he flew gently round the bed, fanning the boy's forehead with his wings. "How cool I feel," said the boy, "I must be getting better;" and he sank into a delicious slumber.

Then the Swallow flew back to the Happy Prince, and told him what he had done. "It is curious," he remarked, "but I feel quite warm now, although it is so cold."

"That is because you have done a good action," said the Prince. And the little Swallow began to think, and then he fell asleep. Thinking always made him sleepy.

When day broke he flew down to the river and had a bath. "What a remarkable phenomenon," said the Professor of Ornithology as he was passing over the bridge. "A swallow in winter!" And he wrote a long letter about it to the local newspaper. Every one quoted it, it was full of so many words that they could not understand.

"To-night I go to Egypt," said the Swallow, and

he was in high spirits at the prospect. He visited all the public monuments, and sat a long time on top of the church steeple. Wherever he went the Sparrows chirruped, and said to each other, "What a distinguished stranger!" so he enjoyed himself very much.

When the moon rose he flew back to the Happy Prince. "Have you any commissions for Egypt?" he cried; "I am just starting."

"Swallow, Swallow, little Swallow," said the Prince, "will you not stay with me one night longer?"

"I am waited for in Egypt," answered the Swallow. "To-morrow my friends will fly up to the Second Cataract. The river-horse couches there among the bulrushes, and on a great granite throne sits the God Memnon. All night long he watches the stars, and when the morning star shines he utters one cry of joy, and then he is silent. At noon the yellow lions come down to the water's edge to drink. They have eyes like green beryls, and their roar is louder than the roar of the cataract."

"Swallow, Swallow, little Swallow," said the Prince, "far away across the city I see a young man in a garret. He is leaning over a desk covered with papers, and in a tumbler by his side there is a bunch of withered violets. His hair is brown and crisp, and his lips are red as a pomegranate, and he has large and dreamy eyes. He is trying to finish a play for the Director of the Theatre, but he is too cold to write any more. There is no fire in the grate, and hunger has made him faint."

"I will wait with you one night longer," said the Swallow, who really had a good heart. "Shall I take him another ruby?"

"Alas! I have no ruby now," said the Prince; "my eyes are all that I have left. They are made of rare sapphires, which were brought out of India a thousand years ago. Pluck out one of them and take it to him. He will sell it to the jeweller, and buy food and firewood, and finish his play."

"Dear Prince," said the Swallow, "I cannot do that;" and he began to weep.

"Swallow, Swallow, little Swallow," said the Prince, "do as I command you."

So the Swallow plucked out the Prince's eye, and flew away to the student's garret. It was easy enough to get in, as there was a hole in the roof. Through this he darted, and came into the room. The young man had his head buried in his hands, so he did not hear the flutter of the bird's wings, and when he looked up he found the beautiful sapphire lying on the withered violets.

"I am beginning to be appreciated," he cried;

"this is from some great admirer. Now I can finish my play," and he looked quite happy.

The next day the Swallow flew down to the harbour. He sat on the mast of a large vessel and watched the sailors hauling big chests out of the hold with ropes. "Heave a-hoy!" they shouted as each chest came up. "I am going to Egypt!" cried the Swallow, but nobody minded, and when the moon rose he flew back to the Happy Prince.

"I am come to bid you good-bye," he cried.

"Swallow, Swallow, little Swallow," said the Prince, "will you not stay with me one night longer?"

"It is winter," answered the Swallow, "and the chill snow will soon be here. In Egypt the sun is warm on the green palm-trees, and the crocodiles lie in the mud and look lazily about them. My companions are building a nest in the Temple of Baalbec, and the pink and white doves are watching them, and cooing to each other. Dear Prince, I must leave you, but I will never forget you, and next spring I will bring you back two beautiful jewels in place of those you have given away. The ruby shall be redder than a red rose, and the sapphire shall be as blue as the great sea."

"In the square below," said the Happy Prince, "there stands a little match-girl. She has let her matches fall in the gutter, and they are all spoiled.

Her father will beat her if she does not bring home some money, and she is crying. She has no shoes or stockings, and her little head is bare. Pluck out my other eye, and give it to her, and her father will not beat her."

"I will stay with you one night longer," said the Swallow, "but I cannot pluck out your eye. You would be quite blind then."

"Swallow, Swallow, little Swallow," said the Prince, "do as I command you."

So he plucked out the Prince's other eye, and darted down with it. He swooped past the match-girl, and slipped the jewel into the palm of her hand. "What a lovely bit of glass," cried the little girl; and she ran home, laughing.

Then the Swallow came back to the Prince. "You are blind now," he said, "so I will stay with you always."

"No, little Swallow," said the poor Prince, "you must go away to Egypt."

"I will stay with you always," said the Swallow, and he slept at the Prince's feet.

All the next day he sat on the Prince's shoulder, and told him stories of what he had seen in strange lands. He told him of the red ibises, who stand in long rows on the banks of the Nile, and catch gold fish in their beaks; of the Sphinx, who is as old as the world itself, and lives in the desert, and knows everything; of the merchants, who walk slowly by the side of their camels, and carry amber beads in their hands; of the King of the Mountains of the Moon, who is as black as ebony, and worships a large crystal; of the great green snake that sleeps in a palm-tree, and has twenty priests to feed it with honey-cakes; and of the pygmies who sail over a big lake on large flat leaves, and are always at war with the butterflies.

"Dear little Swallow," said the Prince, "you tell me of marvellous things, but more marvellous than anything is the suffering of men and of women. There is no Mystery so great as Misery. Fly over my city, little Swallow, and tell me what you see there."

So the Swallow flew over the great city, and saw the rich making merry in their beautiful houses, while the beggars were sitting at the gates. He flew into dark lanes, and saw the white faces of starving children looking out listlessly at the black streets. Under the archway of a bridge two little boys were lying in one another's arms to try and keep themselves warm. "How hungry we are!" they said. "You must not lie here," shouted the Watchman, and they wandered out into the rain.

Then he flew back and told the Prince what he had seen.

"I am covered with fine gold," said the Prince, "you must take it off, leaf by leaf, and give it to my poor; the living always think that gold can make them happy."

Leaf after leaf of the fine gold the Swallow picked off, till the Happy Prince looked quite dull and grey. Leaf after leaf of the fine gold he brought to the poor, and the children's faces grew rosier, and they laughed and played games in the street. "We have bread now!" they cried.

Then the snow came, and after the snow came the frost. The streets looked as if they were made of silver, they were so bright and glistening; long icicles like crystal daggers hung down from the eaves of the houses, everybody went about in furs, and the little boys wore scarlet caps and skated on the ice.

The poor little Swallow grew colder and colder, but he would not leave the Prince, he loved him too well. He picked up crumbs outside the baker's door when the baker was not looking, and tried to keep himself warm by flapping his wings.

But at last he knew that he was going to die. He had just strength to fly up to the Prince's shoulder once more. "Good-bye, dear Prince!" he murmured, "will you let me kiss your hand?"

"I am glad that you are going to Egypt at last, little Swallow," said the Prince, "you have stayed too long here; but you must kiss me on the lips, for I love you."

"It is not to Egypt that I am going," said the Swallow. "I am going to the House of Death. Death is the brother of Sleep, is he not?"

And he kissed the Happy Prince on the lips, and fell down dead at his feet.

At that moment a curious crack sounded inside the statue, as if something had broken. The fact is that the leaden heart had snapped right in two. It certainly was a dreadfully hard frost.

Early the next morning the Mayor was walking in the square below in company with the Town Councillors. As they passed the column he looked up at the statue: "Dear me! how shabby the Happy Prince looks!" he said.

"How shabby indeed!" cried the Town Councillors, who always agreed with the Mayor, and they went up to look at it.

"The ruby has fallen out of his sword, his eyes are gone, and he is golden no longer," said the Mayor; "in fact, he is little better than a beggar!"

"Little better than a beggar," said the Town Councillors.

"And here is actually a dead bird at his feet!" continued the Mayor. "We must really issue a proclamation that birds are not to be allowed to die here." And the Town Clerk made a note of the suggestion.

So they pulled down the statue of the Happy Prince. "As he is no longer beautiful he is no longer useful," said the Art Professor at the University.

Then they melted the statue in a furnace, and the Mayor held a meeting of the Corporation to decide what was to be done with the metal. "We must have another statue, of course," he said, "and it shall be a statue of myself."

"Of myself," said each of the Town Councillors, and they quarrelled. When I last heard of them they were quarrelling still.

"What a strange thing!" said the overseer of the workmen at the foundry. "This broken lead heart will not melt in the furnace. We must throw it away." So they threw it on a dust-heap where the dead Swallow was also lying.

"Bring me the two most precious things in the city," said God to one of His Angels; and the Angel brought Him the leaden heart and the dead bird.

"You have rightly chosen," said God, "for in my garden of Paradise this little bird shall sing for ever-more, and in my city of gold the Happy Prince shall praise me."

RICHARD GARNETT

Richard Garnett (1835–1906) started work as an assistant librarian at the British Museum in 1851, and ended up as the Chief Keeper of the Printed Books. Garnett's literary activity included translations from Greek, German, Italian, Spanish, and Portuguese and several books of verse. He wrote biographies of Thomas Carlyle, John Milton, William Blake and many others and was a contributor to the *Encyclopaedia Britannica* and the *Dictionary of National Biography*. He also edited unpublished poems of Shelley and had a strong interest in astrology. The connection between all of these activities is that most of the authors concerned wrote fantastical works of some kind. In 1888, he published *The Twilight of the Gods and Other Tales*, a collection of fables and fantasy stories.

"So you won't sell me your soul?" said the devil.

"Thank you," replied the student, "I had rather keep it myself, if it's all the same to you."

"But it's not all the same to me. I want it very particularly. Come, I'll be liberal. I said twenty years. You can have thirty."

The student shook his head.

"Forty!"

Another shake.

"Fifty!"

As before.

"Now," said the devil, "I know I'm going to do a foolish thing, but I cannot bear to see a clever, spirited young man throw himself away. I'll make you another kind of offer. We won't have any bargain at present, but I will push you on in the world for the next forty years. This day forty years I come back and ask you for a boon; not your soul, mind, or anything not perfectly in your power to grant. If you give it, we are quits; if not, I fly away with you. What say you to this?"

The student reflected for some minutes. "Agreed," he said at last.

Scarcely had the devil disappeared, which he did instantaneously, ere a messenger reined in his smoking steed at the gate of the University of Cordova (the judicious reader will already have remarked that Lucifer could never have been allowed inside a Christian seat of learning), and, inquiring for the student Gerbert, presented him with the Emperor Otho's nomination to the Abbacy of Bobbio, in consideration, said the document, of his virtue and learning, well-nigh miraculous in one so young. Such messengers were frequent visitors during Gerbert's prosperous career. Abbot, bishop, archbishop, cardinal, he was ultimately enthroned Pope on April 2, 999, and assumed the appellation of Silvester the Second. It was then a general belief that the world would come to an end in the following year, a catastrophe which to many seemed the more imminent from the election of a chief pastor whose celebrity as a theologian, though not inconsiderable, by no means equalled his reputation as a necromancer.

The world, notwithstanding, revolved scatheless through the dreaded twelvemonth, and early in the first year of the eleventh century Gerbert was sitting peacefully in his study, perusing a book of magic. Volumes of algebra, astrology, alchemy, Aristotelian philosophy, and other such light reading filled his bookcase; and on a table stood an improved clock of his invention, next to his introduction of the Arabic numerals his chief legacy to posterity. Suddenly a sound of wings was heard, and Lucifer stood by his side.

"It is a long time," said the fiend, "since I have had the pleasure of seeing you. I have now called to remind you of our little contract, concluded this day forty years."

"You remember," said Silvester, "that you are not to ask anything exceeding my power to perform."

"I have no such intention," said Lucifer. "On the contrary, I am about to solicit a favour which can be bestowed by you alone. You are Pope, I desire that you would make me a Cardinal."

"In the expectation, I presume," returned Gerbert, "of becoming Pope on the next vacancy."

"An expectation," replied Lucifer, "which I may most reasonably entertain, considering my enormous wealth, my proficiency in intrigue, and the present condition of the Sacred College."

"You would doubtless," said Gerbert, "endeavour to subvert the foundations of the Faith, and, by a course of profligacy and licentiousness, render the Holy See odious and contemptible."

"On the contrary," said the fiend, "I would extirpate heresy, and all learning and knowledge as inevitably tending thereunto. I would suffer no man to read but the priest, and confine his reading to his breviary. I would burn your books together with your bones on the first convenient opportunity. I would observe an austere propriety of conduct, and be especially careful not to loosen one rivet in the tremendous yoke I was forging for the minds and consciences of mankind."

"If it be so," said Gerbert, "let's be off!"

"What!" exclaimed Lucifer, "you are willing to accompany me to the infernal regions!"

"Assuredly, rather than be accessory to the burning of Plato and Aristotle, and give place to the darkness against which I have been contending all my life."

"Gerbert," replied the demon, "this is arrant trifling. Know you not that no good man can enter my dominions? that, were such a thing possible, my empire would become intolerable to me, and I should be compelled to abdicate?"

"I do know it," said Gerbert, "and hence I have been able to receive your visit with composure."

"Gerbert," said the devil, with tears in his eyes, "I put it to you—is this fair, is this honest? I undertake to promote your interests in the world; I fulfil my promise abundantly. You obtain through my instrumentality a position to which you could never otherwise have aspired. Often have I had a hand in the election of a Pope, but never before have I contributed to confer the tiara on one eminent for virtue and learning. You profit by my assistance to the full, and now take advantage of an adventitious circumstance to deprive me of my reasonable guerdon. It is my constant experience that the good people are much more slippery than the sinners, and drive much harder bargains."

"Lucifer," answered Gerbert, "I have always sought to treat you as a gentleman, hoping that you would approve yourself such in return. I will not inquire whether it was entirely in harmony with this character to seek to intimidate me into compliance with your demand by threatening me with a penalty which you well knew could not be enforced. I will overlook this little irregularity, and concede even more than you have requested. You have asked to be a Cardinal. I will make you Pope——"

"Ha!" exclaimed Lucifer, and an internal glow suffused his sooty hide, as the light of a fading ember is revived by breathing upon it.

"For twelve hours," continued Gerbert. "At the expiration of that time we will consider the matter further; and if, as I anticipate, you are more anxious to divest yourself of the Papal dignity than you were to assume it, I promise to bestow upon you any boon you may ask within my power to grant, and not plainly inconsistent with religion or morals."

"Done!" cried the demon. Gerbert uttered some

cabalistic words, and in a moment the apartment held two Pope Silvesters, entirely indistinguishable save by their attire, and the fact that one limped slightly with the left foot.

"You will find the Pontifical apparel in this cupboard," said Gerbert, and, taking his book of magic with him, he retreated through a masked door to a secret chamber. As the door closed behind him he chuckled, and muttered to himself, "Poor old Lucifer! Sold again!"

If Lucifer was sold he did not seem to know it. He approached a large slab of silver which did duty as a mirror, and contemplated his personal appearance with some dissatisfaction.

"I certainly don't look half so well without my horns," he soliloquised, "and I am sure I shall miss my tail most grievously."

A tiara and a train, however, made fair amends for the deficient appendages, and Lucifer now looked every inch a Pope. He was about to call the master of the ceremonies, and summon a consistory, when the door was burst open, and seven cardinals, brandishing poniards, rushed into the room.

"Down with the sorcerer!" they cried, as they seized and gagged him.

"Death to the Saracen!"

"Practises algebra, and other devilish arts!"

"Knows Greek!"

"Talks Arabic!"

"Reads Hebrew!"

"Burn him!"

"Smother him!"

"Let him be deposed by a general council," said a young and inexperienced Cardinal.

"Heaven forbid!" said an old and wary one, *sotto voce*.

Lucifer struggled frantically, but the feeble frame he was doomed to inhabit for the next eleven hours was speedily exhausted. Bound and helpless, he swooned away.

"Brethren," said one of the senior cardinals, "it hath been delivered by the exorcists that a sorcerer or other individual in league with the demon doth usually bear upon his person some visible token of his infernal compact. I propose that we forthwith institute a search for this stigma, the discovery of which may contribute to justify our proceedings in the eyes of the world."

"I heartily approve of our brother Anno's proposition," said another, "the rather as we cannot possibly fail to discover such a mark, if, indeed, we desire to find it."

The search was accordingly instituted, and had not proceeded far ere a simultaneous yell from all the seven cardinals indicated that their investigation had brought more to light than they had ventured to expect.

The Holy Father had a cloven foot!

For the next five minutes the Cardinals remained utterly stunned, silent, and stupefied with amazement. As they gradually recovered their faculties it would have become manifest to a nice observer that the Pope had risen very considerably in their good opinion.

"This is an affair requiring very mature deliberation," said one.

"I always feared that we might be proceeding too precipitately," said another.

"It is written, 'the devils believe,'" said a third: "the Holy Father, therefore, is not a heretic at any rate."

"Brethren," said Anno, "this affair, as our brother Benno well remarks, doth indeed call for mature deliberation. I therefore propose that, instead of smothering his Holiness with cushions, as originally contemplated, we immure him for the present in the dungeon adjoining hereunto, and, after spending the night in meditation and prayer, resume the consideration of the business tomorrow morning."

"Informing the officials of the palace," said

Benno, "that his Holiness has retired for his devotions, and desires on no account to be disturbed."

"A pious fraud," said Anno, "which not one of the Fathers would for a moment have scrupled to commit."

The Cardinals accordingly lifted the still insensible Lucifer, and bore him carefully, almost tenderly, to the apartment appointed for his detention. Each would fain have lingered in hopes of his recovery, but each felt that the eyes of his six brethren were upon him: and all, therefore, retired simultaneously, each taking a key of the cell.

Lucifer regained consciousness almost immediately afterwards. He had the most confused idea of the circumstances which had involved him in his present scrape, and could only say to himself that if they were the usual concomitants of the Papal dignity, these were by no means to his taste, and he wished he had been made acquainted with them sooner. The dungeon was not only perfectly dark, but horribly cold, and the poor devil in his present form had no latent store of infernal heat to draw upon. His teeth chattered, he shivered in every limb, and felt devoured with hunger and thirst. There is much probability in the assertion of some of his biographers that it was on this occasion that he invented ardent spirits; but, even if he did, the mere conception of a glass of brandy could only increase his sufferings. So the long January night wore wearily on, and Lucifer seemed likely to expire from inanition, when a key turned in the lock, and Cardinal Anno cautiously glided in, bearing a lamp, a loaf, half a cold roast kid, and a bottle of wine.

"I trust," he said, bowing courteously, "that I may be excused any slight breach of etiquette of which I may render myself culpable from the difficulty under which I labour of determining whether, under present circumstances, 'Your Holiness,' or 'Your Infernal Majesty' be the form of address most befitting me to employ."

"Bub-ub-bub-boo," went Lucifer, who still had the gag in his mouth.

"Heavens!" exclaimed the Cardinal, "I crave your Infernal Holiness's forgiveness. What a lamentable oversight!"

And, relieving Lucifer from his gag and bonds, he set out the refection, upon which the demon fell voraciously.

"Why the devil, if I may so express myself," pursued Anno, "did not your Holiness inform us that you *were* the devil? Not a hand would then have been raised against you. I have myself been seeking all my life for the audience now happily vouchsafed me. Whence this mistrust of your faithful Anno, who has served you so loyally and zealously these many years?"

Lucifer pointed significantly to the gag and fetters.

"I shall never forgive myself," protested the Cardinal, "for the part I have borne in this unfortunate transaction. Next to ministering to your Majesty's bodily necessities, there is nothing I have so much at heart as to express my penitence. But I entreat your Majesty to remember that I believed myself to be acting in your Majesty's interest by overthrowing a magician who was accustomed to send your Majesty upon errands, and who might at any time enclose you in a box, and cast you into the sea. It is deplorable that your Majesty's most devoted servants should have been thus misled."

"Reasons of State," suggested Lucifer.

"I trust that they no longer operate," said the Cardinal. "However, the Sacred College is now fully possessed of the whole matter: it is therefore unnecessary to pursue this department of the subject further. I would now humbly crave leave to confer with your Majesty, or rather, perhaps, your Holiness, since I am about to speak of spiritual things, on the important and delicate point of your Holiness's successor. I am ignorant how long your Holiness proposes to occupy the Apostolic chair; but of course you are aware that public opinion will not suffer you to hold it for a term exceeding that of the pontificate of Peter. A vacancy, therefore, must one day occur; and I am humbly to represent that the office could not be filled by one more congenial than myself to the present incumbent, or on whom he could more fully rely to carry out in every respect his views and intentions."

And the Cardinal proceeded to detail various circumstances of his past life, which certainly seemed to corroborate his assertion. He had not, however, proceeded far ere he was disturbed by the grating of another key in the lock, and had just time to whisper impressively, "Beware of Benno," ere he dived under a table.

Benno was also provided with a lamp, wine, and cold viands. Warned by the other lamp and the remains of Lucifer's repast that some colleague had been beforehand with him, and not knowing how many more might be in the field, he came briefly to the point as regarded the Papacy, and preferred his claim in much the same manner as Anno. While he was earnestly cautioning Lucifer against this Cardinal as one who could and would cheat the very Devil himself, another key turned in the lock, and Benno escaped under the table, where Anno immediately inserted his finger into his right eye. The little squeal consequent upon this occurrence Lucifer successfully smothered by a fit of coughing.

Cardinal No. 3, a Frenchman, bore a Bayonne ham, and exhibited the same disgust as Benno on seeing himself forestalled. So far as his requests transpired they were moderate, but no one knows where he would have stopped if he had not been scared by the advent of Cardinal No. 4. Up to this time he had only asked for an inexhaustible purse, power to call up the Devil *ad libitum*, and a ring of invisibility to allow him free access to his mistress, who was unfortunately a married woman.

Cardinal No. 4 chiefly wanted to be put into the way of poisoning Cardinal No. 5; and Cardinal No. 5 preferred the same petition as respected Cardinal No. 4.

Cardinal No. 6, an Englishman, demanded the reversion of the Archbishoprics of Canterbury and York, with the faculty of holding them together, and of unlimited non-residence. In the course of his harangue he made use of the phrase *non obstantibus*, of which Lucifer immediately took a note.

What the seventh Cardinal would have solicited is not known, for he had hardly opened his mouth when the twelfth hour expired, and Lucifer, regaining his vigour with his shape, sent the Prince of the Church spinning to the other end of the room, and split the marble table with a single stroke of his tail. The six crouched and huddling Cardinals cowered revealed to one another, and at the same time enjoyed the spectacle of his Holiness darting through the stone ceiling, which yielded like a film to his passage, and closed up afterwards as if nothing had happened. After the first shock of dismay they unanimously rushed to the door, but found it bolted on the outside. There was no other exit, and no means of giving an alarm. In this emergency the demeanour of the Italian Cardinals set a bright example to their ultramontane colleagues. "*Bisogna, pazienzia,*" they said, as they shrugged their shoulders. Nothing could exceed the mutual politeness of Cardinals Anno and Benno, unless that of the two who had sought to poison each other. The Frenchman was held to have gravely derogated from good manners by alluding to this circumstance, which had reached his ears while he was under the table: and the Englishman swore so outrageously at the plight in which he found himself that the Italians then and there silently registered a vow that none of his nation should ever be Pope, a maxim which, with one exception, has been observed to this day.

Lucifer, meanwhile, had repaired to Silvester, whom he found arrayed in all the insignia of his dignity; of which, as he remarked, he thought his visitor had probably had enough.

"I should think so indeed," replied Lucifer. "But at the same time I feel myself fully repaid for all I have undergone by the assurance of the loyalty of my friends and admirers, and the conviction that it is needless for me to devote any considerable amount of personal attention to ecclesiastical affairs. I now claim the promised boon, which it will be in no way inconsistent with thy functions to grant, seeing that it is a work of mercy. I demand that the Cardinals be released, and that their conspiracy against thee, by which I alone suffered, be buried in oblivion."

"I hoped you would carry them all off," said Gerbert, with an expression of disappointment.

"Thank you," said the Devil. "It is more to my interest to leave them where they are."

So the dungeon-door was unbolted, and the Cardinals came forth, sheepish and crestfallen. If, after all, they did less mischief than Lucifer had expected from them, the cause was their entire bewilderment by what had passed, and their utter inability to penetrate the policy of Gerbert, who henceforth devoted himself even with ostentation to good works. They could never quite satisfy themselves whether they were speaking to the Pope or to the Devil, and when under the latter impression habitually emitted propositions which Gerbert justly stigmatised as rash, temerarious, and scandalous. They plagued him with allusions to certain matters mentioned in their interviews with Lucifer, with which they naturally but erroneously supposed him to be conversant, and worried him by continual nods and titterings as they glanced at his nether extremities. To abolish this nuisance, and at the same time silence sundry unpleasant rumours which had somehow got abroad, Gerbert devised the ceremony of kissing the Pope's feet, which, in a grievously mutilated form, endures to this day. The stupefaction of the Cardinals on discovering that the Holy Father had lost his hoof surpasses all description, and they went to their graves without having obtained the least insight into the mystery.

H. P. BLAVATSKY

Madame Blavatsky (Helena Petrovna Blavatsky[a], née Hahn von Rottenstern, 1831–1891) was a Russian mystic who co-founded the Theosophical Society in 1875, which still exists today. Blavatsky's mother was a writer, and both her parents seem to have been interested in alternative religions. Blavatsky was well travelled in Europe and she also claimed to have travelled in Asia and to have trained in Tibet. These claims were probably fictitious but they have become part of the fantasy tropes of 'ancient wisdom' and 'mystics in the mountains' now so common that they are a source of reliable humour in the fantasies of Terry Pratchett. In the 1870s, Madame Blavatsky practised as a spirit medium, and in the 1880s she moved to India and then to Ceylon, and although very much influenced by Hinduism, became a Buddhist. She remains an influence on the New Age movements. It is easy to dismiss Blavatsky as a charlatan, but there was a spiritual truth to her teachings that influenced many, and that she could be so influential was in part due to her talents as a writer. Here is a piece of her fiction.

The Ensouled Violin

In the year 1828, an old German, a music teacher, came to Paris with his pupil and settled unostentatiously in one of the quiet faubourgs of the metropolis. The first rejoiced in the name of Samuel Klaus; the second answered to the more poetical appellation of Franz Stenio. The younger man was a violinist, gifted, as rumour went, with extraordinary, almost miraculous talent. Yet as he was poor and had not hitherto made a name for himself in Europe, he remained for several years in the capital of France—the heart and pulse of capricious continental fashion—unknown and unappreciated. Franz was a Styrian by birth, and, at the time of the event to be presently described, he was a young man considerably under thirty. A philosopher and a dreamer by nature, imbued with all the mystic oddities of true genius, he reminded one of some of the heroes in Hoffmann's *Contes Fantastiques*. His earlier existence had been a very unusual, in fact, quite an eccentric one, and its history must be briefly told—for the better understanding of the present story.

Born of very pious country people, in a quiet burg among the Styrian Alps; nursed "by the native gnomes who watched over his cradle"; growing up in the weird atmosphere of the ghouls and vampires who play such a prominent part in the household of every Styrian and Slavonian in Southern Austria; educated later, as a student, in the shadow of the old Rhenish castles of Germany; Franz from his childhood had passed through every emotional stage on the plane of the so-called "supernatural." He had also studied at one time the "occult arts" with an enthusiastic disciple of Paracelsus and Kunrath; alchemy had few theoretical secrets for him; and he had dabbled in "ceremonial magic" and "sorcery" with some Hungarian Tziganes. Yet he loved above all else music, and above music—his violin.

At the age of twenty-two he suddenly gave up his practical studies in the occult, and from that day, though as devoted as ever in thought to the beautiful Grecian Gods, he surrendered himself entirely to his art. Of his classic studies he had retained only that which related to the muses—Euterpe especially, at whose altar he worshipped—and Orpheus whose magic lyre he tried to emulate with his violin. Except his dreamy belief in the nymphs and the sirens, on account probably of the double relationship of the latter to the muses through Calliope and Orpheus, he was interested but little in the matters of this sublunary world. All his aspirations mounted, like incense, with the wave of the heavenly harmony that he drew from his instrument, to a higher and a nobler sphere. He dreamed awake, and lived a real though an enchanted life only during those hours when his magic bow carried him along the wave of sound to the Pagan Olympus, to the feet of Euterpe. A strange child he had ever been in his own home, where tales of magic and witchcraft grow out of every inch of the soil; a still stranger boy he had become, until finally he had blossomed into manhood, without one single characteristic of youth. Never had a fair face attracted his attention; not for one moment had his thoughts turned from his solitary studies to a life beyond that of a mystic Bohemian. Content with his own company, he had thus passed the best years of his youth and manhood with his violin for his chief idol, and with the Gods and Goddesses of old Greece for his audience, in perfect ignorance of practical life. His whole existence had been one long day of dreams, of melody and sunlight, and he had never felt any other aspirations.

How useless, but oh, how glorious those dreams! how vivid! and why should he desire any better fate? Was he not all that he wanted to be, transformed in a second of thought into one or another hero; from Orpheus, who held all nature breathless, to the urchin who piped away under the plane tree to the naiads of Calirrhoë's crystal fountain? Did not the swift-footed nymphs frolic at his beck and call to the sound of the magic flute of the Arcadian shepherd—who was himself? Behold, the Goddess of Love and Beauty herself descending from on high, attracted by the sweet-voiced notes of his violin! . . . Yet there came a time when he preferred Syrinx to Aphrodite—not as the fair nymph pursued by Pan, but after her transformation by the merciful Gods into the reed out of which the frustrated God of the Shepherds had made his magic pipe. For also, with time, ambition grows and is rarely satisfied. When he tried to emulate on his violin the enchanting sounds that resounded in his mind, the whole of Parnassus kept silent under the spell, or joined in heavenly chorus; but the audience he finally craved was composed of more than the Gods sung by Hesiod, verily of the most appreciative *mélomanes* of European capitals. He felt jealous of the magic pipe, and would fain have had it at his command.

"Oh! that I could allure a nymph into my beloved violin!"—he often cried, after awakening from one of his day-dreams. "Oh, that I could only span in spirit flight the abyss of Time! Oh, that I could find myself for one short day a partaker of the secret arts of the Gods, a God myself, in the sight and hearing of enraptured humanity; and, having learned the mystery of the lyre of Orpheus, or secured within my violin a siren, thereby benefit mortals to my own glory!"

Thus, having for long years dreamed in the company of the Gods of his fancy, he now took to dreaming of the transitory glories of fame upon this earth. But at this time he was suddenly called home by his widowed mother from one of the German universities where he had lived for the last year or two. This was an event which brought his plans to an end, at least so far as the immediate future was concerned, for he had hitherto drawn upon her alone for his meagre pittance, and his means were not sufficient for an independent life outside his native place.

His return had a very unexpected result. His mother, whose only love he was on earth, died soon after she had welcomed her Benjamin back; and the good wives of the burg exercised their swift tongues for many a month after as to the real causes of that death.

Frau Stenio, before Franz's return, was a healthy, buxom, middle-aged body, strong and hearty. She was a pious and a God-fearing soul too, who had never failed in saying her prayers, nor had missed an early mass for years during his absence. On the first Sunday after her son had settled at home—a day that she had been longing for and had anticipated for months in joyous visions, in which she saw him kneeling by her side in the little church on the hill— she called him from the foot of the stairs. The hour had come when her pious dream was to be realized, and she was waiting for him, carefully wiping the dust from the prayer-book he had used in his boyhood. But instead of Franz, it was his violin that responded to her call, mixing its sonorous voice with the rather cracked tones of the peal of the merry Sunday bells. The fond mother was somewhat shocked at hearing the prayer-inspiring sounds drowned by the weird, fantastic notes of the "Dance of the Witches"; they seemed to her so unearthly and mocking. But she almost fainted upon hearing the definite refusal of her well-beloved son to go to church. He never went to church, he coolly remarked. It was loss of time; besides which, the loud peals of the old church organ jarred on his nerves. Nothing should induce him to submit to the torture of listening to that cracked organ. He was firm, and nothing could move him. To her supplications and remonstrances he put an end by offering to play for her a "Hymn to the Sun" he had just composed.

From that memorable Sunday morning, Frau Stenio lost her usual serenity of mind. She hastened to lay her sorrows and seek for consolation at the foot of the confessional; but that which she heard in response from the stern priest filled her gentle and unsophisticated soul with dismay and almost with despair. A feeling of fear, a sense of profound terror, which soon became a chronic state with her, pursued her from that moment; her nights became disturbed and sleepless, her days passed in prayer and lamentations. In her maternal anxiety for the salvation of her beloved son's soul, and for his *post mortem* welfare, she made a series of rash vows. Finding that neither the Latin petition to the Mother of God written for her by her spiritual adviser, nor yet the humble supplications in German, addressed by herself to every saint she had reason to believe was residing in Paradise, worked the desired effect, she took to pilgrimages to distant shrines. During one of these journeys to a holy chapel situated high up in the mountains, she caught cold, amidst the glaciers of the Tyrol, and redescended only to take to a sick bed, from which she arose no more. Frau Stenio's vow had led her, in one sense, to the desired result. The poor woman was now given an opportunity of seeking out in *propriâ personâ* the saints she had believed in so well, and of pleading face to face for the recreant son, who refused adherence to them and to the Church, scoffed at monk and confessional, and held the organ in such horror.

Franz sincerely lamented his mother's death. Unaware of being the indirect cause of it, he felt no remorse; but selling the modest household goods and chattels, light in purse and heart, he resolved to travel on foot for a year or two, before settling down to any definite profession.

A hazy desire to see the great cities of Europe, and to try his luck in France, lurked at the bottom of this travelling project, but his Bohemian habits of life were too strong to be abruptly abandoned. He placed his small capital with a banker for a rainy day, and started on his pedestrian journey *viâ* Germany and Austria. His violin paid for his board and lodging in the inns and farms on his way, and he passed his days in the green fields and in the solemn silent woods, face to face with Nature, dreaming all the time as usual with his eyes open. During the three months of his pleasant travels to and fro, he never descended for one moment from Parnassus; but, as an alchemist transmutes lead into gold, so he transformed everything on his way into a song of Hesiod or Anacreon. Every evening, while fiddling for his supper and bed, whether on a green lawn or in the hall of a rustic inn, his fancy changed the whole scene for him. Village swains and maidens became transfigured into Arcadian shepherds and nymphs. The sand-covered floor was now a green sward; the uncouth couples spinning round in a measured waltz with the wild grace of tamed bears became priests and priestesses of Terpsichore; the bulky, cherry-cheeked and blue-eyed daughters of rural Germany were the Hesperides circling around the trees laden with the golden apples. Nor did the melodious strains of the Arcadian demi-gods piping on their syrinxes, and audible but to his own enchanted ear, vanish with the dawn. For no sooner was the curtain of sleep raised from his eyes than he would sally forth into a new magic realm of day-dreams. On his way to some dark and solemn pine-forest, he played incessantly, to himself and to everything else. He fiddled to the green hill, and forthwith the mountain and the moss-covered rocks moved forward to hear him the better, as they had done at the sound of the Orphean lyre. He fiddled to the merry-voiced brook, to the hurrying river, and both slackened their speed and stopped their waves, and, becoming silent, seemed to listen to him in an entranced rapture. Even the long-legged stork who stood meditatively on one leg on the thatched top of the rustic mill, gravely resolving unto himself the problem of his too-long existence, sent out after him a long and strident cry, screeching, "Art thou Orpheus himself, O Stenio?"

It was a period of full bliss, of a daily and almost hourly exaltation. The last words of his dying mother, whispering to him of the horrors of eternal condemnation, had left him unaffected, and the only vision her warning evoked in him was that of Pluto. By a ready association of ideas, he saw the lord of the dark nether kingdom greeting him as he had greeted the husband of Eurydice before him. Charmed with the magic sounds of his violin, the wheel of Ixion was at a standstill once more, thus affording relief to the wretched seducer of Juno, and giving the lie to those who claim eternity for the duration of the punishment of condemned sinners. He perceived Tantalus forgetting his never-ceasing thirst, and smacking his lips as he drank in the heaven-born melody; the stone of Sisyphus becoming motionless, the Furies themselves smiling on him, and the sovereign of the gloomy regions delighted, and awarding preference to his violin over the lyre of Orpheus. Taken *au sérieux*, mythology thus seems a decided antidote to fear, in the face of theological threats, especially when strengthened with an insane and passionate love of music; with Franz, Euterpe proved always victorious in every contest, aye, even with Hell itself!

But there is an end to everything, and very soon Franz had to give up uninterrupted dreaming. He had reached the university town where dwelt his old violin teacher, Samuel Klaus. When this antiquated musician found that his beloved and favourite pupil, Franz, had been left poor in purse and still poorer in earthly affections, he felt his strong attachment to the boy awaken with tenfold force. He took Franz to his heart, and forthwith adopted him as his son.

The old teacher reminded people of one of those grotesque figures which look as if they had just stepped out of some mediæval panel. And yet Klaus, with his fantastic *allures* of a night-goblin, had the most loving heart, as tender as that of a woman, and the self-sacrificing nature of an old Christian martyr. When Franz had briefly narrated to him the history of his last few years, the professor took him by the hand, and leading him into his study simply said:

"Stop with me, and put an end to your Bohemian life. Make yourself famous. I am old and childless and will be your father. Let us live together and forget all save fame."

And forthwith he offered to proceed with Franz to Paris, *viâ* several large German cities, where they would stop to give concerts.

In a few days Klaus succeeded in making Franz forget his vagrant life and its artistic independence, and reawakened in his pupil his now dormant ambition and desire for worldly fame. Hitherto, since his mother's death, he had been content to receive applause only from the Gods and Goddesses who inhabited his vivid fancy; now he began to crave once more for the admiration of mortals. Under the clever and careful training of old Klaus his remarkable talent gained in strength and powerful charm with every day, and his reputation grew and expanded with every city and town wherein he made himself heard. His ambition was being rapidly realized; the presiding genii of various musical centres to whose patronage his talent was submitted soon proclaimed him *the one* violinist of the day, and the public declared loudly that he stood unrivalled by any one whom they had ever heard. These laudations very soon made both master and pupil completely lose their heads.

But Paris was less ready with such appreciation. Paris makes reputations for itself, and will take none on faith. They had been living in it for almost three years, and were still climbing with difficulty the artist's Calvary, when an event occurred which put an end even to their most modest expectations. The first arrival of Niccolo Paganini was suddenly heralded, and threw Lutetia into a convulsion of expectation. The unparalleled artist arrived, and— all Paris fell at once at his feet.

II.

Now it is a well-known fact that a superstition born in the dark days of mediæval superstition, and surviving almost to the middle of the present century, attributed all such abnormal, out-of-the-way talent as that of Paganini to "supernatural" agency. Every great and marvellous artist had been accused in his day of dealings with the devil. A few instances will suffice to refresh the reader's memory.

Tartini, the great composer and violinist of the XVIIth century, was denounced as one who got his best inspirations from the Evil One, with whom he was, it was said, in regular league. This accusation was, of course, due to the almost magical impression he produced upon his audiences. His inspired performance on the violin secured for him in his native country the title of "Master of Nations." The *Sonate du Diable*, also called "Tartini's Dream"—as every one who has heard it will be ready to testify—is the most weird melody ever heard or invented: hence, the marvellous composition has become the source of endless legends. Nor were they entirely baseless, since it was he, himself, who was shown to have originated them. Tartini confessed to having written it on awakening from a dream, in which he had heard his sonata performed by Satan, for his benefit, and in consequence of a bargain made with his infernal majesty.

Several famous singers, even, whose exceptional voices struck the hearers with superstitious admiration, have not escaped a like accusation. Pasta's splendid voice was attributed in her day to the fact that, three months before her birth, the diva's mother was carried during a trance to heaven, and there treated to a vocal concert of seraphs. Malibran was indebted for her voice to St. Cecilia, while others said she owed it to a demon who watched over her cradle and sung the baby to sleep. Finally, Paganini—the unrivalled performer, the mean Italian, who like Dryden's Jubal striking on the "chorded shell" forced the throngs that followed him to worship the divine sounds produced, and made people say that "less than a God could not dwell within the hollow of his violin"—Paganini left a legend too.

The almost supernatural art of the greatest violin-player that the world has ever known was often speculated upon, never understood. The effect produced by him on his audience was literally marvellous, overpowering. The great Rossini is said to have wept like a sentimental German maiden on hearing him play for the first time. The Princess Elisa of Lucca, a sister of the great Napoleon, in whose service Paganini was, as director of her private orchestra, for a long time was unable to hear him play without fainting. In women he produced nervous fits and hysterics at his will; stout-hearted men he drove to frenzy. He changed cowards into heroes and made the bravest soldiers feel like so many nervous school-girls. Is it to be wondered at, then, that hundreds of weird tales circulated for long years about and around the mysterious Genoese, that modern Orpheus of Europe? One of these was especially ghastly. It was rumoured, and was believed by more people than would probably like to confess it, that the strings of his violin were made of *human intestines, according to all the rules and requirements of the Black Art.*

Exaggerated as this idea may seem to some, it has nothing impossible in it; and it is more than probable that it was this legend that led to the extraordinary events which we are about to narrate. Human organs are often used by the Eastern Black Magician, so-called, and it is an averred fact that some Bengâlî Tântrikas (reciters of *tantras,* or "invocations to the demon," as a reverend writer has described them) use human corpses, and certain internal and external organs pertaining to them, as powerful magical agents for bad purposes.

However this may be, now that the magnetic and

mesmeric potencies of hypnotism are recognized as facts by most physicians, it may be suggested with less danger than heretofore that the extraordinary effects of Paganini's violin-playing were not, perhaps, entirely due to his talent and genius. The wonder and awe he so easily excited were as much caused by his external appearance, "which had something weird and demoniacal in it," according to certain of his biographers, as by the inexpressible charm of his execution and his remarkable mechanical skill. The latter is demonstrated by his perfect imitation of the flageolet, and his performance of long and magnificent melodies on the G string alone. In this performance, which many an artist has tried to copy without success, he remains unrivalled to this day.

It is owing to this remarkable appearance of his—termed by his friends eccentric, and by his too nervous victims, diabolical—that he experienced great difficulties in refuting certain ugly rumours. These were credited far more easily in his day than they would be now. It was whispered throughout Italy, and even in his own native town, that Paganini had murdered his wife, and, later on, a mistress, both of whom he had loved passionately, and both of whom he had not hesitated to sacrifice to his fiendish ambition. He had made himself proficient in magic arts, it was asserted, and had succeeded thereby in imprisoning the souls of his two victims in his violin—his famous Cremona.

It is maintained by the immediate friends of Ernst T. W. Hoffmann, the celebrated author of *Die Elixire des Teufels*, *Meister Martin*, and other charming and mystical tales, that Councillor Crespel, in the *Violin of Cremona*, was taken from the legend about Paganini. It is, as all who have read it know, the history of a celebrated violin, into which the voice and the soul of a famous diva, a woman whom Crespel had loved and killed, had passed, and to which was added the voice of his beloved daughter, Antonia.

Nor was this superstition utterly ungrounded, nor was Hoffmann to be blamed for adopting it, after he had heard Paganini's playing. The extraordinary facility with which the artist drew out of his instrument, not only the most unearthly sounds, but positively human voices, justified the suspicion. Such effects might well have startled an audience and thrown terror into many a nervous heart. Add to this the impenetrable mystery connected with a certain period of Paganini's youth, and the most wild tales about him must be found in a measure justifiable, and even excusable; especially among a nation whose ancestors knew the Borgias and the Medicis of Black Art fame.

III.

In those pre-telegraphic days, newspapers were limited, and the wings of fame had a heavier flight than they have now.

Franz had hardly heard of Paganini; and when he did, he swore he would rival, if not eclipse, the Genoese magician. Yes, he would either become the most famous of all living violinists, or he would break his instrument and put an end to his life at the same time.

Old Klaus rejoiced at such a determination. He rubbed his hands in glee, and jumping about on his lame leg like a crippled satyr, he flattered and incensed his pupil, believing himself all the while to be performing a sacred duty to the holy and majestic cause of art.

Upon first setting foot in Paris, three years before, Franz had all but failed. Musical critics pronounced him a rising star, but had all agreed that he required a few more years' practice, before he could hope to carry his audiences by storm. Therefore, after a desperate study of over two years and uninterrupted preparations, the Styrian artist had finally made himself ready for his first serious appearance in the great Opera House where a public concert before the most exacting critics of the old world was to be held; at this critical moment Pagani-ni's arrival in the European metropolis placed an obstacle in the way of the realization of his hopes, and the old German professor wisely postponed his pupil's *début*. At first he had simply smiled at the wild enthusiasm, the laudatory hymns sung about the Genoese violinist, and the almost superstitious awe with which his name was pronounced. But very soon Paganini's name became a burning iron in the hearts of both the artists, and a threatening phantom in the mind of Klaus. A few days more, and they shuddered at the very mention of their great rival, whose success became with every night more unprecedented.

The first series of concerts was over, but neither Klaus nor Franz had as yet had an opportunity of hearing him and of judging for themselves. So great and so beyond their means was the charge for admission, and so small the hope of getting a free pass from a brother artist justly regarded as the meanest of men in monetary transactions, that they had to wait for a chance, as did so many others. But the day came when neither master nor pupil could control their impatience any longer; so they pawned their watches, and with the proceeds bought two modest seats.

Who can describe the enthusiasm, the triumphs, of this famous, and at the same time fatal night! The audience was frantic; men wept and women screamed and fainted, while both Klaus and Stenio sat looking paler than two ghosts. At the first touch of Paganini's magic bow, both Franz and Samuel felt as if the icy hand of death had touched them. Carried away by an irresistible enthusiasm, which turned into a violent, unearthly mental torture, they dared neither look into each other's faces, nor exchange one word during the whole performance.

At midnight, while the chosen delegates of the Musical Societies and the Conservatory of Paris unhitched the horses, and dragged the carriage of the grand artist home in triumph, the two Germans returned to their modest lodging, and it was a pitiful sight to see them. Mournful and desperate, they placed themselves in their usual seats at the fire-corner, and neither for a while opened his mouth.

"Samuel!" at last exclaimed Franz, pale as death itself. "Samuel—it remains for us now but to die! . . . Do you hear me? . . . We are worthless! We were two madmen to have ever hoped that any one in this world would ever rival . . . him!"

The name of Paganini stuck in his throat, as in utter despair he fell into his arm chair.

The old professor's wrinkles suddenly became

purple. His little greenish eyes gleamed phosphores-
cently as, bending toward his pupil, he whispered to
him in hoarse and broken tones:

"*Nein, nein!* Thou art wrong, my Franz! I have
taught thee, and thou hast learned all of the great
art that a simple mortal, and a Christian by baptism,
can learn from another simple mortal. Am I to
blame because these accursed Italians, in order to
reign unequalled in the domain of art, have recourse
to Satan and the diabolical effects of Black Magic?"

Franz turned his eyes upon his old master. There
was a sinister light burning in those glittering orbs;
a light telling plainly, that, to secure such a power,
he, too, would not scruple to sell himself, body and
soul, to the Evil One.

But he said not a word, and, turning his eyes
from his old master's face, gazed dreamily at the
dying embers.

The same long-forgotten incoherent dreams,
which, after seeming such realities to him in his
younger days, had been given up entirely, and had
gradually faded from his mind, now crowded back
into it with the same force and vividness as of old.
The grimacing shades of Ixion, Sisyphus and Tantalus resurrected and stood before him, saying:

"What matters hell—in which thou believest not.
And even if hell there be, it is the hell described by

the old Greeks, not that of the modern bigots—a locality full of conscious shadows, to whom thou canst be a second Orpheus."

Franz felt that he was going mad, and, turning instinctively, he looked his old master once more right in the face. Then his bloodshot eye evaded the gaze of Klaus.

Whether Samuel understood the terrible state of mind of his pupil, or whether he wanted to draw him out, to make him speak, and thus to divert his thoughts, must remain as hypothetical to the reader as it is to the writer. Whatever may have been in his mind, the German enthusiast went on, speaking with a feigned calmness:

"Franz, my dear boy, I tell you that the art of the accursed Italian is not natural; that it is due neither to study nor to genius. It never was acquired in the usual, natural way. You need not stare at me in that wild manner, for what I say is in the mouth of millions of people. Listen to what I now tell you, and try to understand. You have heard the strange tale whispered about the famous Tartini? He died one fine Sabbath night, strangled by his familiar demon, who had taught him how to endow his violin with a human voice, by shutting up in it, by means of incantations, the soul of a young virgin. Paganini did more. In order to endow his instrument with the faculty of emitting human sounds, such as sobs, despairing cries, supplications, moans of love and fury—in short, the most heart-rending notes of the human voice—Paganini became the murderer not only of his wife and his mistress, but also of a friend, who was more tenderly attached to him than any other being on this earth. He then made the four chords of his magic violin out of the intestines of his last victim. This is the secret of his enchanting talent, of that overpowering melody, that combination of sounds, which you will never be able to master unless . . ."

The old man could not finish the sentence. He staggered back before the fiendish look of his pupil, and covered his face with his hands.

Franz was breathing heavily, and his eyes had an expression which reminded Klaus of those of a hyena. His pallor was cadaverous. For some time he could not speak, but only gasped for breath. At last he slowly muttered:

"Are you in earnest?"

"I am, as I hope to help you."

"And . . . and do you really believe that had I only the means of obtaining human intestines for strings, I could rival Paganini?" asked Franz, after a moment's pause, and casting down his eyes.

The old German unveiled his face, and, with a strange look of determination upon it, softly answered:

"Human intestines alone are not sufficient for our purpose; they must have belonged to some one who had loved us well, with an unselfish, holy love. Tartini endowed his violin with the life of a virgin; but that virgin had died of unrequited love for him. The fiendish artist had prepared beforehand a tube, in which he managed to catch her last breath as she expired, pronouncing his beloved name, and he then transferred this breath to his violin. As to Paganini, I have just told you his tale. It was with the consent of his victim, though, that he murdered him to get possession of his intestines.

"Oh, for the power of the human voice!" Samuel went on, after a brief pause. "What can equal the eloquence, the magic spell of the human voice? Do you think, my poor boy, I would not have taught you this great, this final secret, were it not that it throws one right into the clutches of him . . . who must remain unnamed at night?" he added, with a sudden return to the superstitions of his youth.

Franz did not answer; but with a calmness awful to behold, he left his place, took down his violin from the wall where it was hanging, and, with one powerful grasp of the chords, he tore them out and flung them into the fire.

Samuel suppressed a cry of horror. The chords were hissing upon the coals, where, among the blazing logs, they wriggled and curled like so many living snakes.

"By the witches of Thessaly and the dark arts of Circe!" he exclaimed, with foaming mouth and his eyes burning like coals; "by the Furies of Hell and Pluto himself, I now swear, in thy presence, O Samuel, my master, never to touch a violin again until I can string it with four human chords. May I be accursed for ever and ever if I do!" He fell senseless on the floor, with a deep sob, that ended like a funeral wail; old Samuel lifted him up as he would have lifted a child, and carried him to his bed. Then he sallied forth in search of a physician.

IV.

For several days after this painful scene Franz was very ill, ill almost beyond recovery. The physician declared him to be suffering from brain fever and said that the worst was to be feared. For nine long days the patient remained delirious; and Klaus, who was nursing him night and day with the solicitude of the tenderest mother, was horrified at the work of his own hands. For the first time since their acquaintance began, the old teacher, owing to the wild ravings of his pupil, was able to penetrate into the darkest corners of that weird, superstitious, cold, and, at the same time, passionate nature; and—he trembled at what he discovered. For he saw that which he had failed to perceive before—Franz as he was in reality, and not as he seemed to superficial observers. Music was the life of the young man, and adulation was the air he breathed, without which that life became a burden; from the chords of his violin alone, Stenio drew his life and being, but the applause of men and even of Gods was necessary to its support. He saw unveiled before his eyes a genuine, artistic, *earthly* soul, with its divine counterpart totally absent, a son of the Muses, all fancy and brain poetry, but without a heart. While listening to the ravings of that delirious and unhinged fancy Klaus felt as if he were for the first time in his long life exploring a marvellous and untravelled region, a human nature not of this world but of some incomplete planet. He saw all this, and shuddered. More than once he asked himself whether it would not be doing a kindness to his "boy" to let him die before he returned to consciousness.

But he loved his pupil too well to dwell for long on such an idea. Franz had bewitched his truly artistic nature, and now old Klaus felt as though their two lives were inseparably linked together. That he could thus feel was a revelation to the old man; so he decided to save Franz, even at the expense of his own old and, as he thought, useless life.

The seventh day of the illness brought on a most terrible crisis. For twenty-four hours the patient never closed his eyes, nor remained for a moment silent; he raved continuously during the whole time. His visions were peculiar, and he minutely described each. Fantastic, ghastly figures kept slowly swimming out of the penumbra of his small, dark room, in regular and uninterrupted procession, and he greeted each by name as he might greet old acquaintances. He referred to himself as Prometheus, bound to the rock by four bands made of human intestines. At the foot of the Caucasian Mount the black waters of the river Styx were running . . . They had deserted Arcadia, and were now endeavouring to encircle within a seven-fold embrace the rock upon which he was suffering . . .

"Wouldst thou know the name of the Promethean rock, old man?" he roared into his adopted father's ear . . . "Listen then, . . . its name is . . . called . . . Samuel Klaus . . ."

"Yes, yes! . . ." the German murmured disconsolately. "It is I who killed him, while seeking to console. The news of Paganini's magic arts struck his fancy too vividly . . . Oh, my poor, poor boy!"

"Ha, ha, ha, ha!" The patient broke into a loud and discordant laugh. "Aye, poor old man, sayest thou? . . . So, so, thou art of poor stuff, anyhow, and wouldst look well only when stretched upon a fine Cremona violin! . . ."

Klaus shuddered, but said nothing. He only bent over the poor maniac, and with a kiss upon his brow, a caress as tender and as gentle as that of a doting mother, he left the sick-room for a few instants, to seek relief in his own garret. When he returned, the ravings were following another channel. Franz was singing, trying to imitate the sounds of a violin.

Toward the evening of that day, the delirium of the sick man became perfectly ghastly. He saw spirits of fire clutching at his violin. Their skeleton hands, from each finger of which grew a flaming claw, beckoned to old Samuel . . . They approached and surrounded the old master, and were preparing to rip him open . . . him, "the only man on this earth who loves me with an unselfish, holy love, and . . . whose intestines can be of any good at all!" he went on whispering, with glaring eyes and demon laugh . . .

By the next morning, however, the fever had disappeared, and by the end of the ninth day Stenio had left his bed, having no recollection of his illness, and no suspicion that he had allowed Klaus to read his inner thought. Nay; had he himself any knowledge that such a horrible idea as the sacrifice of his old master to his ambition had ever entered his mind? Hardly. The only immediate result of his fatal illness was, that as, by reason of his vow, his artistic passion could find no issue, another passion awoke, which might avail to feed his ambition and his insatiable fancy. He plunged headlong into the study of the Occult Arts, of Alchemy and of Magic. In the practice of Magic the young dreamer sought to stifle the voice of his passionate longing for his, as he thought, for ever lost violin . . .

Weeks and months passed away, and the conversation about Paganini was never resumed between the master and the pupil. But a profound melancholy had taken possession of Franz, the two hardly exchanged a word, the violin hung mute, chordless, full of dust, in its habitual place. It was as the presence of a soulless corpse between them.

The young man had become gloomy and sarcastic, even avoiding the mention of music. Once, as his old professor, after long hesitation, took out his own violin from its dust-covered case and prepared to play, Franz gave a convulsive shudder, but said nothing. At the first notes of the bow, however, he glared like a madman, and rushing out of the house, remained for hours, wandering in the streets. Then old Samuel in his turn threw his instrument down, and locked himself up in his room till the following morning.

One night as Franz sat, looking particularly pale and gloomy, old Samuel suddenly jumped from his seat, and after hopping about the room in a magpie fashion, approached his pupil, imprinted a fond kiss upon the young man's brow, and squeaked at the top of his shrill voice:

"Is it not time to put an end to all this?" . . .

Whereupon, starting from his usual lethargy, Franz echoed, as in a dream:

"Yes, it is time to put an end to this."

Upon which the two separated, and went to bed.

On the following morning, when Franz awoke, he was astonished not to see his old teacher in his usual place to greet him. But he had greatly altered during the last few months, and he at first paid no attention to his absence, unusual as it was. He dressed and went into the adjoining room, a little parlour where they had their meals, and which separated their two bedrooms. The fire had not been lighted since the embers had died out on the previous night, and no sign was anywhere visible of the professor's busy hand in his usual housekeeping duties. Greatly puzzled, but in no way dismayed, Franz took his usual place at the corner of the now cold fire-place, and fell into an aimless reverie. As he stretched himself in his old arm-chair, raising both his hands to clasp them behind his head in a favourite posture of his, his hand came into contact with something on a shelf at his back; he knocked against a case, and brought it violently on the ground.

It was old Klaus' violin-case that came down to the floor with such a sudden crash that the case opened and the violin fell out of it, rolling to the feet of Franz. And then the chords, striking against the brass fender emitted a sound, prolonged, sad and mournful as the sigh of an unrestful soul; it seemed to fill the whole room, and reverberated in the head and the very heart of the young man. The effect of that broken violin-string was magical.

"Samuel!" cried Stenio, with his eyes starting from their sockets, and an unknown terror suddenly taking possession of his whole being. "Samuel! what has happened? . . . My good, my dear old master!" he called out, hastening to the professor's little room, and throwing the door violently open. No one answered, all was silent within.

He staggered back, frightened at the sound of his own voice, so changed and hoarse it seemed to him at this moment. No reply came in response to his call. Naught followed but a dead silence . . . that stillness which, in the domain of sounds, usually denotes death. In the presence of a corpse, as in the lugubrious stillness of a tomb, such silence acquires a mysterious power, which strikes the sensitive soul with a nameless terror . . . The little room was dark, and Franz hastened to open the shutters.

*

Samuel was lying on his bed, cold, stiff, and lifeless . . . At the sight of the corpse of him who had loved him so well, and had been to him more than a father, Franz experienced a dreadful revulsion of feeling, a terrible shock. But the ambition of the fanatical artist got the better of the despair of the man, and smothered the feelings of the latter in a few seconds.

A note bearing his own name was conspicuously placed upon a table near the corpse. With trembling hand, the violinist tore open the envelope, and read the following:

MY BELOVED SON, FRANZ,

When you read this, I shall have made the greatest sacrifice, that your best and only friend and teacher could have accomplished for your fame. He, who loved you most, is now but an inanimate lump of clay. Of your old teacher there now remains but a clod of cold organic matter. I need not prompt you as to what you have to do with it. Fear not stupid prejudices. It is for your future fame that I have made an offering of my body, and you would be guilty of the blackest ingratitude were you now to render useless this sacrifice. When you shall have replaced the chords upon your violin, and these chords a portion of my own self, under your touch it will acquire the power of that accursed sorcerer, all the magic voices of Paganini's instrument. You will find therein my voice, my sighs and groans, my song of welcome, the prayerful sobs of my infinite and sorrowful sympathy, my love for you. And now, my Franz, fear nobody! Take your instrument with you, and dog the steps of him who filled our lives with bitterness and despair! . . . Appear in every arena, where, hitherto, he has reigned without a rival, and bravely throw the gauntlet of defiance in his face. O Franz! then only wilt thou hear with what a magic power the full notes of unselfish love will issue forth from thy violin. Perchance, with a last caressing touch of its chords, thou wilt remember that they once formed a portion of thine old teacher, who now embraces and blesses thee for the last time.

SAMUEL.

Two burning tears sparkled in the eyes of Franz,

but they dried up instantly. Under the fiery rush of passionate hope and pride, the two orbs of the future magician-artist, riveted to the ghastly face of the dead man, shone like the eyes of a demon.

Our pen refuses to describe that which took place on that day, after the legal inquiry was over. As another note, written with the view of satisfying the authorities, had been prudently provided by the loving care of the old teacher, the verdict was, "Suicide from causes unknown"; after this the coroner and the police retired, leaving the bereaved heir alone in the death-room, with the remains of that which had once been a living man.

*

Scarcely a fortnight had elapsed from that day, ere the violin had been dusted, and four new, stout strings had been stretched upon it. Franz dared not look at them. He tried to play, but the bow trembled in his hand like a dagger in the grasp of a novice-brigand. He then determined not to try again, until the portentous night should arrive, when he should have a chance of rivalling, nay, of surpassing, Paganini.

The famous violinist had meanwhile left Paris, and was giving a series of triumphant concerts at an old Flemish town in Belgium.

V.

One night, as Paganini, surrounded by a crowd of admirers, was sitting in the dining-room of the hotel at which he was staying, a visiting card, with a few words written on it in pencil, was handed to him by a young man with wild and staring eyes.

Fixing upon the intruder a look which few persons could bear, but receiving back a glance as calm and determined as his own, Paganini slightly bowed, and then dryly said:

"Sir, it shall be as you desire. Name the night. I am at your service."

On the following morning the whole town was startled by the appearance of bills posted at the corner of every street, and bearing the strange notice:

On the night of . . . , at the Grand Theatre of . . . , and for the first time, will appear before the public, Franz Stenio, a German violinist, arrived purposely to throw down the gauntlet to the world-famous Paganini and to challenge him to a duel—upon their violins. He purposes to compete with the great "virtuoso" in the execution of the most difficult of his compositions. The famous Paganini has accepted the challenge. Franz Stenio will play, in competition with the unrivalled violinist, the celebrated "Fantaisie Caprice" of the latter, known as "The Witches."

The effect of the notice was magical. Paganini, who, amid his greatest triumphs, never lost sight of a profitable speculation, doubled the usual price of admission, but still the theatre could not hold the crowds that flocked to secure tickets for that memorable performance.

At last the morning of the concert day dawned, and the "duel" was in every one's mouth. Franz Stenio, who, instead of sleeping, had passed the whole long hours of the preceding midnight in walking up and down his room like an encaged panther, had, toward morning, fallen on his bed from mere physical exhaustion. Gradually he passed into a death-like and dreamless slumber. At the gloomy winter dawn he awoke, but finding it too early to rise he fell asleep again. And then he had a vivid dream—so vivid indeed, so life-like, that from its terrible realism he felt sure that it was a vision rather than a dream.

He had left his violin on a table by his bedside, locked in its case, the key of which never left him. Since he had strung it with those terrible chords he never let it out of his sight for a moment. In accordance with his resolution he had not touched it since his first trial, and his bow had never but once touched the human strings, for he had since always practised on another instrument. But now in his sleep he saw himself looking at the locked case. Something in it was attracting his attention, and he found himself incapable of detaching his eyes from it. Suddenly he saw the upper part of the case slowly rising, and, within the chink thus produced, he perceived two small, phosphorescent green eyes—eyes but too familiar to him—fixing themselves on his, lovingly, almost beseechingly. Then a thin, shrill voice, as if issuing from these ghastly orbs—the voice and orbs of Samuel Klaus himself—resounded in Stenio's horrified ear, and he heard it say:

"Franz, my beloved boy . . . Franz, I cannot, no, *I cannot* separate myself from . . . *them!*"

And "they" twanged piteously inside the case.

Franz stood speechless, horror-bound. He felt his blood actually freezing, and his hair moving and standing erect on his head . . .

"It's but a dream, an empty dream!" he attempted to formulate in his mind.

"I have tried my best, Franzchen . . . I have tried my best to sever myself from these accursed strings, without pulling them to pieces . . ." pleaded the same shrill, familiar voice. "Wilt thou help me to do so? . . ."

Another twang, still more prolonged and dismal, resounded within the case, now dragged about the table in every direction, by some interior power, like some living, wriggling thing, the twangs becoming sharper and more jerky with every new pull.

It was not for the first time that Stenio heard those sounds. He had often remarked them before—indeed, ever since he had used his master's viscera as a footstool for his own ambition. But on every occasion a feeling of creeping horror had prevented him from investigating their cause, and he had tried to assure himself that the sounds were only a hallucination.

But now he stood face to face with the terrible fact, whether in dream or in reality he knew not, nor did he care, since the hallucination—if hallucination it were—was far more real and vivid than any reality. He tried to speak, to take a step forward; but, as often happens in nightmares, he could neither utter a word nor move a finger . . . He felt hopelessly paralyzed.

The pulls and jerks were becoming more desperate with each moment, and at last something inside the case snapped violently. The vision of his Stradivarius, devoid of its magical strings, flashed before his eyes, throwing him into a cold sweat of mute and unspeakable terror.

He made a superhuman effort to rid himself of the incubus that held him spell-bound. But as the last supplicating whisper of the invisible Presence repeated:

"Do, oh, do . . . help me to cut myself off——"

Franz sprang to the case with one bound, like an enraged tiger defending its prey, and with one frantic effort breaking the spell.

"Leave the violin alone, you old fiend from hell!" he cried, in hoarse and trembling tones.

He violently shut down the self-raising lid, and while firmly pressing his left hand on it, he seized with the right a piece of rosin from the table and drew on the leather-covered top the sign of the six-pointed star—the seal used by King Solomon to bottle up the rebellious djins inside their prisons.

A wail, like the howl of a she-wolf moaning over her dead little ones, came out of the violin-case:

"Thou art ungrateful . . . very ungrateful, my Franz!" sobbed the blubbering "spirit-voice." "But I forgive . . . for I still love thee well. Yet thou canst not shut me in . . . boy. Behold!"

And instantly a grayish mist spread over and covered case and table, and rising upward formed itself first into an indistinct shape. Then it began growing, and as it grew, Franz felt himself gradually enfolded in cold and damp coils, slimy as those of a huge snake. He gave a terrible cry and—awoke; but, strangely enough, not on his bed, but near the table, just as he had dreamed, pressing the violin case desperately with both his hands.

"It was but a dream, . . . after all," he muttered, still terrified, but relieved of the load on his heaving breast.

With a tremendous effort he composed himself, and unlocked the case to inspect the violin. He found it covered with dust, but otherwise sound and in order, and he suddenly felt himself as cool and as determined as ever. Having dusted the instrument he carefully rosined the bow, tightened the strings and tuned them. He even went so far as to try upon it the first notes of "The Witches"; first cautiously and timidly, then using his bow boldly and with full force.

The sound of that loud, solitary note—defiant as the war trumpet of a conqueror, sweet and majestic as the touch of a seraph on his golden harp in the fancy of the faithful—thrilled through the very soul of Franz. It revealed to him a hitherto unsuspected potency in his bow, which ran on in strains that filled the room with the richest swell of melody, unheard by the artist until that night. Commencing in uninterrupted *legato* tones, his bow sang to him of sun-bright hope and beauty, of moonlit nights, when the soft and balmy stillness endowed every blade of grass and all things animate and inanimate with a voice and a song of love. For a few brief moments it was a torrent of melody, the harmony of which, "tuned to soft woe," was calculated to make mountains weep, had there been any in the room, and to soothe

... even th' inexorable powers of hell,

the presence of which was undeniably felt in this modest hotel room. Suddenly, the solemn *legato* chant, contrary to all laws of harmony, quivered, became *arpeggios*, and ended in shrill *staccatos*, like the notes of a hyena laugh. The same creeping sensation of terror, as he had before felt, came over him, and Franz threw the bow away. He had recognized the familiar laugh, and would have no more of it. Dressing, he locked the bedevilled violin securely in its case, and, taking it with him to the dining-room, determined to await quietly the hour of trial.

VI.

The terrible hour of the struggle had come, and Stenio was at his post—calm, resolute, almost smiling.

The theatre was crowded to suffocation, and there was not even standing room to be got for any amount of hard cash or favouritism. The singular challenge had reached every quarter to which the post could carry it, and gold flowed freely into Paganini's unfathomable pockets, to an extent almost satisfying even to his insatiate and venal soul.

It was arranged that Paganini should begin. When he appeared upon the stage, the thick walls of the theatre shook to their foundations with the applause that greeted him. He began and ended his famous composition "The Witches" amid a storm of cheers. The shouts of public enthusiasm lasted so long that Franz began to think his turn would never come. When, at last, Paganini, amid the roaring applause of a frantic public, was allowed to retire behind the scenes, his eye fell upon Stenio, who was tuning his violin, and he felt amazed at the serene calmness, the air of assurance, of the unknown German artist.

When Franz approached the footlights, he was received with icy coldness. But for all that, he did not feel in the least disconcerted. He looked very pale, but his thin white lips wore a scornful smile as response to this dumb unwelcome. He was sure of his triumph.

At the first notes of the prelude of "The Witches" a thrill of astonishment passed over the audience. It was Paganini's touch, and—it was something more.

Some—and they were the majority—thought that never, in his best moments of inspiration, had the Italian artist himself, in executing that diabolical composition of his, exhibited such an extraordinary diabolical power. Under the pressure of the long muscular fingers of Franz, the chords shivered like the palpitating intestines of a disembowelled victim under the vivisector's knife. They moaned melodiously, like a dying child. The large blue eye of the artist, fixed with a satanic expression upon the sounding-board, seemed to summon forth Orpheus himself from the infernal regions, rather than the musical notes supposed to be generated in the depths of the violin. Sounds seemed to transform themselves into objective shapes, thickly and precipitately gathering as at the evocation of a mighty magician, and to be whirling around him, like a host of fantastic, infernal figures, dancing the witches' "goat dance." In the empty depths of the shadowy background of the stage, behind the artist, a nameless phantasmagoria, produced by the concussion of unearthly vibrations, seemed to form pictures of shameless orgies, of the voluptuous hymens of a real witches' Sabbat . . . A collective hallucination took hold of the public. Panting for breath, ghastly, and trickling with the icy perspiration of an inexpressible horror, they sat spell-bound, and unable to break the spell of the music by the slightest motion. They experienced all the illicit enervating delights of the paradise of Mahommed, that come into the disordered fancy of an opium-eating Mussulman, and felt at the same time the abject terror, the agony of one who struggles against an attack of *delirium tremens* . . . Many ladies shrieked aloud, others fainted, and strong men gnashed their teeth in a state of utter helplessness . . .

Then came the *finale*. Thundering uninterrupted applause delayed its beginning, expanding the momentary pause to a duration of almost a quarter of an hour. The bravos were furious, almost hysterical. At last, when after a profound and last bow, Stenio, whose smile was as sardonic as it was triumphant, lifted his bow to attack the famous *finale*, his eye fell upon Paganini, who, calmly seated in the manager's box, had been behind none in zealous applause. The small and piercing black eyes of the Genoese artist were riveted to the Stradivarius in the hands of Franz, but otherwise he seemed quite cool and unconcerned. His rival's face troubled him for one short instant, but he regained his self-possession and, lifting once more his bow, drew the first note.

Then the public enthusiasm reached its acme, and soon knew no bounds. The listeners heard and saw indeed. The witches' voices resounded in the air, and beyond all the other voices, one voice was heard—

> Discordant, and unlike to human sounds;
> It seem'd of dogs the bark, of wolves the howl;
> The doleful screechings of the midnight owl;
> The hiss of snakes, the hungry lion's roar;
> The sounds of billows beating on the shore;
> The groan of winds among the leafy wood,
> And burst of thunder from the rending cloud;—
> 'Twas these, all these in one . . .

The magic bow was drawing forth its last quivering sounds—famous among prodigious musical feats—imitating the precipitate flight of the witches before bright dawn; of the unholy women saturated with the fumes of their nocturnal Saturnalia, when—a strange thing came to pass on the stage. Without the slightest transition, the notes suddenly changed. In their aerial flight of ascension and descent, their melody was unexpectedly altered in character. The sounds became confused, scattered, disconnected . . . and then—it seemed from the sounding-board of the violin—came out squeaking, jarring tones, like those of a street Punch, screaming at the top of a senile voice:

"Art thou satisfied, Franz, my boy? . . . Have not I gloriously kept my promise, eh?"

The spell was broken. Though still unable to realize the whole situation, those who heard the voice and the *Punchinello*-like tones, were freed, as by enchantment, from the terrible charm under which they had been held. Loud roars of laughter, mocking exclamations of half-anger and half-irritation were now heard from every corner of the vast theatre. The musicians in the orchestra, with faces still blanched from weird emotion, were now seen shaking with laughter, and the whole audience rose, like one man, from their seats, unable yet to solve the enigma; they felt, nevertheless, too disgusted, too disposed to laugh to remain one moment longer in the building.

But suddenly the sea of moving heads in the stalls and the pit became once more motionless, and stood petrified as though struck by lightning. What all saw was terrible enough—the handsome though wild face of the young artist suddenly aged, and his graceful, erect figure bent down, as though under the weight of years; but this was nothing to that which some of the most sensitive clearly perceived. Franz Stenio's person was now entirely enveloped in a semi-transparent mist, cloud-like, creeping with serpentine motion, and gradually tightening round the living form, as though ready to engulf him. And there were those also who discerned in this tall and ominous pillar of smoke a clearly-defined figure, a form showing the unmistakable outlines of a grotesque and grinning, but terribly awful-looking old man, whose viscera were protruding and the ends of the intestines stretched on the violin.

Within this hazy, quivering veil, the violinist was then seen, driving his bow furiously across the human chords, with the contortions of a demoniac, as we see them represented on mediæval cathedral paintings!

An indescribable panic swept over the audience, and breaking now, for the last time, through the spell which had again bound them motionless, every living creature in the theatre made one mad rush towards the door. It was like the sudden outburst of a dam, a human torrent, roaring amid a shower of discordant notes, idiotic squeakings, prolonged and whining moans, cacophonous cries of frenzy, above which, like the detonations of pistol shots, was heard the consecutive bursting of the four strings stretched upon the sound-board of that bewitched violin.

When the theatre was emptied of the last man of the audience, the terrified manager rushed on the stage in search of the unfortunate performer. He was found dead and already stiff, behind the footlights, twisted up into the most unnatural of postures, with the "catguts" wound curiously around his neck, and his violin shattered into a thousand fragments . . .

When it became publicly known that the unfortunate would-be rival of Niccolo Paganini had not left a cent to pay for his funeral or his hotel-bill, the Genoese, his proverbial meanness notwithstanding, settled the hotel-bill and had poor Stenio buried at his own expense.

He claimed, however, in exchange, the fragments of the Stradivarius—as a memento of the strange event.

E. Nesbit

Edith Nesbit (1858–1924) was an English playwright, poet and author whose fame has lived on as a writer of children's books, both realist and fantastical. Her best-known children's books are the realist *The Story of the Treasure Seekers* (1899) and *The Railway Children* (1905), but close behind is *Five Children and It* (1902), in which five children meet a sand fairy and learn the danger of ill thought-through wishes. The book is very much beloved and emulated. Alongside this, Nesbit also wrote supernatural fiction for adults, much of it rather dark and weird. The key trope Nesbit offered to fantasy is the ordinariness in which the fantastic takes place. Nesbit was a Fabian socialist, and her work reflected the arbitrariness of luck in an unjust world, but also the ways in which humans could exert control.

The Dragon Tamers

There was once an old, old castle—it was so old that its walls and towers and turrets and gateways and arches had crumbled to ruins, and of all its old splendour there were only two little rooms left; and it was here that John the blacksmith had set up his forge. He was too poor to live in a proper house, and no one asked any rent for the rooms in the ruin, because all the lords of the castle were dead and gone this many a year. So there John blew his bellows, and hammered his iron, and did all the work which came his way. This was not much, because most of the trade went to the mayor of the town, who was also a blacksmith in quite a large way of business, and had his huge forge facing the square of the town, and had twelve apprentices, all hammering like a nest of woodpeckers, and twelve journeymen to order the apprentices about, and a patent forge and a self-acting hammer and electric bellows, and all things handsome about him. So that of course the townspeople, whenever they wanted a horse shod or a shaft mended, went to the mayor. And John the blacksmith struggled on as best he could, with a few odd jobs from travellers and strangers who did not know what a superior forge the mayor's was. The two rooms were warm and weather-tight, but not very large; so the blacksmith got into the way of keeping his old iron, and his odds and ends, and his fagots, and his twopenn'orths of coal in the great dungeon down under the castle. It was a very fine dungeon indeed, with a handsome vaulted roof and big iron rings, whose staples were built into the wall, very strong and convenient for tying captives up to, and at one end was a broken flight of wide steps leading down no one knew where. Even the lords of the castle in the good old times had never known where those steps led to, but every now and then they would kick a prisoner down the steps in their light-hearted, hopeful way, and, sure enough, the prisoners never came back. The blacksmith had never dared to go beyond the seventh step, and no more have I—so I know no more than he did what was at the bottom of those stairs.

John the blacksmith had a wife and a little baby. When his wife was not doing the house-work she used to nurse the baby and cry, remembering the happy days when she lived with her father, who kept seventeen cows and lived quite in the country, and when John used to come courting her in the summer evenings, as smart as smart, with a posy in his button-hole. And now John's hair was getting grey, and there was hardly ever enough to eat.

As for the baby, it cried a good deal at odd times;

but at night, when its mother had settled down to sleep, it would always begin to cry, quite as a matter of course, so that she hardly got any rest at all. This made her very tired. The baby could make up for its bad nights during the day, if it liked, but the poor mother couldn't. So whenever she had nothing to do she used to sit and cry, because she was tired out with work and worry.

One evening the blacksmith was busy with his forge. He was making a goat-shoe for the goat of a very rich lady, who wished to see how the goat liked being shod, and also whether the shoe would come to fivepence or sevenpence before she ordered the whole set. This was the only order John had had that week. And as he worked his wife sat and nursed the baby, who, for a wonder, was not crying.

Presently, over the noise of the bellows, and over the clank of the iron, there came another sound. The blacksmith and his wife looked at each other.

"I heard nothing," said he.

"Neither did I," said she.

But the noise grew louder—and the two were so anxious not to hear it that he hammered away at the goat-shoe harder than he had ever hammered in his life, and she began to sing to the baby—a thing she had not had the heart to do for weeks.

But through the blowing and hammering and

singing the noise came louder and louder—and the more they tried not to hear it, the more they had to. It was like the noise of some great creature purring, purring, purring—and the reason they did not want to believe they really heard it was, that it came from the great dungeon down below, where the old iron was, and the firewood and the twopenn'orth of coal, and the broken steps that went down into the dark and ended no one knew where.

"It *can't* be anything in the dungeon," said the blacksmith, wiping his face. "Why, I shall have to go down there after more coals in a minute."

"There isn't anything there, of course. How could there be?" said his wife. And they tried so hard to believe that there could be nothing there that presently they very nearly did believe it.

Then the blacksmith took his shovel in one hand and his riveting hammer in the other, and hung the old stable lantern on his little finger, and went down to get the coals.

"I am not taking the hammer because I think there is anything there," said he, "but it is handy for breaking the large lumps of coal."

"I quite understand," said his wife, who had brought the coal home in her apron that very afternoon, and knew that it was all coal-dust.

So he went down the winding stairs to the

dungeon, and stood at the bottom of the steps holding the lantern above his head just to see that the dungeon really *was* empty, as usual. Half of it was empty as usual, except for the old iron and odds and ends, and the firewood and the coals. But the other side was not empty. It was quite full, and what it was full of was *Dragon*.

"It must have come up those nasty broken steps from goodness knows where," said the blacksmith to himself, trembling all over, as he tried to creep back up the winding stairs.

But the dragon was too quick for him—it put out a great claw and caught him by the leg, and as it moved it rattled like a great bunch of keys, or like the sheet-iron they make thunder out of in the pantomime.

"No you don't," said the dragon, in a spluttering voice, like a damp squib.

"Deary, deary me," said poor John, trembling more than ever in the claw of the dragon; "here's a nice end for a respectable blacksmith!"

The dragon seemed very much struck by this remark.

"Do you mind saying that again?" said he, quite politely.

So John said again, very distinctly:—

"Here—Is—A—Nice—End—For—A—Respectable—Blacksmith."

"I didn't know," said the dragon. "Fancy now! You're the very man I wanted."

"So I understood you to say before," said John, his teeth chattering.

"Oh, I don't mean what you mean," said the dragon; "but I should like you to do a job for me. One of my wings has got some of the rivets out of it just above the joint. Could you put that to rights?"

"I might, sir," said John, politely, for you must always be polite to a possible customer, even if he be a dragon.

"A master craftsman—you *are* a master, of course?—can see in a minute what's wrong," the dragon went on. "Just come round here and feel of my plates, will you?"

John timidly went round when the dragon took his claw away; and, sure enough, the dragon's off wing was hanging loose and all anyhow, and several of the plates near the joint certainly wanted riveting.

The dragon seemed to be made almost entirely of iron armour—a sort of tawny, red-rust colour it was; from damp, no doubt—and under it he seemed to be covered with something furry.

All the blacksmith welled up in John's heart, and he felt more at ease.

"You could certainly do with a rivet or two, sir," said he; "in fact, you want a good many."

"Well, get to work, then," said the dragon. "You mend my wing, and then I'll go out and eat up all the town, and if you make a really smart job of it I'll eat you last. There!"

"I don't want to be eaten last, sir," said John.

"Well, then, I'll eat you *first*," said the dragon.

"I don't want that, sir, either," said John.

"Go on with you, you silly man," said the dragon; "you don't know your own silly mind. Come, set to work."

"I don't like the job, sir," said John, "and that's the truth. I know how easily accidents happen. It's all fair and smooth, and 'Please rivet me, and I'll eat you last'—and then you get to work and you give a gentleman a bit of a nip or a dig under his rivets—and then it's fire and smoke, and no apologies will meet the case."

"Upon my word of honour as a dragon," said the other.

"I know you wouldn't do it on purpose, sir," said John; "but any gentleman will give a jump and a sniff if he's nipped, and one of your sniffs would be enough for me. Now, if you'd just let me fasten you up?"

"It would be so undignified," objected the dragon.

"We always fasten a horse up," said John, "and he's the 'noble animal.'"

"It's all very well," said the dragon, "but how do I know you'd untie me again when you'd riveted me? Give me something in pledge. What do you value most?"

"My hammer," said John. "A blacksmith is nothing without a hammer."

"But you'd want that for riveting me. You must think of something else, and at once, or I'll eat you first."

At this moment the baby in the room above began to scream. Its mother had been so quiet that it thought she had settled down for the night, and that it was time to begin.

"Whatever's that?" said the dragon—starting so that every plate on his body rattled.

"It's only the baby," said John.

"What's that?" asked the dragon—"something you value?"

"Well, yes, sir, rather," said the blacksmith.

"Then bring it here," said the dragon; "and I'll take care of it till you've done riveting me, and you shall tie me up."

"All right, sir," said John; "but I ought to warn you. Babies are poison to dragons, so I don't deceive you. It's all right to touch—but don't you go putting it into your mouth. I shouldn't like to see any harm come to a nice-looking gentleman like you."

The dragon purred at this compliment and said:—

"All right, I'll be careful. Now go and fetch the thing, whatever it is."

So John ran up the steps as quickly as he could, for he knew that if the dragon got impatient before it was fastened up, it could heave up the roof of the dungeon with one heave of its back, and kill them all in the ruins. His wife was asleep, in spite of the baby's cries; and John picked up the baby and took it down and put it between the dragon's front paws.

"You just purr to it, sir," he said, "and it'll be as good as gold."

So the dragon purred, and his purring pleased the baby so much that it left off crying.

Then John rummaged among the heap of old iron and found there some heavy chains and a great collar that had been made in the days when men sang over their work and put their hearts into it, so that the things they made were strong enough to bear the weight of a thousand years, let alone a dragon.

John fastened the dragon up with the collar and the chains, and when he had padlocked them all on safely he set to work to find out how many rivets would be needed.

"Six, eight, ten—twenty, forty," said he: "I

haven't half enough rivets in the shop. If you'll excuse me, sir, I'll step round to another forge and get a few dozen. I won't be a minute."

And off he went, leaving the baby between the dragon's fore-paws, laughing and crowing with pleasure at the very large purr of it.

John ran as hard as he could into the town, and found the mayor and corporation.

"There's a dragon in my dungeon," he said; "I've chained him up. Now come and help to get my baby away."

And he told them all about it.

But they all happened to have engagements for that evening; so they praised John's cleverness, and said they were quite content to leave the matter in his hands.

"But what about my baby?" said John.

"Oh, well," said the mayor, "if anything should happen, you will always be able to remember that your baby perished in a good cause."

So John went home again, and told his wife some of the tale.

"You've given the baby to the dragon!" she cried. "Oh, you unnatural parent!"

"Hush," said John, and he told her some more.

"Now," he said, "I'm going down. After I've been

down you can go, and if you keep your head the boy will be all right."

So down went the blacksmith, and there was the dragon purring away with all his might to keep the baby quiet.

"Hurry up, can't you?" he said. "I can't keep up this noise all night."

"I'm very sorry, sir," said the blacksmith, "but all the shops are shut. The job must wait till the morning. And don't forget you've promised to take care of that baby. You'll find it a little wearing, I'm afraid. Good-night, sir."

The dragon had purred till he was quite out of breath—so now he stopped, and as soon as everything was quiet the baby thought everyone must have settled for the night, and that it was time to begin to scream. So it began.

"Oh, dear," said the dragon, "this is awful."

He patted the baby with his claw, but it screamed more than ever.

"And I am so tired, too," said the dragon. "I did so hope I should have had a good night."

The baby went on screaming.

"There'll be no peace for me after this," said the dragon; "it's enough to ruin one's nerves. Hush, then—did 'ums, then." And he tried to quiet the baby as if it had been a young dragon. But when he began to sing "Hush-a-by, dragon," the baby screamed more and more and more. "I can't keep it quiet," said the dragon; and then suddenly he saw a woman sitting on the steps. "Here, I say," said he, "do you know anything about babies?"

"I do, a little," said the mother.

"Then I wish you'd take this one, and let me get some sleep," said the dragon, yawning. "You can bring it back in the morning before the blacksmith comes."

So the mother picked up the baby and took it upstairs and told her husband, and they went to bed happy, for they had caught the dragon and saved the baby.

And next day John went down and explained carefully to the dragon exactly how matters stood, and he got an iron gate with a grating to it, and set it up at the foot of the steps, and the dragon mewed furiously for days and days, but when he found it was no good he was quiet.

So now John went to the mayor and said:—

"I've got the dragon and I've saved the town."

"Noble preserver," cried the mayor, "we will get up a subscription for you, and crown you in public with a laurel wreath."

So the mayor put his name down for five pounds, and the corporation each gave three, and other people gave their guineas and half-guineas, and half-crowns and crowns, and while the subscription was being made the mayor ordered three poems at his own expense from the town poet to celebrate the occasion. The poems were very much admired, especially by the mayor and corporation.

The first poem dealt with the noble conduct of the mayor in arranging to have the dragon tied up. The second described the splendid assistance rendered by the corporation. And the third expressed the pride and joy of the poet in being permitted to sing such deeds, beside which the actions of St. George must appear quite commonplace to all with a feeling heart or a well-balanced brain.

When the subscription was finished there was a thousand pounds, and a committee was formed to settle what should be done with it. A third of it went to pay for a banquet to the mayor and corporation; another third was spent in buying a gold collar with a dragon on it for the mayor, and gold medals with dragons on them for the corporation; and what was left went in committee expenses.

So there was nothing for the blacksmith except the laurel wreath, and the knowledge that it really *was* he who had saved the town. But after this things went a little better with the blacksmith. To begin with, the baby did not cry so much as it had before.

Then the rich lady who owned the goat was so touched by John's noble action that she ordered a complete set of shoes at 2s. 4d., and even made it up to 2s. 6d. in grateful recognition of his public-spirited conduct.

Then tourists used to come in breaks from quite a long way off, and pay two-pence each to go down the steps and peep through the iron grating at the rusty dragon in the dungeon—and it was threepence extra for each party if the blacksmith let off coloured fire to see it by, which, as the fire was extremely short, was twopence-halfpenny clear profit every time. And the blacksmith's wife used to provide teas at ninepence a head, and altogether things grew brighter week by week.

The baby—named John, after his father, and called Johnnie for short—began presently to grow up. He was great friends with Tina, the daughter of the whitesmith, who lived nearly opposite. She was a dear little girl, with yellow pigtails and blue eyes, and she was never tired of hearing the story of how Johnnie, when he was a baby, had been minded by a real dragon.

The two children used to go together to peep through the iron grating at the dragon, and sometimes they would hear him mew piteously. And they would light a halfpennyworth of coloured fire to look at him by. And they grew older and wiser.

Now, at last one day the mayor and corporation, hunting the hare in their gold gowns, came screaming back to the town gates with the news that a lame, humpy giant, as big as a tin church, was coming over the marshes towards the town.

"We're lost," said the mayor. "I'd give a thousand pounds to anyone who could keep that giant out of the town. *I* know what he eats—by his teeth."

No one seemed to know what to do. But Johnnie and Tina were listening, and they looked at each other, and then ran off as fast as their boots would carry them.

They ran through the forge, and down the dungeon steps, and knocked at the iron door.

"Who's there?" said the dragon.

"It's only us," said the children.

And the dragon was so dull from having been alone for ten years that he said:—

"Come in, dears."

"You won't hurt us, or breathe fire at us or anything?" asked Tina. And the dragon said, "Not for worlds."

So they went in and talked to him, and told him what the weather was like outside, and what there was in the papers, and at last Johnnie said:—

"There's a lame giant in the town. He wants you."

"Does he?" said the dragon, showing his teeth. "If only I were out of this!"

"If we let you loose you might manage to run away before he could catch you."

"Yes, I *might*," answered the dragon, "but then again I mightn't."

"Why—you'd never fight him?" said Tina.

"No," said the dragon; "I'm all for peace, I am. You let me out, and you'll see."

So the children loosed the dragon from the chains and the collar, and he broke down one end of the dungeon and went out—only pausing at the forge door to get the blacksmith to rivet his wing.

He met the lame giant at the gate of the town, and the giant banged on the dragon with his club as if he were banging an iron foundry, and the dragon behaved like a smelting works—all fire and smoke. It was a fearful sight, and people watched it from a distance, falling off their legs with the shock of every bang, but always getting up to look again.

At last the dragon won, and the giant sneaked away across the marshes, and the dragon, who was very tired, went home to sleep, announcing his intention of eating the town in the morning. He went back into his old dungeon because he was a stranger in the town, and he did not know of any other respectable lodging. Then Tina and Johnnie went to the mayor and corporation and said, "The giant is settled. Please give us the thousand pounds reward."

But the mayor said, "No, no, my boy. It is not you who have settled the giant, it is the dragon. I suppose you have chained him up again? When *he* comes to claim the reward he shall have it."

"He isn't chained up yet," said Johnnie. "Shall I send him to claim the reward?"

But the mayor said he need not trouble; and now he offered a thousand pounds to anyone who would get the dragon chained up again.

"I don't trust you," said Johnnie. "Look how you treated my father when he chained up the dragon."

But the people who were listening at the door interrupted, and said that if Johnnie could fasten up the dragon again they would turn out the mayor and let Johnnie be mayor in his place. For they had been dissatisfied with the mayor for some time, and thought they would like a change.

So Johnnie said, "Done," and off he went, hand-in-hand with Tina, and they called on all their little friends and said:—

"Will you help us to save the town?"

And all the children said, "Yes, of course we will. What fun!"

"Well, then," said Tina, "you must all bring your

basins of bread and milk to the forge to-morrow at breakfast time."

"And if ever I am mayor," said Johnnie, "I will give a banquet, and you shall be invited. And we'll have nothing but sweet things from beginning to end."

All the children promised, and next morning Tina and Johnny rolled the big washing-tub down the winding stair.

"What's that noise?" asked the dragon.

"It's only a big giant breathing," said Tina; "he's gone by, now."

Then, when all the town children brought their bread and milk, Tina emptied it into the wash-tub, and when the tub was full Tina knocked at the iron door with the grating in it, and said:—

"May we come in?"

"Oh, yes," said the dragon; "it's very dull here."

So they went in, and with the help of nine other children they lifted the washing-tub in and set it down by the dragon. Then all the other children went away, and Tina and Johnnie sat down and cried.

"What's this?" asked the dragon, "and what's the matter?"

"*This* is bread and milk," said Johnnie; "it's our breakfast—all of it."

"Well," said the dragon, "I don't see what you

E. NESBIT

want with breakfast. I'm going to eat every one in the town as soon as I've rested a little."

"Dear Mr. Dragon," said Tina, "I wish you wouldn't eat us. How would you like to be eaten yourself?"

"Not at all," the dragon confessed, "but nobody will eat me."

"I don't know," said Johnnie, "there's a giant——"

"I know. I fought with him, and licked him——"

"Yes, but there's another come now—the one you fought was only this one's little boy. This one is half as big again."

"He's seven times as big," said Tina.

"No, nine times," said Johnnie. "He's bigger than the steeple."

"Oh, dear," said the dragon. "I never expected this."

"And the mayor has told him where you are," Tina went on, "and he is coming to eat you as soon as he has sharpened his big knife. The mayor told him you were a wild dragon—but he didn't mind. He said he only ate wild dragons—with bread sauce."

"That's tiresome," said the dragon, "and I suppose this sloppy stuff in the tub is the bread sauce?"

The children said it was. "Of course," they added, "bread sauce is only served with wild dragons. Tame ones are served with apple sauce and

252

onion stuffing. What a pity you're not a tame one: he'd never look at you then," they said. "Good-bye, poor dragon, we shall never see you again, and now you'll know what it's like to be eaten." And they began to cry again.

"Well, but look here," said the dragon, "couldn't you pretend I was a tame dragon? Tell the giant that I'm just a poor little, timid tame dragon that you kept for a pet."

"He'd never believe it," said Johnnie. "If you were our tame dragon we should keep you tied up, you know. We shouldn't like to risk losing such a dear, pretty pet."

Then the dragon begged them to fasten him up at once, and they did so: with the collar and chains that were made years ago—in the days when men sang over their work and made it strong enough to bear any strain.

And then they went away and told the people what they had done, and Johnnie was made mayor, and had a glorious feast exactly as he had said he would—with nothing in it but sweet things. It began with Turkish delight and halfpenny buns, and went on with oranges, toffee, cocoanut-ice, pepper-mints, jam-puffs, raspberry-noyeau, ice-creams, and meringues, and ended with bull's-eyes and ginger-bread and acid-drops.

This was all very well for Johnnie and Tina; but if you are kind children with feeling hearts you will perhaps feel sorry for the poor deceived, deluded dragon—chained up in the dull dungeon, with nothing to do but to think over the shocking untruths that Johnnie had told him.

When he thought how he had been tricked the poor captive dragon began to weep—and the large tears fell down over his rusty plates. And presently he began to feel faint, as people sometimes do when they have been crying, especially if they have not had anything to eat for ten years or so.

And then the poor creature dried his eyes and looked about him, and there he saw the tub of bread and milk. So he thought, "If giants like this damp, white stuff, perhaps *I* should like it too," and he tasted a little, and liked it so much that he ate it all up.

And the next time the tourists came, and Johnnie let off the coloured fire, the dragon said, shyly:—

"Excuse my troubling you, but could you bring me a little more bread and milk?"

So Johnnie arranged that people should go round with carts every day to collect the children's bread and milk for the dragon. The children were fed at the town's expense—on whatever they liked; and they ate nothing but cake and buns and sweet

things, and they said the poor dragon was very welcome to their bread and milk.

Now, when Johnnie had been mayor ten years or
so he married Tina, and on their wedding morning
they went to see the dragon. He had grown quite
tame, and his rusty plates had fallen off in places,
and underneath he was soft and furry to stroke. So
now they stroked him.

And he said, "I don't know how I could ever have
liked eating anything but bread and milk. I *am* a
tame dragon, now, aren't I?" And when they said
"Yes, he was," the dragon said:—

"I am so tame, won't you undo me?" And some
people would have been afraid to trust him, but
Johnnie and Tina were so happy on their wedding
day that they could not believe any harm of
anyone in the world. So they loosed the chains, and
the dragon said, "Excuse me a moment, there are
one or two little things I should like to fetch," and
he moved off to those mysterious steps and went
down them, out of sight into the darkness. And
as he moved more and more of his rusty plates
fell off.

In a few minutes they heard him clanking up the
steps. He brought something in his mouth—it was a
bag of gold.

"It's no good to me," he said; "perhaps you might

find it come in useful." So they thanked him very kindly.

"More where that came from," said he, and fetched more and more and more, till they told him to stop. So now they were rich, and so were their fathers and mothers. Indeed, everyone was rich, and there were no more poor people in the town. And they all got rich without working, which is very wrong; but the dragon had never been to school, as you have, so he knew no better.

And as the dragon came out of the dungeon, following Johnnie and Tina into the bright gold and blue of their wedding day, he blinked his eyes as a cat does in the sunshine, and he shook himself, and the last of his plates dropped off, and his wings with them, and he was just like a very, very extra-sized cat. And from that day he grew furrier and furrier, and he was the beginning of all cats. Nothing of the dragon remained except the claws, which all cats have still, as you can easily ascertain.

And I hope you see now how important it is to feed your cat with bread and milk. If you were to let it have nothing to eat but mice and birds it might grow larger and fiercer, and scalier and tailier, and get wings and turn into the beginning of dragons. And then there would be all the bother over again.

WILLIAM MORRIS

William Morris (1834–1896) is probably best remembered today through his design work: his wallpapers, fabrics and furniture. He was a passionate utopian socialist who decried the ugliness of modern life and set out to offer something different in the art he created: he saw the Middle Ages as a time when craftspeople combined utility with beauty. Morris was partially responsible for the Arthurian revival – his early writing included a poem, 'The Defence of Guenevere', which would become one of the key narrative sources for modern fantasy, and through translations he also brought medieval Icelandic sagas to the attention of Victorian readers. He virtually created the modern heroic fantasy, in novels like *The Well at the World's End* (1896) and *The Water of the Wondrous Isles* (1897). Even today, the epic or heroic fantasy is by default 'medieval'. Narnia and Middle Earth, the fantasy worlds of C. S. Lewis and J. R. R. Tolkien, have their origins in childhood readings of Morris's fantasies.

Of old time, in the days of the kings, there was a king of folk, a mighty man in battle, a man deemed lucky by the wise, who ruled over a folk that begrudged not his kingship, whereas they knew of his valour and wisdom and saw how by his means they prevailed over other folks, so that their land was wealthy and at peace save about its uttermost borders. And this folk was called the Folk of the Mountain Door, or more shortly, of the Door.

Strong of body was this king, tall and goodly to look on, so that the hearts of women fluttered with desire when he passed them by. In the prime and flower of his age he wedded a wife, a seemly mate, a woman of the Earl-kin, tall and white-skinned, golden haired and grey-eyed; healthy, sweet-breathed, and soft-spoken, courteous of manners, wise of heart, kind to all folk, well-beloved of little children. In early spring-tide was the wedding, and a little after Yule she was brought to bed of a man-child of whom the midwives said they had never seen a fairer. He was sprinkled with water and was named Host-lord after the name of his kindred of old.

Great was the feast of his name-day, and much people came thereto, the barons of the land, and the lords of the neighbouring folk who would fain stand

258

well with the king; and merchants and craftsmen and sages and bards; and the king took them with both hands and gave them gifts, and hearkened to their talk and their tales, as if he were their very earthly fellow; for as fierce as he was afield with the sword in his fist, even so meek and kind he was in the hall amongst his folk and the strangers that sought to him.

Now amongst the guests that ate and drank in the hall on the even of the Name-day, the king as he walked amidst the tables beheld an old man as tall as any champion of the king's host, but far taller had he been, but that he was bowed with age. He was so clad that he had on him a kirtle of lambswool undyed and snow-white, and a white cloak, lined with ermine and welted with gold; a golden fillet set with gems was on his head, and a gold-hilted sword by his side; and the king deemed as he looked on him that he had never seen any man more like to the Kings of the Ancient World than this man. By his side sat a woman old and very old, but great of stature, and noble of visage, clad, she also, in white wool raiment embroidered about with strange signs of worms and fire-drakes, and the sun and the moon and the host of heaven.

So the king stayed his feet by them, for already he had noted that at the table whereat they sat there had been this long time at whiles greater laughter and more joyous than anywhere else in the hall, and whiles the hush of folk that hearken to what delights the inmost of their hearts. So now he greeted those ancients and said to them: "Is it well with you, neighbours?" And the old carle hailed the king, and said, "There is little lack in this house today."

"What lack at all do ye find therein?" said the king. Then there came a word into the carle's mouth and he sang in a great voice:

Erst was the earth
Fulfilled of mirth:
Our swords were sheen
In the summer green;
And we rode and ran
Through winter wan,
And long and wide
Was the feast-hall's side.
And the sun that was sunken
Long under the wold
Hung ere we were drunken
High over the gold;
And as fowl in the bushes
Of summer-tide sing
So glad as the thrushes
Sang earl-folk and king.

Though the wild wind might splinter
The oak-tree of Thor,
The hand of mid-winter
But beat on the door.

"Yea," said the king, "and dost thou say that winter hath come into my hall on the Name-day of my first-born?"

"Not so," said the carle.

"What is amiss then?" said the king. Then the carle sang again:

Were many men
In the feast-hall then,
And the worst on bench
Ne'er thought to blench
When the storm arose
In the war-god's close;
And for Tyr's high-seat,
Were the best full meet:
And who but the singer
Was leader and lord,
I steel-god, I flinger
Of adder-watched hoard?
Aloft was I sitting
Amidst of the place
And watched men a-flitting

261

All under my face.
And hushed for mere wonder
Were great men and small
As my voice in rhyme-thunder
Went over the hall.

"Yea," said the king, "thou hast been a mighty lord in days gone past, I thought no less when first I set eyes on thee. And now I bid thee stand up and sit on the high-seat beside me, thou and thy mate. Is she not thy very speech-friend?"

Therewith a smile lit up the ancient man's face, and the woman turned to him and he sang:

Spring came of old
In the days of gold,
In the thousandth year
Of the thousands dear,
When we twain met
And the mead was wet
With the happy tears
Of the best of the years.
But no cloud hung over
The eyes of the sun
That looked down on the lover
Ere eve was begun.
Oft, oft came the greeting

Of spring and her bliss

To the mead of our meeting,

The field of our kiss.

Is spring growing older?

Is earth on the wane

As the bold and the bolder

That come not again?

"O king of a happy land," said [the ancient man], "I will take thy bidding, and sit beside thee this night that thy wisdom may wax and the days that are to come may be better for thee than the days that are."

So he spake and rose to his feet, and the ancient woman with him, and they went with the king up to the high-seat, and all men in the feast-hall rose up and stood to behold them, and they deemed them wonderful and their coming a great thing.

But now when they were set down on the right hand and the left hand of the king, he turned to the ancient man and said to him: "O Lord of the days gone past, and of the battles that have been, wilt thou now tell me of thy name, and the name of thy mate, that I may call a health for thee first of all great healths that shall be drunk tonight."

But the old man said and sang:

King, hast thou thought
How nipped and nought
Is last year's rose
Of the snow-filled close?
Or dost thou find
Last winter's wind
Will yet avail
For thy hall-glee's tale?
E'en such and no other
If spoken tonight
Were the name of the brother
Of war-gods of might.
Yea the word that hath shaken
The walls of the house
When the warriors half waken
To battle would rouse
Ye should drowse if ye heard it
Nor turn in the chair.
O long long since they feared it
Those foemen of fear!
Unhelpful, unmeaning
Its letters are left;
For the man overweening
Of manhood is reft.

This word the king hearkened, and found no
word in his mouth to answer: but he sat pondering

heavy things, and sorrowful with the thought of the lapse of years, and the waning of the blossom of his youth. And all the many guests of the great feast-hall sat hushed, and the hall-glee died out amongst them.

But the old man raised his head and smiled, and he stood on his feet, and took the cup in his hand and cried out aloud: "What is this my masters, are ye drowsy with meat and drink in this first hour of the feast? Or have tidings of woe without words been borne amongst you, that ye sit like men given over to wan hope, awaiting the coming of the doom that none may gainsay, and the foe that none may overcome? Nay then, nay; but if ye be speechless I will speak; and if ye be joyless I will rejoice and bid the good wine welcome home. But first will I call a health over the cup:

> Pour, white-armed ones,
> As the Rhine flood runs!
> And O thanes in hall
> I bid you all
> Rise up, and stand
> With the horn in hand,
> And hearken and hear
> The old name and the dear.
> To HOST-LORD the health is
> Who guarded of old

The House where the wealth is
The Home of the gold.
And again the Tree bloometh
Though winter it be
And no heart of man gloometh
From mountain to sea.
Come thou Lord, the rightwise,
Come Host-lord once more
To thy Hall-fellows, fightwise
The Folk of the Door!

Huge then was the sudden clamour in the hall, and the shouts of men and clatter of horns and clashing of weapons as all folk old and young, great and little, carle and quean, stood up on the Night of the Name-day. And once again there was nought but joy in the hall of the Folk of the Door.

But amidst the clamour the inner doors of the hall were thrown open, and there came in women clad most meetly in coloured raiment, and amidst them a tall woman in scarlet, bearing in her arms the babe new born clad in fine linen and wrapped in a golden cloth, and she bore him up thus toward the high-seat, while all men shouted even more if it were possible, and set down cup and horn from their lips, and took up sword and shield and raised the shield-roar in the hall.

But the [king] rose up with a joyful countenance, and got him from out of his chair, and stood there by: and the women stayed at the foot of the dais all but the nurse, who bore up the child to the king, and gave it into his arms; and he looked fondly on the youngling for a short space, and then raised him aloft so that all men in the hall might see him, and so laid him on the board before them and took his great spear from the wall behind him and drew the point thereof across and across the boy's face so that it well nigh grazed his flesh: at the first and at the last did verily graze it as little as might be, but so that the blood started; and while the babe wailed and cried, as was to be looked for, the king cried aloud with a great voice:

"Here mark I thee to Odin even as were all thy kin marked from of old from the time that the Gods were first upon the earth."

Then he took the child up in his arms and laid him in his own chair, and cried out: "This is Host-lord the son of Host-lord King and Duke of the Folk of the Door, who sitteth in his father's chair and shall do when I am gone to Odin, unless any of the Folk gainsay it."

When he had spoken there came a man in at the door of the hall clad in all his war-gear with a great spear in his hand, and girt with a sword, and he strode clashing through the hall up to the high-seat and stood by the chair of the king and lifted up his helm a little and cried out:

"Where are now the gainsayers, or where is the champion of the gainsayers? Here stand I Host-rock of the Falcons of the Folk of the Door, ready to meet the gainsayers."

And he let his helm fall down again so that his face was hidden. And a man one-eyed and huge rose up from the lower benches and cried out in a loud voice: "O champion, hast thou hitherto foregone thy meat and drink to sing so idle a song over the hall-glee? Come down amongst us, man, and put off thine armour and eat and drink and be merry; for [of] thine hunger and thirst am I full certain. Here be no gainsayers, but brethren all, the sons of one Mother and one Father, though they be grown somewhat old by now."

Then was there a clamour again, joyous with laughter and many good words. And some men say, that when this man had spoken, the carle and quean ancient of days who sat beside the king's chair, were all changed and seemed to men's eyes as if they were in the flower of their days, mighty, and lovely and of merry countenance: and it is told that no man knew that big-voiced speaker, nor whence he came, and that presently when men looked for him he was gone from the hall, and they knew not how.

Be this as it may, the two ancient ones each stooped down over the chair whereas lay the little one and kissed him; and the old man took his cup and wetted the lips of the babe with red wine, and the old woman took a necklace from her neck of amber and silver and gold and did it on the youngling's neck and spake; and her voice was very sweet though she were old; and many heard the speech of her:

"O Host-lord of this even, Live long and hale! Many a woman shall look on thee and few that see thee shall forbear to love thee."

Then the nurse took up the babe again and bore him out to the bower where lay his mother, and the folk were as glad as glad might be, and no man hath told of mirth greater and better than the hall-glee of that even. And the old carle sat yet beside the king and was blithe with him and of many words, and told him tales that he had never known before; and all these were of the valiant deeds and the lives of his fathers before him, and strange stories of the Folk of the Door and what they had done, and the griefs which they had borne and the joys which they had won from the earth and the heavens and the girdling waters of the world. And the king waxed exceeding glad as he heard it all, and thought he would try to bear it in mind as long as he lived; for it seemed to him that when he had parted from those two ancient ones, that night, he should never see them again.

So wore the time and the night was so late, that had it been summer-tide, it had been no night but early day. And the king looked up from the board and those two old folk, and beheld the hall, that there were few folk therein, save those that lay along by the walls of the aisles, so swiftly had the night gone and all folk were departed or asleep. Then was he like a man newly wakened from a dream, and he turned about to the two ancients almost looking to see their places empty. But they abode there yet beside him on the right hand and on the left; so he said: "Guests, I give you all thanks for your company and the good words and noble tales wherewith ye have beguiled this night of winter, and surely tomorrow shall I rise up wiser than I was yesterday. And now meseemeth ye are old and doubtless weary with the travel and the noisy mirth of the feast-hall, nor may I ask you to abide bedless any longer, though it be great joy to me to hearken to your speech. Come then to the bower aloft and I will show you the best of beds and the soft and kind place to abide the uprising of tomorrow's sun; and late will he arise, for this is now the very midwinter, and the darkest of all days in the year."

Then answered the old man: "I thank thee, O son of the Kindred; but so it is that we have further to

wend than thou mightest deem; yea, back to the land
whence we came many a week of years ago and
before the building of houses in the land, between
the mountain and the sea. Wherefore if thou would-
est do aught to honour us, come thou a little way on
the road and see us off in the open country without
the walls of thy Burg: then shall we depart in such
wise that we shall be dear friends as long as we live,
thou and thine, and I and mine."

"This is not so great an asking," said the king,
"but that I would do more for thee; yet let it be as
thou wilt."

And he arose from table and they with him, and
they went down the hall amidst the sleeping folk and
the benches that had erst been so noisy and merry,
and out a-doors they went all three and into the
street of the Burg. Open were the Burg-gates and
none watched there, for there was none to break the
Yule-tide peace; so the king went forth clad in his
feasting-raiment, and those twain went, one on
either side of him. The midwinter frost was hard
upon the earth, so that few waters were running, and
all the face of the world was laid under snow: high
was the moon and great and round in a cloudless
sky, so that the stars looked but little.

The king set his face toward the mountains and
strode with great strides over the white highway

betwixt the hidden fruitfulness of the acres, and he was as one wending on an errand which he may not forego; but at last he said: "Whither wend we and how far?" Then spake the old man: "Whither should we wend save to the Mountain Door, and the entrance to the land whence the folk came forth, when great were its warriors and little was the tale of them."

Then the king spake no more, but it seemed to him as if his feet sped on faster than their wont was, and as if those twain bore him up so that his feet were but light on the face of the earth.

Thus wise they passed the plain and the white-clad ridges at the mountain feet in no long while, and were come before the yawning gap and strait way into the heart of the mountains, and there was no other way thereinto save this; for otherwhere, the cliffs rose like a wall from the plain-country. Grim was that pass, and high were the sides of it beneath the snow, which lay heaped up high, so now there were smooth white slopes on either side of the narrow road of the pass; while the wind had whistled the said road in most places well nigh clear of snow, which even now went whirling and drifting about beneath the broad moon. For the wind yet blew though the night was old, and the sound of it in the clefts of the rocks and the windings of the pass was like the rolling of the summer thunder.

Up the pass they went till it widened, and there was a wide space before them, the going up whereto was as by stairs, and also the going up from it to the higher pass; and all around it the rocks were high and sheer, so that there was no way over them save for the fowl flying; and were it not winter there had been a trickling stream running round about the eastern side of the cliff wall which lost itself in the hollow places of the rocks at the lower end of that round hall of the mountain, unroofed and unpillared. Amidmost the place the snow was piled up high; for there in summer was a grassy mound amidst of a little round meadow of sweet grass, treeless, bestrewn here and there with blocks that had been borne down thitherward by the waters from the upper mountain; and for ages beyond what the memory of men might tell of this had been the Holy place and Motestead of the Folk of the Door.

Now all three went up on to the snow-covered mound, and those two turned about and faced the king and he saw their faces clearly, so bright as the moon was, and now it was so that they were no more wrinkled and hollow-cheeked and sunken-eyed, though scarce might a man say that they looked young, but exceeding fair they were, and they looked on him with eyes of love, and the carle said: "Lord of the Folk of the Door, father of the son new born whom the Folk this night have taken for their father, and the image of those that have been, we have brought thee to the Holy Place that we might say a word to thee and give thee a warning of the days to come, so that if it may be thou mightest eschew the evil and ensue the good. For thou art our dear son, and thy son is yet dearer to us, since his days shall be longer if weird will so have it. Hearken to this by the token that under the grass, beneath this snow, lieth the first of the Folk of the Door of those that come on the earth and go thence; and this was my very son begotten on this woman that here standeth. For wot thou that I am Host-lord of the Ancient Days, and from me is all the blood of you come; and dear is the blood of my sons and my name even as that which I have seen spilt on field and in fold, on grass and in grange, without the walls of the watches and about the lone wells of the desert places. Hearken then, Host-lord the Father of Host-lord, for we have looked into the life of thy son; and this we say is the weird of him; childless shall he be unless he wed as his will is; for of all his kindred none is wilfuller than he. Who then shall he wed, and where is the House that is lawful to him that thou hast not heard of? For as to wedding with his will in the House whereof thou wottest, and the Line of the Sea-dwellers, look not for it. Where then is the House of his wedding, lest the Folk of the Door lose their Chieftain and become the servants of those that are worser than they? I may not tell thee; and if I did, it would help thee nought. But this I will tell thee, when thy fair son is of fifteen winters, until the time that he is twenty winters and two, evil waylayeth on him: evil of the sword, evil of the cord, evil of the shaft, evil of the draught, evil of the cave, evil of the wave. O Son and father of my son, heed my word and let him be so watched that while as none hath been watched and warded of all thy kindred who have gone before, lest when his time come and he depart from this land he wander about the further side of the bridge that goeth to the Hall of the Gods, for very fear of shaming amongst the bold warriors and begetters of kindred and fathers of the sons that I love, that shall one day sit and play at the golden tables in the Plains of Ida."

So he spake, but the king spake: "O Host-lord of the Ancients I had a deeming of what thou wert, and that thou hadst a word for me. Wilt thou now tell me one thing more? In what wise shall I ward our son from the evil till his soul is strengthened, and the Wise-wights and the Ancients are become his friends, and the life of the warrior is in his hands and the days of a chieftain of our folk?"

Then the carle smiled on him and sang:

Wide is the land
Where the houses stand,
There bale and bane
Ye scarce shall chain;
There the sword is ground
And wounds abound;
And women fair
Weave the love-nets there.
Merry hearts in the Mountain
Dales shepherd-men keep,
And about the Fair Fountain
Need more than their sheep.
Of the Dale of the Tower
Where springeth the well
In the sun-slaying hour
They talk and they tell;
And often they wonder
Whence cometh the name
And what tale lies thereunder
For honour or shame.
For beside the fount welling
No castle now is;
Yet seldom foretelling
Of weird wends amiss.

Quoth the king, "I have heard tell of the Fair Fountain and the Dale of the Tower; though I have never set eyes thereon, and I deem it will be hard to find. But dost thou mean that our son who is born the Father of the Folk shall dwell there during that while of peril?"

Again sang the carle:

> Good men and true,
> They deal and do
> In the grassy dales
> Of that land of the tales;
> Where dale and down
> Yet wears the crown
> Of the flower and fruit
> From our kinship's root.
> There little man sweateth
> In trouble and toil,
> And in joy he forgetteth
> The feud and the foil.
> The weapon he wendeth
> Achasing the deer,
> And in peace the moon endeth
> That endeth the year.
> Yet there dwell our brothers,
> And should they but know
> They thy stem of all others

Were planted to grow
Beside the Fair Fountain,
How fain were those men
Of the God of the Mountain
So come back again.

Then the king said: "Shall I fulfill the weird and build a Tower in the Dale for our Son? And deemest thou he shall dwell there happily till the time of peril is overpast?"

But the carle cried out, "Look, look! Who is the shining one who cometh up the pass?"

And the king turned hastily and drew his sword, but beheld neither man nor mare in the mountain, and when he turned back again to those twain, lo! they were clean gone, and there was nought in the pass save the snow and the wind, and the long shadows cast by the sinking moon. So he turned about again and went down the pass; and by then he was come into the first of the plain-country once more, the moon was down and the stars shone bright and big; but even in the dead midwinter there was a scent abroad of the coming of the dawn. So went the king as speedily as he might back to the Burg and his High House; and he was glad in his inmost heart that he had seen the God and Father of his Folk.

Arthur Machen

Arthur Machen (1863–1947) was born Arthur Llewellyn Jones but when he was two, his father changed his surname from Jones to Machen-Jones and Machen adopted the first part of that name for his writing. He moved to London and scraped a living as a tutor as well as working for publishers, and in 1890 began publishing stories, often with a fantastic theme. His first success was with his novella *The Great God Pan* (1894), which Stephen King described in 2008 as 'one of the best horror stories ever written. Maybe the best in the English language.' The other stories he wrote in the 1890s and early twentieth century were mostly horror, and they influenced H. P. Lovecraft, Alfred Hitchcock and much of the twentieth-century Gothic. In 1910, despairing of obtaining a decent income, he began work for Lord Northcliffe's *Evening Post*, and it was there he published 'The Bowmen' and other propagandistic stories that suited the mood of the time (and of his employer).

The Bowmen

It was during the Retreat of the Eighty Thousand, and the authority of the Censorship is sufficient excuse for not being more explicit. But it was on the most awful day of that awful time, on the day when ruin and disaster came so near that their shadow fell over London far away; and, without any certain news, the hearts of men failed within them and grew faint; as if the agony of the army in the battlefield had entered into their souls.

On this dreadful day, then, when three hundred thousand men in arms with all their artillery swelled like a flood against the little English company, there was one point above all other points in our battle line that was for a time in awful danger, not merely of defeat, but of utter annihilation. With the permission of the Censorship and of the military expert, this corner may, perhaps, be described as a salient, and if this angle were crushed and broken, then the English force as a whole would be shattered, the Allied left would be turned, and Sedan would inevitably follow.

All the morning the German guns had thundered and shrieked against this corner, and against the thousand or so of men who held it. The men joked at the shells, and found funny names for them, and had bets about them, and greeted them with scraps of music-hall songs. But the shells came on and burst, and tore good Englishmen limb from limb, and tore brother from brother, and as the heat of the day increased so did the fury of that terrific cannon-ade. There was no help, it seemed. The English artillery was good, but there was not nearly enough of it; it was being steadily battered into scrap iron.

There comes a moment in a storm at sea when people say to one another, "It is at its worst; it can blow no harder," and then there is a blast ten times more fierce than any before it. So it was in these British trenches.

There were no stouter hearts in the whole world than the hearts of these men; but even they were appalled as this seven-times-heated hell of the German cannonade fell upon them and overwhelmed them and destroyed them. And at this very moment they saw from their trenches that a tremendous host was moving against their lines. Five hundred of the thousand remained, and as far as they could see the German infantry was pressing on against them, column upon column, a grey world of men, ten thou-sand of them, as it appeared afterwards.

There was no hope at all. They shook hands, some of them. One man improvised a new version of the battle-song, "Good-bye, good-bye to Tipperary," ending with "And we shan't get there." And they all went on firing steadily. The officers pointed out that such an opportunity for high-class fancy shooting might never occur again; the Germans dropped line after line; the Tipperary humorist asked, "What price Sidney Street?" And the few machine guns did their best. But everybody knew it was of no use. The dead grey bodies lay in companies and battalions, as others came on and on and on, and they swarmed and stirred and advanced from beyond and beyond.

"World without end. Amen," said one of the British soldiers with some irrelevance as he took aim and fired. And then he remembered—he says he cannot think why or wherefore—a queer vegetarian restaurant in London where he had once or twice eaten eccentric dishes of cutlets made of lentils and nuts that pretended to be steak. On all the plates in this restaurant there was printed a figure of St. George in blue, with the motto, *Adsit Anglis Sanctus Georgius*— May St. George be a present help to the English. This soldier happened to know Latin and other useless things, and now, as he fired at his man in the grey advancing mass—three hundred yards away—he uttered the pious vegetarian motto. He went on firing to the end, and at last Bill on his right had to clout him cheerfully over the head to make him stop, pointing out as he did so that the King's ammunition cost money and was not lightly to be wasted in drilling funny patterns into dead Germans.

For as the Latin scholar uttered his invocation he felt something between a shudder and an electric shock pass through his body. The roar of the battle died down in his ears to a gentle murmur; instead of it, he says, he heard a great voice and a shout louder than a thunder-peal crying, "Array, array, array!"

His heart grew hot as a burning coal, it grew cold as ice within him, as it seemed to him that a tumult of voices answered to his summons. He heard, or seemed to hear, thousands shouting: "St. George! St. George!"

"Ha! messire; ha! sweet Saint, grant us good deliverance!"

"St. George for merry England!"

"Harow! Harow! Monseigneur St. George, succour us."

"Ha! St. George! Ha! St. George! a long bow and a strong bow."

"Heaven's Knight, aid us!"

And as the soldier heard these voices he saw before him, beyond the trench, a long line of shapes, with a shining about them. They were like men who drew the bow, and with another shout, their cloud of arrows flew singing and tingling through the air towards the German hosts.

*

The other men in the trench were firing all the while. They had no hope; but they aimed just as if they had been shooting at Bisley.

Suddenly one of them lifted up his voice in the plainest English.

"Gawd help us!" he bellowed to the man next to him, "but we're blooming marvels! Look at those grey . . . gentlemen, look at them! D'ye see them? They're not going down in dozens nor in 'undreds; it's thousands, it is. Look! look! there's a regiment gone while I'm talking to ye."

"Shut it!" the other soldier bellowed, taking aim, "what are ye gassing about?"

But he gulped with astonishment even as he spoke, for, indeed, the grey men were falling by the thousands. The English could hear the guttural scream of the German officers, the crackle of their revolvers as they shot the reluctant; and still line after line crashed to the earth.

*

All the while the Latin-bred soldier heard the cry:

"Harow! Harow! Monseigneur, dear saint, quick to our aid! St. George help us!"

"High Chevalier, defend us!"

The singing arrows fled so swift and thick that they darkened the air; the heathen horde melted from before them.

*

"More machine guns!" Bill yelled to Tom.

"Don't hear them," Tom yelled back. "But, thank God, anyway; they've got it in the neck."

In fact, there were ten thousand dead German soldiers left before that salient of the English army, and consequently there was no Sedan. In Germany, a country ruled by scientific principles, the Great General Staff decided that the contemptible English must have employed shells containing an unknown gas of a poisonous nature, as no wounds were discernible on the bodies of the dead German soldiers. But the man who knew what nuts tasted like when they called themselves steak knew also that St. George had brought his Agincourt Bowmen to help the English.

REGINA MIRIAM BLOCH

Regina Miriam Bloch (1888–1938) was a German Jewish author, born in Sondershausen in present-day Thuringia and educated in Berlin and London. Bloch settled in London after the First World War and made a public appeal for the establishment of a Jewish arts and crafts movement. Bloch wrote for both the Jewish and the Gentile press and contributed to a number of anthologies, including *New Songs* (1907), edited by Fred G. Bowles, *The Book of the Poet's Club* (1909), which includes early poetry by Ezra Pound and *The Real Jew* (1925), edited by H. Newman. Her best-known publication is *The Confessions of Inayat Khan* (1915), a study of the Indian philosopher and musician, whose mission was to bring Sufi mysticism to Europe and America. In her fiction, Bloch blended mysticism and the occult.

The Swine-Gods

In my dream I wandered along an endless lane, gray as the smoke of twilight ere night hath kindled the fires of her stars upon God's hearthplace. It wound ceaselessly on and on as a grey serpent uncoiling; the trees were lean and dismal, and gloomed like clouds through the besetting mists.

I grew weary wandering its arid spaces; my feet saddened and my heart sank within me.

And there came by a little child whose face was peaked with sobbing, and whose hair was wild, and that had a broken wing upon its shoulder.

I said: "Where am I?"

It said: "This is the Long Lane of the Lost, and I am a Lost Love."

And it passed on.

And there came another child, with an elfin face that held a ruined laughter, and whose rose-red robe was tattered.

I said: "Who art thou?"

She said: "I am a lost Hour of Delight and there is mud upon my feet."

And she went on.

She was followed by a third child in a gown that had once been skyey-blue, but was faded to drabness by wind and weather. She bare withered lilies in her arm and at her kirtle hung a broken lute.

I said: "Who art thou?"

And she looked at me with eyes wherein the violets had paled and said: "I am a Lost Illusion, for all things lost wander along this Lane."

I said: "Is there no house within it? For I am weary of my bitter wayfaring, and it hath no end."

She made answer: "There is no rest-house but one."

I said: "Where?"

Then she pointed, saying: "Yonder," and passed by also.

I looked where she had shewn to me and saw, beyond the mist, a palace with mighty walls frowning on high and pinnaces and towers that were fashioned curiously.

I went on towards it and lo! the bridge fell clashing from invisible hands above a river that ran murk and drear about it. The gates and doorways of bronze stood wide and nowhere was there a keeper and straightway I entered in.

As I passed I heard from afar, a moaning as of one in pain and the baying of a distant pack. I wondered who it was that hunted a-down the Long Lane of the Lost.

And I went marvelling into the silent palace.

I found myself within a hall greater than any dreamed of by men, and built entirely with pillars and walls of black porphyry and basalt.

The heavy columns frowned stupendously; a sable dome seemed to soar above me in its giddy heights, where beasts and bats with harpy faces and dusk wings circled without cess, flapping and screaming. The floors were of black jade that shimmered like a haunted mere. And from the pillars hung pendants of black crystal shining frostily, while in the crevices of the flags, the pediments and colonnades, raven flowers like creatures of death moved and spread their petals until they seemed as greedy, voracious mouths. At either end of the hall there was a furnace of red fire, in the midst whereof, beyond steps of black marble, loomed a terrific Baal of iron to which many acolytes were sacrificing.

I went towards the Baal at the right end of the hall.

The glow of the fires in all that surrounding opaqueness dazzled me. For a time I stood deafened by the crackle and roar of the flames from the core of the furnace. Then as my sight cleared, I saw a huge Moloch, with wide-open jaws and molten flaring hands and a head fashioned in the image of a Swine, whose snout belched fire.

Before him were priests with shaven heads and

leering faces, attired also in black. And each one bare a little silent flame of blue or white or red or green towards a High-Priest, who stood in the centre of the uppermost step before the Baal.

The High-Priest towered above the others and his robes shone with black jade. I could not see his face, but upon his head there were eagle-feathers and his foot was cloven.

And the High-Priest chanted, saying: "Master Mammon, O God Mammon, alway we find thy fuel and thy eternal fires never die, although thy hands are burnt unto white embers. O God above the other Gods of whom the world craves grace, since the dawning hath thy house been set upon sure foundations. Thy lures are deeper than the sockets of the sea; thy pride is ever fed, thy tents spread out their mighty camps in mockery of the Lord.

Behold! begetter of men, we do thine ancient service."

And one of the priests came forward and the little flame that burnt upon the platter in his hands was white.

And he gave it to him of the cloven foot, droning: "Arch-Flamen, this is the soul of a very young maid. Her limbs and body are as folded flowers, but her parents have sold her to an old man who hath much gold in his coffers. His lips are frore and blue, his breath is as the odour of death and his heart is as a satyr's."

Then the Arch-Priest lifted the white flame high, so that it lay close beneath the searing fire of the Swine-Baal's snout.

And crying: "O Mammon, the sweet savour of thy Virgin-bride!" he cast it down into the molten hands.

The fire hissed up once and crackled and burnt on.

Now there came a second priest, with a little blue flame, saying:

"This is the soul of a poet who dreamt exquisite dreams and went hungerful and there were very few to hearken.

Yet desire came to him, so he cast away his dreams and sang of vileness and abominable things. But the people flocked to hear and cried: 'More! More!'

He said: 'Verily, I will give ye more of my obscenities, if ye will give me your gold.'

Then they laughed, and stripped the coins from their hair and the bracelets from their arms.

And he sang on."

And the High-Priest cast the blue flame in, saying: "All the dreams and songs, the ideals and quests of the world are thine, O Master Mammon."

Next there came one bearing a red flame, who said: "This is the heart of a man who loved a maiden dearly.

She had only one gown and no jewels for her anklets, but her soul was pure as the dews of the dawn.

And he came unto a house wherein there dwelt a harlot, who had been the dancing-woman of the Caliphs. Her bed was hung with silk, her tables were of chalcedony, her ewers of silver and she had pearls upon her kirtle-zone.

And she said: 'I lust for thy youth and strength. Thou art as an oak and I as a palm that is broken. Abide with me!'

Then he looked upon her pearls and the chalcedony and barred the doors of her house against his love in the robe of white linen.

And her heart brake, but he drank of the wine in the ewers and forgat."

The red flame fell into the crimson fire and the Arch-Priest said: "O Master Mammon, O Breaker and Maker of hearts, O shaper of ways and wielder of destinies!"

Thereon came a priest bearing a yellow flame and he said:

"This is the soul of a man who was the favourite

Vizier of the King, who had raised him up from the poor of his city and set him within his gates.

The King gave him of his lands and much power besides, wherefore his house was almost as rich as the palace of his master.

But this Vizier had a wife who had also been of the poor of the King's city and could not rise to fit her place. And the Vizier left her and she grew old as a crone.

Then he cast his eyes upon the King's wife, who was fair and wore a tiar of emeralds on her head. And the King's wife looked upon him and he won her favours, for she was vain and his tongue was subtil.

And one night as he was secretly in the Queen's closet, he gazed about him at the rare traceries of gems and gold, and said:

'My house is not so great nor my wife so young and lovely. There is priceless treasure within the treasure-chambers. Why should not I wear the royal cloak and crown and make this woman my Queen?'

Then he rose up from her arms and stole privily into the bed-chamber of the King and stabbed him to death in his sleep."

And the Arch-Priest cast the yellow flame into the scarlet pit, chanting: "All the flowers of the world's envy and the fruits of the world's passion are woven into thy garland, Master Mammon!"

But I was sickened, and turned away and went over to the Baal that stood in the fiery furnace at the left end of the hall.

And lo! here too were priests bearing the soul-flames. Only their vessels were not of gold and silver, but of iron and steel. And the head of the Moloch was different, for it was that of a boar. From his jaws protruded two great tusks like spikes and from them burst alternate flame and smoke, amid an angry roaring that clattered through all his tremendous iron bulk.

But the High-Priest before him was as the one before the image of Mammon and had a cloven foot also.

And he chanted: "O Master Mars, O Master Mars, all nature is thy pawn. Thou battenest upon the weak in the numberless degrees of thy strength. Thou art the lord of the sharp fang, the ravenous maw, the piercing beak, the leaping beast. The Christs, Messiahs and prophets, the priests and angels fail before thee. The rot of thy carrion and the stench of thy carcasses ascend unto the portals of Heaven and their hellish incense defies the rose-haunted closes of Paradise . . .

Thou art the lord of the Valley of the Shadow, the moving scythe of death; thy arms grapple with youth immortally. Thou art the despoiler of the divine in

Man; thou demandest unending sacrifice and lo! it is given. For every son of woman, every creature of earth and sea and air are thine, thou Ravisher of the Eternities!"

And there came a priest bearing a flame, who said: "Lord, this is the soul of a young man who was the only son of his mother and she a widow.

They dwelt happily together, for he tilled her field and gat her oil and cracknels with the labour of his hands; while she gloried in the strength of him and the hair which was a gold fleece on his head and as the hair of the lover of her youth.

But the great Kings quarrelled in high places. They carried division into the land and laid it waste and despoiled its maidens.

Then the young husbandman said: 'My mother, I must lay by the plough-share and the pruning-hook and seize a lance and buckler in their stead. Farewell!'

She clung to him, tearless and numb for the greatness of her sorrow, and said: 'Haste home to me again. For thou art my all in the world and there is no other footfall that comes to me over the hills.'

He said: 'I will return.'

But he never came, for the sling-stone of a foeman struck his temple and he was trampled out of human semblance and into blood and mire by the stampeding chargers of the King's horsemen.

And his mother died alone of her broken heart."

Then the Arch-Priest seized the flame and hurled it in, saying:

"May this fair fume arise to thee, my Sire! Thine is the sweet first-fruit of all manhood, thine the eye-apple of maternity, thine the throne-jewels of a Sultan's vassalry."

Next there came a second priest, with a blood-red flame.

He said: "This is the soul of one who was the maker of machines of torment and torture.

He pored by night and by day to evolve strange gases that slay and metal monsters that devour.

He joyed when the fields ran foul with gore and entrails, where myriads of men had stood an hour a-gone, because of his devices.

He was crowned with glory and given great rewards by the ruler of his land."

And the Arch-Priest cast it in, saying: "O Mars, thou unknitter of bones, thou destroyer of flesh, thou glutton of limbs, thou wine-bibber of blood: accept thy sacrament!"

Yet there came another priest, bearing a flame that was almost black upon a platter of iron.

He spake: "This is the soul of a mighty King.

His palaces were gemmed with the riches of the world, his ships traversed the seven seas, his merchants sate in conclave, his armies were strong as the hosts of heaven, his throne was firm as the plinth of the sun.

He dreamed long beneath his canopies of his exceeding wealth, all things were at his service and decree. One day as he sat thus upon the dais of his pleasure-palace, idly toying with his sceptre, he said unto his minister: 'Hast thou ever seen a greater ruby or one of more brilliance than that upon my head-band?'

The counsellor replied: 'Yea, my Liege, for there is a larger one of more surpassing lustre in the fillet of the King of the Yonder-Land.'

The King said: 'Have it brought unto me!'

But the minister replied: 'I cannot, for it belongeth to this King and is the heirloom of his heritage.'

The King asked: 'Hath he other jewels?'

The counsellor answered: 'His is the only realm which rivalleth thine. His caskets overflow, his daughters are fair, his kingdom is peaceful, his people happy and toil pleasantly in the fertile fields.'

But the King's face grew dark with envy and his nostrils distended.

He said: 'Call out my guards and mariners, for I

will wrest his kingdom from him. There shall be no other King but me, no other Empire but mine own; I will rule unto the four ends of the earth.'

And he sent his rushing armies upon the Yonder-Land. Its rich fields were turned to seas of mud, its houses and temples to ruins, its castles looted, its Kings and young men slain, its Virgins defiled, its children and old women murdered.

But the ruby of the Yonder-Land glowed beside the other ruby in the head-band of the baleful King.

And he cried to his overseers and chamberlains: 'My Empire hath grown greater and there are now no other Kings on land or sea.

Whip up my slaves with your scourges, O over-seers; tax my people, O satraps, and let them rebuild the Yonder-Land and found new palaces unto my paramours and temples to my gods.'"

And the Arch-Priest cast the flame into the fire, saying: "Thou art the King of the blood-stained places, of the desolate and razëd cities; thine are the women killed with child, the ravished, the brutally slaughtered. Thine are tyranny and persecution, the anguish of wounded beasts, the offerings of the oppressed and tithed. Thine are the groans of slaves, the whistle of whips, the sweats of exceeding labour, O Master Mars, O God of War!"

Then sorrow seized upon me and I ran forth as

one possessed from that sable House of Mammon and Mars, with its dirging priests, its jeering litanies, its ceaseless sacrifices of human souls, its molten Swine-Gods amid its howling, insatiable fires.

As I sped out through the brazen gates and over the drawbridge, I heard again the baying of dogs and the monotonous moaning.

And as I reached the Long Lane of the Lost, there swept past me a pack of hounds in full cry.

Some were yellow as flame, some red as fire and others black as night. And they belled and raced like the wind.

As I gazed at them aghast, there came a clattering of hooves and behold! upon a great white horse, which had a crystal jewel set between its eyes and whose mane flew out in the storm, rode an Angel clad in black, who blew that wailing music upon a silver horn.

He had neither saddle nor stirrup nor rein, and yet rode fleetly after the manner of God's legionaries.

I caught at his robe, crying: "Huntsman! Huntsman!"

He paused a moment, saying: "What wouldst thou?"

And I saw that his face was white and sad as that

of one whom chill winds have beaten. His hair was dewy and his great wings draggled with rain.

I said: "What pack be this?"

He said: "The sleuth-hounds of God are passing down the Long Lane of the Lost. The black hounds are the moments of Pain, the red of Passion and the yellow of Remorse. We are hard upon the heels of a human soul that is seeking for the House of Mammon and Mars."

I said: "O Huntsman, who art thou?"

Then he smiled upon me with the sadness of his eyes, and answered: "The Eternal Conscience."

And blowing a mournful "Halloo! Hallo!" upon his silver horn, he shook me loose and was gone after the yelping pack.

And I cried out in terror and awoke.

RABINDRANATH TAGORE

Rabindranath Tagore (1861–1941) was a Bengali poet, playwright, composer, philosopher and social reformer. Tagore was educated at home in an intensely cultured family – his siblings all made their own reputations in poetry, music and prose. When he was sixteen, Tagore published his first poems under a pseudonym and these were mistaken as lost classics. In the late nineteenth century Tagore's work in poetry and prose was central to the emergence of Bengali modernism, and he won the Nobel prize for Literature in 1913. *Gitanjali* (*Song Offerings*), *Gora* (*Fair-Faced*) and *Ghare Baire* (*The Home and the World*) are his best-known works. Two of Tagore's compositions were chosen by two nations as national anthems: India's 'Jana Gana Mana' and Bangladesh's 'Amar Shonar Bangla'. In 1915, Tagore was awarded a knighthood but he renounced it in 1919, after the massacre at Jallianwala Bagh (also known as the Amritsar massacre) by the British. In 1922, he set up the Institute for Rural Reconstruction, and in the 1930s he attacked and lectured against caste consciousness. Tagore was anti-imperialist and pro-nationalist. His career spanned seventy years and every aspect of cultural endeavour.

Once There Was a King

"Once upon a time there was a king."

When we were children there was no need to know who the king in the fairy story was. It didn't matter whether he was called Shiladitya or Shaliban, whether he lived at Kashi or Kanauj. The thing that made a seven-year-old boy's heart go thump, thump with delight was this one sovereign truth, this reality of all realities: "Once there was a king."

But the readers of this modern age are far more exact and exacting. When they hear such an opening to a story, they are at once critical and suspicious. They apply the searchlight of science to its legendary haze and ask: "Which king?"

The story-tellers have become more precise in their turn. They are no longer content with the old indefinite, "There was a king," but assume instead a look of profound learning, and begin: "Once there was a king named Ajatasatru."

The modern reader's curiosity, however, is not so easily satisfied. He blinks at the author through his scientific spectacles, and asks again: "Which Ajatasatru?"

"Every schoolboy knows," the author proceeds, "that there were three Ajatasatrus. The first was born in the twentieth century B.C., and died at the tender age of two years and eight months. I deeply regret that it is impossible to find, from any trustworthy source, a detailed account of his reign. The second Ajatasatru is better known to historians. If you refer to the new Encyclopedia of History . . ."

By this time the modern reader's suspicions are dissolved. He feels he may safely trust his author. He says to himself: "Now we shall have a story that is both improving and instructive."

Ah! how we all love to be deluded! We have a secret dread of being thought ignorant. And we end by being ignorant after all, only we have done it in a long and roundabout way.

There is an English proverb: "Ask me no questions, and I will tell you no lies." The boy of seven who is listening to a fairy story understands that perfectly well; he withholds his questions, while the story is being told. So the pure and beautiful falsehood of it all remains naked and innocent as a babe; transparent as truth itself; limpid as a fresh bubbling spring. But the ponderous and learned lie of our moderns has to keep its true character draped and veiled. And if there is discovered anywhere the least little peep-hole of deception, the reader turns away with a prudish disgust, and the author is discredited.

When we were young, we understood all sweet

things; and we could detect the sweets of a fairy story by an unerring science of our own. We never cared for such useless things as knowledge. We only cared for truth. And our unsophisticated little hearts knew well where the Crystal Palace of Truth lay and how to reach it. But to-day we are expected to write pages of facts, while the truth is simply this:

"There was a king."

I remember vividly that evening in Calcutta when the fairy story began. The rain and the storm had been incessant. The whole of the city was flooded. The water was knee-deep in our lane. I had a straining hope, which was almost a certainty, that my tutor would be prevented from coming that evening. I sat on the stool in the far corner of the veranda looking down the lane, with a heart beating faster and faster. Every minute I kept my eye on the rain, and when it began to grow less I prayed with all my might: "Please, God, send some more rain till half-past seven is over." For I was quite ready to believe that there was no other need for rain except to protect one helpless boy one evening in one corner of Calcutta from the deadly clutches of his tutor.

If not in answer to my prayer, at any rate according to some grosser law of physical nature, the rain did not give up.

But, alas! nor did my teacher.

Exactly to the minute, in the bend of the lane, I saw his approaching umbrella. The great bubble of hope burst in my breast, and my heart collapsed. Truly, if there is a punishment to fit the crime after death, then my tutor will be born again as me, and I shall be born as my tutor.

As soon as I saw his umbrella I ran as hard as I could to my mother's room. My mother and my grandmother were sitting opposite one another playing cards by the light of a lamp. I ran into the room, and flung myself on the bed beside my mother, and said:

"Mother dear, the tutor has come, and I have such a bad headache; couldn't I have no lessons today?"

I hope no child of immature age will be allowed to read this story, and I sincerely trust it will not be used in text-books or primers for schools. For what I did was dreadfully bad, and I received no punishment whatever. On the contrary, my wickedness was crowned with success.

My mother said to me: "All right," and turning to the servant added: "Tell the tutor that he can go back home."

It was perfectly plain that she didn't think my illness very serious, as she went on with her game as before, and took no further notice. And I also, burying my head in the pillow, laughed to my heart's content. We perfectly understood one another, my mother and I.

But every one must know how hard it is for a boy of seven years old to keep up the illusion of illness for a long time. After about a minute I got hold of Grandmother, and said: "Grannie, do tell me a story."

I had to ask this many times. Grannie and Mother went on playing cards, and took no notice. At last Mother said to me: "Child, don't bother. Wait till we've finished our game." But I persisted: "Grannie, do tell me a story." I told Mother she could finish her game to-morrow, but she must let Grannie tell me a story there and then.

At last Mother threw down the cards and said: "You had better do what he wants. I can't manage him." Perhaps she had it in her mind that she would have no tiresome tutor on the morrow, while I should be obliged to be back to those stupid lessons.

As soon as ever Mother had given way, I rushed at Grannie. I got hold of her hand, and, dancing with delight, dragged her inside my mosquito curtain on to the bed. I clutched hold of the bolster with both hands in my excitement, and jumped up and down with joy, and when I had got a little quieter, said: "Now, Grannie, let's have the story!"

Grannie went on: "And the king had a queen." That was good to begin with. He had only one.

It is usual for kings in fairy stories to be extravagant in queens. And whenever we hear that there are two queens, our hearts begin to sink. One is sure to be unhappy. But in Grannie's story that danger was past. He had only one queen.

We next hear that the king had not got any son. At the age of seven I didn't think there was any need to bother if a man had had no son. He might only have been in the way.

Nor are we greatly excited when we hear that the king has gone away into the forest to practise austerities in order to get a son. There was only one thing that would have made me go into the forest, and that was to get away from my tutor!

But the king left behind with his queen a small girl, who grew up into a beautiful princess.

Twelve years pass away, and the king goes on practising austerities, and never thinks all this while of his beautiful daughter. The princess has reached the full bloom of her youth. The age of marriage has passed, but the king does not return. And the queen pines away with grief and cries: "Is my golden daughter destined to die unmarried? Ah me! What a fate is mine."

Then the queen sent men to the king to entreat

him earnestly to come back for a single night and take one meal in the palace. And the king consented.

The queen cooked with her own hand, and with the greatest care, sixty-four dishes, and made a seat for him of sandal-wood, and arranged the food in plates of gold and cups of silver. The princess stood behind with the peacock-tail fan in her hand. The king, after twelve years' absence, came into the house, and the princess waved the fan, lighting up all the room with her beauty. The king looked in his daughter's face, and forgot to take his food.

At last he asked his queen: "Pray, who is this girl whose beauty shines as the gold image of the goddess? Whose daughter is she?"

The queen beat her forehead, and cried: "Ah, how evil is my fate! Do you not know your own daughter?"

The king was struck with amazement. He said at last: "My tiny daughter has grown to be a woman."

"What else?" the queen said with a sigh. "Do you not know that twelve years have passed by?"

"But why did you not give her in marriage?" asked the king.

"You were away," the queen said. "And how could I find her a suitable husband?"

The king became vehement with excitement.

"The first man I see to-morrow," he said, "when I come out of the palace shall marry her."

The princess went on waving her fan of peacock feathers, and the king finished his meal.

The next morning, as the king came out of his palace, he saw the son of a Brahman gathering sticks in the forest outside the palace gates. His age was about seven or eight.

The king said: "I will marry my daughter to him."

Who can interfere with a king's command? At once the boy was called, and the marriage garlands were exchanged between him and the princess.

At this point I came up close to my wise Grannie and asked her eagerly: "What then?"

In the bottom of my heart there was a devout wish to substitute myself for that fortunate wood-gatherer of seven years old. The night was resonant with the patter of rain. The earthen lamp by my bedside was burning low. My grandmother's voice droned on as she told the story. And all these things served to create in a corner of my credulous heart the belief that I had been gathering sticks in the dawn of some indefinite time in the kingdom of some unknown king, and in a moment garlands had been exchanged between me and the princess, beautiful as the Goddess of Grace. She had a gold band on her hair and gold earrings in her ears. She had a necklace and bracelets of gold, and a golden waist-chain round her waist, and a pair of golden anklets tinkled above her feet.

If my grandmother were an author how many explanations she would have to offer for this little story! First of all, every one would ask why the king remained twelve years in the forest? Secondly, why should the king's daughter remain unmarried all that while? This would be regarded as absurd.

Even if she could have got so far without a quarrel, still there would have been a great hue and cry about the marriage itself. First, it never happened. Secondly, how could there be a marriage between a princess of the Warrior Caste and a boy of the priestly Brahman Caste? Her readers would have imagined at once that the writer was preaching against our social customs in an underhand way. And they would write letters to the papers.

So I pray with all my heart that my grandmother may be born a grandmother again, and not through some cursed fate take birth as her luckless grandson.

So with a throb of joy and delight, I asked Grannie: "What then?"

Grannie went on: Then the princess took her little husband away in great distress, and built a large palace with seven wings, and began to cherish her husband with great care.

I jumped up and down in my bed and clutched at the bolster more tightly than ever and said: "What then?"

Grannie continued: The little boy went to school and learnt many lessons from his teachers, and as he grew up his class-fellows began to ask him: "Who is that beautiful lady who lives with you in the palace with the seven wings?"

The Brahman's son was eager to know who she was. He could only remember how one day he had been gathering sticks, and a great disturbance arose. But all that was so long ago, that he had no clear recollection.

Four or five years passed in this way. His companions always asked him: "Who is that beautiful lady in the palace with the seven wings?" And the Brahman's son would come back from school and sadly tell the princess: "My school companions always ask me who is that beautiful lady in the palace with the seven wings, and I can give them no reply. Tell me, oh, tell me, who you are!"

The princess said: "Let it pass to-day. I will tell you some other day." And every day the Brahman's son would ask: "Who are you?" and the princess would reply: "Let it pass to-day. I will tell you some other day." In this manner four or five more years passed away.

At last the Brahman's son became very impatient, and said: "If you do not tell me to-day who you are, O beautiful lady, I will leave this palace with the seven wings." Then the princess said: "I will certainly tell you to-morrow."

Next day the Brahman's son, as soon as he came home from school, said: "Now, tell me who you are." The princess said: "To-night I will tell you after supper, when you are in bed."

The Brahman's son said: "Very well"; and he began to count the hours in expectation of the night. And the princess, on her side, spread white flowers over the golden bed, and lighted a gold lamp with fragrant oil, and adorned her hair, and dressed herself in a beautiful robe of blue, and began to count the hours in expectation of the night.

That evening when her husband, the Brahman's son, had finished his meal, too excited almost to eat, and had gone to the golden bed in the bed-chamber strewn with flowers, he said to himself: "To-night I shall surely know who this beautiful lady is in the palace with the seven wings."

The princess took for her the food that was left over by her husband, and slowly entered the bed-chamber. She had to answer that night the question, who was the beautiful lady who lived in the palace with the seven wings. And as she went up to the bed to tell him she found a serpent had crept out of the flowers and had bitten the Brahman's son. Her boy-husband was lying on the bed of flowers, with face pale in death.

My heart suddenly ceased to throb, and I asked with choking voice: "What then?"

Grannie said: "Then . . ."

But what is the use of going on any further with the story? It would only lead on to what was more and more impossible. The boy of seven did not know that, if there were some "What then?" after death, no grandmother of a grandmother could tell us all about it.

But the child's faith never admits defeat, and it would snatch at the mantle of death itself to turn him back. It would be outrageous for him to think that such a story of one teacherless evening could so suddenly come to a stop. Therefore the grand-mother had to call back her story from the ever-shut chamber of the great End, but she does it so simply: it is merely by floating the dead body on a banana stem on the river, and having some incantations read by a magician. But in that rainy night and in the dim light of a lamp death loses all its horror in the mind of the boy, and seems nothing more than a deep slumber of a single night. When the story ends the tired eyelids are weighed down with sleep. Thus it is that we send the little body of the child floating on the back of sleep over the still water of time, and then in the morning read a few verses of incantation to restore him to the world of life and light.

W. E. B. Du Bois

William Edward Burghardt Du Bois (1868–1963) was an American sociologist, historian and journalist. He is one of the key figures in the American civil rights movement in the first half of the twentieth century. Du Bois was the first African American to be awarded a doctorate from Harvard University, and in 1909 he co-founded the National Association for the Advancement of Colored People (NAACP). Like many activists, he found in science fiction and fantasy a way to express his critique of the past and his hopes for the future. After the First World War, when the contrast between treatment at home and abroad caused many Black men to challenge the status quo, Du Bois wrote a number of essays and stories. His best-known books are *The Souls of Black Folk* (1903) and *Black Reconstruction in America* (1935), but it is in *Darkwater: Voices from Within the Veil* (1920) that he included a number of fantastical stories.

The Princess of the Hither Isles

Her soul was beautiful, wherefore she kept it veiled in lightly-laced humility and fear, out of which peered anxiously and anon the white and blue and pale-gold of her face,—beautiful as daybreak or as the laughing of a child. She sat in the Hither Isles, well walled between the This and Now, upon a low and silver throne, and leaned upon its armposts, sadly looking upward toward the sun. Now the Hither Isles are flat and cold and swampy, with drear-drab light and all manner of slimy, creeping things, and piles of dirt and clouds of flying dust and sordid scraping and feeding and noise.

She hated them and ever as her hands and busy feet swept back the dust and slime her soul sat silver-throned, staring toward the great hill to the westward, which shone so brilliant-golden beneath the sunlight and above the sea.

The sea moaned and with it moaned the princess' soul, for she was lonely,—very, very lonely, and full weary of the monotone of life. So she was glad to see a moving in Yonder Kingdom on the mountainside, where the sun shone warm, and when the king of Yonder Kingdom, silken in robe and golden-crowned and warded by his hound, walked down along the restless waters and sat beside the armpost

of her throne, she wondered why she could not love
him and fly with him up the shining mountain's side,
out of the dirt and dust that nested between the This
and Now. She looked at him and tried to be glad, for
he was bonny and good to look upon, this king of
Yonder Kingdom,—tall and straight, thin-lipped
and white and tawny. So, again, this last day, she
strove to burn life into his singularly sodden clay,—
to put his icy soul aflame wherewith to warm her
own, to set his senses singing. Vacantly he heard her
winged words, staring and curling his long mus-
taches with vast thoughtfulness. Then he said:

"We've found more gold in Yonder Kingdom."

"Hell seize your gold!" blurted the princess.

"No,—it's mine," he maintained stolidly.

She raised her eyes. "It belongs," she said, "to the
Empire of the Sun."

"Nay,—the Sun belongs to us," said the king
calmly as he glanced to where Yonder Kingdom
blushed above the sea. She glanced, too, and a softness crept into her eyes.

"No, no," she murmured as with hesitating pause
she raised her eyes above the sea, above the hill, up
into the sky where the sun hung silent and splendid.
Its robes were heaven's blue, lined and broidered in
living flame, and its crown was one vast jewel, glistening in glittering glory that made the sun's own

face a blackness,—the blackness of utter light. With blinded, tear-filled eyes she peered into that formless black and burning face and sensed in its soft, sad gleam unfathomed understanding. With sudden, wild abandon she stretched her arms toward it appealing, beseeching, entreating, and lo!

"Niggers and dagoes," said the king of Yonder Kingdom, glancing carelessly backward and lighting in his lips a carefully rolled wisp of fragrant tobacco. She looked back, too, but in half-wondering terror, for it seemed—

A beggar man was creeping across the swamp, shuffling through the dirt and slime. He was little and bald and black, rough-clothed, sodden with dirt, and bent with toil. Yet withal something she sensed about him and it seemed,—

The king of Yonder Kingdom lounged more comfortably beside the silver throne and let curl a tiny trail of light-blue smoke.

"I hate beggars," he said, "especially brown and black ones." And he then pointed at the beggar's retinue and laughed,—an unpleasant laugh, welded of contempt and amusement. The princess looked and shrank on her throne. He, the beggar man, was—was what? But his retinue,—that squalid, sordid, parti-colored band of vacant, dull-faced filth and viciousness—was writhing over the land, and he

and they seemed almost crouching underneath the
scorpion lash of one tall skeleton, that looked like
Death, and the twisted woman whom men called
Pain. Yet they all walked as one.

The king of Yonder Kingdom laughed, but the
princess shrank on her throne, and the king on
seeing her thus took a gold-piece from out of his
purse and tossed it carelessly to the passing throng.
She watched it with fascinated eyes,—how it rose
and sailed and whirled and struggled in the air, then
seemed to burst, and upward flew its light and sheen
and downward dropped its dross. She glanced at
the king, but he was lighting a match. She watched
the dross wallow in the slime, but the sunlight fell
on the back of the beggar's neck, and he turned his
head.

The beggar passing afar turned his head and the
princess straightened on her throne; he turned his
head and she shivered forward on her silver seat; he
looked upon her full and slow and suddenly she saw
within that formless black and burning face the
same soft, glad gleam of utter understanding, seen
so many times before. She saw the suffering of endless years and endless love that softened it. She saw
the burning passion of the sun and with it the cold,
unbending duty-deeds of upper air. All she had seen
and dreamed of seeing in the rising, blazing sun she

saw now again and with it myriads more of human tenderness, of longing, and of love. So, then, she knew. She rose as to a dream come true, with solemn face and waiting eyes.

With her rose the king of Yonder Kingdom, almost eagerly.

"You'll come?" he cried. "You'll come and see my gold?" And then in sudden generosity, he added: "You'll have a golden throne,—up there—when we marry."

But she, looking up and on with radiant face, answered softly: "I come."

So down and up and on they mounted,—the black beggar man and his cavalcade of Death and Pain, and then a space; and then a lone, black hound that nosed and whimpered as he ran, and then a space; and then the king of Yonder Kingdom in his robes, and then a space; and last the princess of the Hither Isles, with face set sunward and lovelight in her eyes.

And so they marched and struggled on and up through endless years and spaces and ever the black beggar looked back past death and pain toward the maid and ever the maid strove forward with lovelit eyes, but ever the great and silken shoulders of the king of Yonder Kingdom arose between the princess and the sun like a cloud of storms.

Now, finally, they neared unto the hillside's top-most shoulder and there most eagerly the king bent to the bowels of the earth and bared its golden entrails,—all green and gray and rusted—while the princess strained her pitiful eyes aloft to where the beggar, set 'twixt Death and Pain, whirled his slim back against the glory of the setting sun and stood somber in his grave majesty, enhaloed and transfig-ured, outstretching his long arms, and around all heaven glittered jewels in a cloth of gold.

A while the princess stood and moaned in mad amaze, then with one wilful wrench she bared the white flowers of her breast and snatching forth her own red heart held it with one hand aloft while with the other she gathered close her robe and poised herself.

The king of Yonder Kingdom looked upward quickly, curiously, still fingering the earth, and saw the offer of her bleeding heart.

"It's a Negro!" he growled darkly; "it may not be." The woman quivered.

"It's a nigger!" he repeated fiercely. "It's neither God nor man, but a nigger!"

The princess stepped forward.

The king grasped his sword and looked north and east; he raised his sword and looked south and west.

"I seek the sun," the princess sang, and started into the west.

"Never!" cried the king of Yonder Kingdom, "for such were blasphemy and defilement and the making of all evil."

So, raising his great sword he struck with all his might, and more. Down hissed the blow and it bit that little, white, heart-holding hand until it flew armless and dis-bodied up through the sunlit air. Down hissed the blow and it clove the whimpering hound until his last shriek shook the stars. Down hissed the blow and it rent the earth. It trembled, fell apart, and yawned to a chasm wide as earth from heaven, deep as hell, and empty, cold, and silent.

On yonder distant shore blazed the mighty Empire of the Sun in warm and blissful radiance, while on this side, in shadows cold and dark, gloomed the Hither Isles and the hill that once was golden, but now was green and slimy dross; all below was the sad and moaning sea, while between the Here and There flew the severed hand and dripped the bleeding heart.

Then up from the soul of the princess welled a cry of dark despair,—such a cry as only babe-raped mothers know and murdered loves. Poised on the crumbling edge of that great nothingness the princess hung, hungering with her eyes and straining her fainting ears against the awful splendor of the sky.

Out from the slime and shadows groped the king, thundering: "Back—don't be a fool!"

But down through the thin ether thrilled the still and throbbing warmth of heaven's sun, whispering "Leap!"

And the princess leapt.

MAY SINCLAIR

Mary Amelia St. Clair (1863–1946) wrote under the name May Sinclair. She wrote modernist novels, short stories, poetry and literary criticism, and was an active suffragist as well as a member of the militant Women's Social and Political Union. In 1914, Sinclair signed a pro-war statement along with the fantasy writer Hope Mirrlees and backed it up by joining the Munro Ambulance Corp (although she served only a few weeks at the front). Sinclair was interested in psychoanalysis, imagism and the relations between the sexes, and she fed these into her fantastical works. Sinclair published two volumes of fantastical stories, *Uncanny Stories* (1923) and *The Intercessor and Other Stories* (1931). Although for many years her work was ignored, by the 1970s she was taking her place as one of the key writers of the 1920s and 1930s.

The Nature of the Evidence

This is the story Marston told me. He didn't want to tell it. I had to tear it from him bit by bit. I've pieced the bits together in their time order, and explained things here and there, but the facts are the facts he gave me. There's nothing that I didn't get out of him somehow.

Out of *him*—you'll admit my source is unimpeachable. Edward Marston, the great K.C., and the author of an admirable work on "The Logic of Evidence." You should have read the chapters on "What Evidence Is and What It Is Not." You may say he lied; but if you knew Marston you'd know he wouldn't lie, for the simple reason that he's incapable of inventing anything. So that, if you ask me whether I believe this tale, all I can say is, I believe the things happened, because he said they happened and because they happened to him. As for what they *were*—well, I don't pretend to explain it, neither would he.

You know he was married twice. He adored his first wife, Rosamund, and Rosamund adored him. I suppose they were completely happy. She was fifteen years younger than he, and beautiful. I wish I could make you see how beautiful. Her eyes and mouth had the same sort of bow, full and wide-sweeping, and they stared out of her face with the same grave, contemplative innocence. Her mouth was finished off at each corner with the loveliest little moulding, rounded like the pistil of a flower. She wore her hair in a solid gold fringe over her forehead, like a child's, and a big coil at the back. When it was let down it hung in a heavy cable to her waist. Marston used to tease her about it. She had a trick of tossing back the rope in the night when it was hot under her, and it would fall smack across his face and hurt him.

There was a pathos about her that I can't describe—a curious, pure, sweet beauty, like a child's; perfect, and perfectly immature; so immature that you couldn't conceive its lasting—like that—any more than childhood lasts. Marston used to say it made him nervous. He was afraid of waking up in the morning and finding that it had changed in the night. And her beauty was so much a part of herself that you couldn't think of her without it. Somehow you felt that if it went she must go too.

Well, she went first.

For a year afterwards Marston existed dangerously, always on the edge of a break-down. If he didn't go over altogether it was because his work saved him. He had no consoling theories. He was one of those bigoted materialists of the nineteenth century type who believe that consciousness is a purely physiological function, and that when your body's dead, *you're* dead. He saw no reason to suppose the contrary. "When you consider," he used to say, "the nature of the evidence!"

It's as well to bear this in mind, so as to realize that he hadn't any bias or anticipation. Rosamund survived for him only in his memory. And in his memory he was still in love with her. At the same time he used to discuss quite cynically the chances of his marrying again.

It seems that in their honeymoon they had gone into that. Rosamund said she hated to think of his being lonely and miserable, supposing she died before he did. She would like him to marry again. If, she stipulated, he married the right woman.

He had put it to her: "And if I marry the wrong one?"

And she had said, That would be different. She couldn't bear that.

He remembered all this afterwards; but there was nothing in it to make him suppose, at the time, that she would take action.

We talked it over, he and I, one night.

"I suppose," he said, "I shall have to marry again. It's a physical necessity. But it won't be anything more. I shan't marry the sort of woman who'll expect anything more. I won't put another woman in Rosamund's place. There'll be no unfaithfulness about it."

And there wasn't. Soon after that first year he married Pauline Silver.

She was a daughter of old Justice Parker, who was a friend of Marston's people. He hadn't seen the girl till she came home from India after her divorce.

Yes, there'd been a divorce. Silver had behaved very decently. He'd let her bring it against *him*, to save her. But there were some queer stories going about. They didn't get round to Marston, because he was so mixed up with her people; and if they had he wouldn't have believed them. He'd made up his mind he'd marry Pauline the first minute he'd seen her. She was handsome; the hard, black, white and vermilion kind, with a little aristocratic nose and a lascivious mouth.

It was, as he had meant it to be, nothing but physical infatuation on both sides. No question of Pauline's taking Rosamund's place.

Marston had a big case on at the time.

They were in such a hurry that they couldn't wait till it was over; and as it kept him in London they agreed to put off their honeymoon till the autumn, and he took her straight to his own house in Curzon Street.

This, he admitted afterwards, was the part he

hated. The Curzon Street house was associated with Rosamund; especially their bedroom—Rosamund's bedroom—and his library. The library was the room Rosamund liked best, because it was his room. She had her place in the corner by the hearth, and they were always alone there together in the evenings when his work was done, and when it wasn't done she would still sit with him, keeping quiet in her corner with a book.

Luckily for Marston, at the first sight of the library Pauline took a dislike to it.

I can hear her. "Br-rr-rh! There's something beastly about this room, Edward. I can't think how you can sit in it."

And Edward, a little caustic:

"*You* needn't, if you don't like it."

"I certainly shan't."

She stood there—I can see her—on the hearth-rug by Rosamund's chair, looking uncommonly handsome and lascivious. He was going to take her in his arms and kiss her vermilion mouth, when, he said, something stopped him. Stopped him clean, as if it had risen up and stepped between them. He supposed it was the memory of Rosamund, vivid in the place that had been hers.

You see it was just that place, of silent, intimate communion, that Pauline would never take. And the rich, coarse, contented creature didn't even want to take it. He saw that he would be left alone there, all right, with his memory.

But the bedroom was another matter. That, Pauline had made it understood from the beginning, she would have to have. Indeed, there was no other he could well have offered her. The drawing-room covered the whole of the first floor. The bedrooms above were cramped, and this one had been formed by throwing the two front rooms into one. It looked south, and the bathroom opened out of it at the back. Marston's small northern room had a door on the narrow landing at right angles to his wife's door. He could hardly expect her to sleep there, still less in any of the tight boxes on the top floor. He said he wished he had sold the Curzon Street house.

But Pauline was enchanted with the wide, three-windowed piece that was to be hers. It had been exquisitely furnished for poor little Rosamund; all seventeenth century walnut wood, Bokhara rugs, thick silk curtains, deep blue with purple linings, and a big, rich bed covered with a purple counter-pane embroidered in blue.

One thing Marston insisted on: that *he* should sleep on Rosamund's side of the bed, and Pauline in his own old place. He didn't want to see Pauline's body where Rosamund's had been. Of course he had to lie about it and pretend he had always slept on the side next the window.

I can see Pauline going about in that room, looking at everything; looking at herself, her black, white and vermilion, in the glass that had held Rosamund's pure rose and gold; opening the wardrobe where Rosamund's dresses used to hang, sniffing up the delicate, flower scent of Rosamund, not caring, covering it with her own thick trail.

And Marston (who cared abominably)—I can see him getting more miserable and at the same time more excited as the wedding evening went on. He took her to the play to fill up the time, or perhaps to get her out of Rosamund's rooms; God knows. I can see them sitting in the stalls, bored and restless, starting up and going out before the thing was half over, and coming back to that house in Curzon Street before eleven o'clock.

It wasn't much past eleven when he went to her room.

I told you her door was at right angles to his, and the landing was narrow, so that anybody standing by Pauline's door must have been seen the minute he opened his. He hadn't even to cross the landing to get to her.

Well, Marston swears that there was nothing there when he opened his own door; but when he came to Pauline's he saw Rosamund standing up before it; and, he said, *"She wouldn't let me in."*

Her arms were stretched out, barring the passage. Oh yes, he saw her face, Rosamund's face; I gathered that it was utterly sweet, and utterly inexorable. He couldn't pass her.

So he turned into his own room, backing, he says, so that he could keep looking at her. And when he stood on the threshold of his own door she wasn't there.

No, he wasn't frightened. He couldn't tell me what he felt; but he left his door open all night because he couldn't bear to shut it on her. And he made no other attempt to go in to Pauline; he was so convinced that the phantasm of Rosamund would come again and stop him.

I don't know what sort of excuse he made to Pauline the next morning. He said she was very stiff and sulky all day; and no wonder. He was still infatuated with her, and I don't think that the phantasm of Rosamund had put him off Pauline in the least. In fact, he persuaded himself that the thing was nothing but a hallucination, due, no doubt, to his excitement.

Anyhow, he didn't expect to see it at the door again the next night.

Yes. It was there. Only, this time, he said, it drew

aside to let him pass. It smiled at him, as if it were saying, "Go in, if you must; you'll see what'll happen."

He had no sense that it had followed him into the room; he felt certain that, this time, it would let him be.

It was when he approached Pauline's bed, which had been Rosamund's bed, that she appeared again, standing between it and him, and stretching out her arms to keep him back.

All that Pauline could see was her bridegroom backing and backing, then standing there, fixed, and the look on his face. That in itself was enough to frighten her.

She said, "What's the matter with you, Edward?"

He didn't move.

"What are you standing there for? Why don't you come to bed?"

Then Marston seems to have lost his head and blurted it out:

"I can't. I can't."

"Can't what?" said Pauline from the bed.

"Can't sleep with you. She won't let me."

"She?"

"Rosamund. My wife. She's there."

"What on earth are you talking about?"

334

"She's there, I tell you. She won't let me. She's pushing me back."

He says Pauline must have thought he was drunk or something. Remember, she *saw* nothing but Edward, his face, and his mysterious attitude. He must have looked very drunk.

She sat up in bed, with her hard, black eyes blazing away at him, and told him to leave the room that minute. Which he did.

The next day she had it out with him. I gathered that she kept on talking about the "state" he was in.

"You came to my room, Edward, in a *disgraceful* state."

I suppose Marston said he was sorry; but he couldn't help it; he wasn't drunk. He stuck to it that Rosamund was there. He had seen her. And Pauline said, if he wasn't drunk then he must be mad, and he said meekly, "Perhaps I *am* mad."

That set her off, and she broke out in a fury. He was no more mad than she was; but he didn't care for her; he was making ridiculous excuses; shamming, to put her off. There was some other woman.

Marston asked her what on earth she supposed he'd married her for. Then she burst out crying and said she didn't know.

Then he seems to have made it up with Pauline. He managed to make her believe he wasn't lying, that he really had seen something, and between them they arrived at a rational explanation of the appearance. He had been overworking. Rosamund's phantasm was nothing but a hallucination of his exhausted brain.

This theory carried him on till bed-time. Then, he says, he began to wonder what would happen, what Rosamund's phantasm would do next. Each morning his passion for Pauline had come back again, increased by frustration, and it worked itself up crescendo, towards night. Supposing he *had* seen Rosamund. He might see her again. He had become suddenly subject to hallucinations. But as long as you *knew* you were hallucinated you were all right.

So what they agreed to do that night was by way of precaution, in case the thing came again. It might even be sufficient in itself to prevent his seeing anything.

Instead of going in to Pauline he was to get into the room before she did, and she was to come to him there. That, they said, would break the spell. To make him feel even safer he meant to be in bed before Pauline came.

Well, he got into the room all right.

It was when he tried to get into bed that—he saw her (I mean Rosamund).

She was lying there, in his place next the window,

her own place, lying in her immature child-like beauty and sleeping, the firm full bow of her mouth softened by sleep. She was perfect in every detail, the lashes of her shut eyelids golden on her white cheeks, the solid gold of her square fringe shining, and the great braided golden rope of her hair flung back on the pillow.

He knelt down by the bed and pressed his forehead into the bedclothes, close to her side. He declared he could feel her breathe.

He stayed there for the twenty minutes Pauline took to undress and come to him. He says the minutes stretched out like hours. Pauline found him still kneeling with his face pressed into the bedclothes. When he got up he staggered.

She asked him what he was doing and why he wasn't in bed. And he said, "It's no use. I can't. I can't."

But somehow he couldn't tell her that Rosamund was there. Rosamund was too sacred; he couldn't talk about her. He only said:

"You'd better sleep in my room to-night."

He was staring down at the place in the bed where he still saw Rosamund. Pauline couldn't have seen anything but the bedclothes, the sheet smoothed above an invisible breast, and the hollow in the pillow. She said she'd do nothing of the sort.

She wasn't going to be frightened out of her own room. He could do as he liked.

He couldn't leave them there; he couldn't leave Pauline with Rosamund, and he couldn't leave Rosamund with Pauline. So he sat up in a chair with his back turned to the bed. No. He didn't make any attempt to go back. He says he knew she was still lying there, guarding his place, which was her place. The odd thing is that he wasn't in the least disturbed or frightened or surprised. He took the whole thing as a matter of course. And presently he dozed off into a sleep.

A scream woke him and the sound of a violent body leaping out of the bed and thudding on to its feet. He switched on the light and saw the bed-clothes flung back and Pauline standing on the floor with her mouth open.

He went to her and held her. She was cold to the touch and shaking with terror, and her jaw dropped as if she was palsied.

She said, "Edward, there's something in the bed."

He glanced again at the bed. It was empty.

"There isn't," he said. "Look."

He stripped the bed to the foot-rail, so that she could see.

"There *was* something."

"Do you see it?"

338

"No. I felt it."

She told him. First something had come swinging, smack across her face. A thick, heavy rope of woman's hair. It had waked her. Then she had put out her hands and felt the body. A woman's body, soft and horrible; her fingers had sunk in the shallow breasts. Then she had screamed and jumped.

And she couldn't stay in the room. The room, she said, was "beastly."

She slept in Marston's room, in his small single bed, and he sat up with her all night, on a chair.

She believed now that he had really seen something, and she remembered that the library was beastly, too. Haunted by something. She supposed that was what she had felt. Very well. Two rooms in the house were haunted; their bedroom and the library. They would just have to avoid those two rooms. She had made up her mind, you see, that it was nothing but a case of an ordinary haunted house; the sort of thing you're always hearing about and never believe in till it happens to yourself. Marston didn't like to point out to her that the house hadn't been haunted till she came into it.

The following night, the fourth night, she was to sleep in the spare room on the top floor, next to the servants, and Marston in his own room.

But Marston didn't sleep. He kept on wondering

339

whether he would or would not go up to Pauline's room. That made him horribly restless, and instead of undressing and going to bed, he sat up on a chair with a book. He wasn't nervous; but he had a queer feeling that something was going to happen, and that he must be ready for it, and that he'd better be dressed.

It must have been soon after midnight when he heard the door knob turning very slowly and softly.

The door opened behind him and Pauline came in, moving without a sound, and stood before him. It gave him a shock; for he had been thinking of Rosamund, and when he heard the door knob turn it was the phantasm of Rosamund that he expected to see coming in. He says, for the first minute, it was this appearance of Pauline that struck him as the uncanny and unnatural thing.

She had nothing, absolutely nothing on but a transparent white chiffony sort of dressing-gown. She was trying to undo it. He could see her hands shaking as her fingers fumbled with the fastenings.

He got up suddenly, and they just stood there before each other, saying nothing, staring at each other. He was fascinated by her, by the sheer glamour of her body, gleaming white through the thin stuff, and by the movement of her fingers. I think

340

I've said she was a beautiful woman, and her beauty at that moment was overpowering.

And still he stared at her without saying anything. It sounds as if their silence lasted quite a long time, but in reality it couldn't have been more than some fraction of a second.

Then she began. "Oh, Edward, for God's sake *say* something. Oughtn't I to have come?"

And she went on without waiting for an answer. "Are you thinking of *her*? Because, if—if you are, I'm not going to let her drive you away from me . . . I'm not going to . . . She'll keep on coming as long as we don't—Can't you see that this is the way to stop it . . . ? When you take me in your arms."

She slipped off the loose sleeves of the chiffon thing and it fell to her feet. Marston says he heard a queer sound, something between a groan and a grunt, and was amazed to find that it came from himself.

He hadn't touched her yet—mind you, it went quicker than it takes to tell, it was still an affair of the fraction of a second—they were holding out their arms to each other, when the door opened again without a sound, and, without visible passage, the phantasm was there. It came incredibly fast, and thin at first, like a shaft of light sliding between them. It didn't do anything; there was no beating of hands, only, as it took on its full form, its perfect likeness of flesh and blood, it made its presence felt like a push, a force, driving them asunder.

Pauline hadn't seen it yet. She thought it was Marston who was beating her back. She cried out: "Oh, don't, don't push me away!" She stooped below the phantasm's guard and clung to his knees, writhing and crying. For a moment it was a struggle between her moving flesh and that still, supernatural being.

And in that moment Marston realized that he hated Pauline. She was fighting Rosamund with her gross flesh and blood, taking a mean advantage of her embodied state to beat down the heavenly, discarnate thing.

He called to her to let go.

"It's not I," he shouted. "Can't you *see* her?"

Then, suddenly, she saw, and let go, and dropped, crouching on the floor and trying to cover herself. This time she had given no cry.

The phantasm gave way; it moved slowly towards the door, and as it went it looked back over its shoulder at Marston, it trailed a hand, signalling to him to come.

He went out after it, hardly aware of Pauline's naked body that still writhed there, clutching at his feet as they passed, and drew itself after him, like a worm, like a beast, along the floor.

She must have got up at once and followed them out on to the landing; for, as he went down the stairs behind the phantasm, he could see Pauline's face, distorted with lust and terror, peering at them above the stairhead. She saw them descend the last flight, and cross the hall at the bottom and go into the library. The door shut behind them.

Something happened in there. Marston never told me precisely what it was, and I didn't ask him. Anyhow, that finished it.

The next day Pauline ran away to her own people. She couldn't stay in Marston's house because it was haunted by Rosamund, and he wouldn't leave it for the same reason.

And she never came back; for she was not only afraid of Rosamund, she was afraid of Marston. And if she *had* come it wouldn't have been any good. Marston was convinced that, as often as he attempted to get to Pauline, something would stop him. Pauline certainly felt that, if Rosamund were pushed to it, she might show herself in some still more sinister and terrifying form. She knew when she was beaten.

And there was more in it than that. I believe he tried to explain it to her; said he had married her on the assumption that Rosamund was dead, but that now he knew she was alive; she was, as he put it, "there." He tried to make her see that if he had Rosamund he couldn't have *her*. Rosamund's presence in the world annulled their contract.

You see I'm convinced that something *did* happen that night in the library. I say, he never told me precisely what it was, but he once let something out. We were discussing one of Pauline's love-affairs (after the separation she gave him endless grounds for divorce).

"Poor Pauline," he said, "she thinks she's so passionate."

"Well," I said, "wasn't she?"

Then he burst out, "No. She doesn't know what passion is. None of you know. You haven't the faintest conception. You'd have to get rid of your bodies first. *I* didn't know until—"

He stopped himself. I think he was going to say, "until Rosamund came back and showed me." For he leaned forward and whispered: "It isn't a localized affair at all . . . If you only knew—"

So I don't think it was just faithfulness to a revived memory. I take it there had been, behind that shut door, some experience, some terrible and exquisite contact. More penetrating than sight or touch. More—more extensive: passion at all points of being.

Perhaps the supreme moment of it, the ecstasy, only came when her phantasm had disappeared.

He couldn't go back to Pauline after *that*.

VERNON LEE

Violet Paget (1856–1935) was born of British
expatriates in France and, although she wrote in
English, she spent most time in France and Italy.
She was a feminist who dressed in men's clothing
and went by the name Vernon Lee. Lee was a travel
writer, proponent of the aesthetic movement, a fol-
lower of the movement's leader, Walter Pater, and a
friend of Oscar Wilde. She had long-term relation-
ships with women but resisted the term lesbian.
During the First World War, Lee was an engaged
pacifist. With partner Kit Anstruther-Thomson, Lee
developed a theory of psychological aesthetics,
which emphasized a visceral relationship to what is
read, with the body changing posture and breathing,
something that is now accepted by students of
horror.

The Doll

I believe that's the last bit of *bric-à-brac* I shall ever buy in my life (she said, closing the Renaissance casket)—that and the Chinese dessert set we have just been using. The passion seems to have left me utterly. And I think I can guess why. At the same time as the plates and the little coffer I bought a thing—I scarcely know whether I ought to call it a thing—which put me out of conceit with ferreting about among dead people's properties. I have often wanted to tell you all about it, and stopped for fear of seeming an idiot. But it weighs upon me sometimes like a secret; so, silly or not silly, I think I should like to tell you the story. There, ring for some more logs, and put that screen before the lamp.

It was two years ago, in the autumn, at Foligno, in Umbria. I was alone at the inn, for you know my husband is too busy for my *bric-à-brac* journeys, and the friend who was to have met me fell ill and came on only later. Foligno isn't what people call an interesting place, but I liked it. There are a lot of picturesque little towns all round; and great savage mountains of pink stone, covered with ilex, where they roll faggots down into the torrent beds, within a drive. There's a full, rushing little river round one side of the walls, which are covered with ivy; and there are fifteenth-century frescoes, which I dare say you know all about. But, what of course I care for most, there are a number of fine old palaces, with gateways carved in that pink stone, and courts with pillars, and beautiful window gratings, mostly in good enough repair, for Foligno is a market town and a junction, and altogether a kind of metropolis down in the valley.

Also, and principally, I liked Foligno because I discovered a delightful curiosity-dealer. I don't mean a delightful curiosity shop, for he had nothing worth twenty francs to sell; but a delightful, enchanting old man. His Christian name was Orestes, and that was enough for me. He had a long white beard and such kind brown eyes, and beautiful hands; and he always carried an earthenware brazier under his cloak. He had taken to the curiosity business from a passion for beautiful things, and for the past of his native place, after having been a master mason. He knew all the old chronicles, lent me that of Matarazzo, and knew exactly where everything had happened for the last six hundred years.

He spoke of the Trincis, who had been local despots, and of St. Angela, who is the local saint, and of the Baglionis and Cæsar Borgia and Julius II, as if he had known them; he showed me the place where St. Francis preached to the birds, and the place where Propertius—was it Propertius or Tibullus?—had had his farm; and when he accompanied me on my rambles in search of *bric-à-brac* he would stop at corners and under arches and say, "This, you see, is where they carried off those Nuns I told you about; that's where the Cardinal was stabbed. That's the place where they razed the palace after the massacre, and passed the ploughshare through the ground and sowed salt." And all with a vague, far-off, melancholy look, as if he lived in those days and not these. Also he helped me to get that little velvet coffer with the iron clasps, which is really one of the best things we have in the house. So I was very happy at Foligno, driving and prowling about all day, reading the chronicles Orestes lent me in the evening; and I didn't mind waiting so long for my friend who never turned up. That is to say, I was perfectly happy until within three days of my departure. And now comes the story of my strange purchase.

Orestes, with considerable shrugging of shoulders, came one morning with the information that a certain noble person of Foligno wanted to sell me a set of Chinese plates. "Some of them are cracked," he said; "but at all events you will see the inside of one of our finest palaces with all its rooms as they used to be—nothing valuable; but I know that

349

the signora appreciates the past wherever it has been let alone."

The palace, by way of exception, was of the late seventeenth century, and looked like a barracks among the neat little carved Renaissance houses. It had immense lions' heads over all the windows, a gateway in which two coaches could have met, a yard where a hundred might have waited, and a colossal staircase with stucco virtues on the vaultings. There was a cobbler in the lodge and a soap factory on the ground floor, and at the end of the colonnaded court a garden with ragged yellow vines and dead sunflowers. "Grandiose, but very coarse—almost eighteenth-century," said Orestes as we went up the sounding, low-stepped stairs. Some of the dessert set had been placed, ready for my inspection, on a great gold console in the immense escutcheoned anteroom. I looked at it, and told them to prepare the rest for me to see the next day. The owner, a very noble person, but half ruined—I should have thought entirely ruined, judging by the state of the house—was residing in the country, and the only occupant of the palace was an old woman, just like those who raise the curtains for you at church doors.

The palace was very grand. There was a ballroom as big as a church, and a number of reception rooms, with dirty floors and eighteenth-century furniture, all tarnished and tattered, and a gala room, all yellow satin and gold, where some emperor had slept; and there were horrible racks of faded photographs on the walls, and twopenny screens, and Berlin wool cushions, attesting the existence of more modern occupants.

I let the old woman unbar one painted and gilded shutter after another, and open window after window, each filled with little greenish panes of glass, and followed her about passively, quite happy, because I was wandering among the ghosts of dead people. "There is the library at the end here," said the old woman, "if the signora does not mind passing through my room and the ironing-room; it's quicker than going back by the big hall." I nodded, and prepared to pass as quickly as possible through an untidy-looking servants' room, when I suddenly stepped back. There was a woman in 1820 costume seated opposite, quite motionless. It was a huge doll. She had a sort of Canova classic face, like the pictures of Mme. Pasta and Lady Blessington. She sat with her hands folded on her lap and stared fixedly.

"It is the first wife of the Count's grandfather," said the old woman. "We took her out of her closet this morning to give her a little dusting."

The Doll was dressed to the utmost detail. She

had on open-work silk stockings, with sandal shoes, and long silk embroidered mittens. The hair was merely painted, in flat bands narrowing the forehead to a triangle. There was a big hole in the back of her head, showing it was cardboard.

"Ah," said Orestes, musingly, "the image of the beautiful countess! I had forgotten all about it. I haven't seen it since I was a lad," and he wiped some cobweb off the folded hands with his red handkerchief, infinitely gently. "She used still to be kept in her own boudoir."

"That was before my time," answered the housekeeper. "I've always seen her in the wardrobe, and I've been here thirty years. Will the signora care to see the old Count's collection of medals?"

Orestes was very pensive as he accompanied me home.

"That was a very beautiful lady," he said shyly, as we came within sight of my inn; "I mean the first wife of the grandfather of the present Count. She died after they had been married a couple of years. The old Count, they say, went half crazy. He had the Doll made from a picture, and kept it in the poor lady's room, and spent several hours in it every day with her. But he ended by marrying a woman he had in the house, a laundress, by whom he had had a daughter."

THE DOLL

"What a curious story!" I said, and thought no more about it.

But the Doll returned to my thoughts, she and her folded hands, and wide open eyes, and the fact of her husband's having ended by marrying the laundress. And next day, when we returned to the palace to see the complete set of old Chinese plates, I suddenly experienced an odd wish to see the Doll once more. I took advantage of Orestes, and the old woman, and the Count's lawyer being busy deciding whether a certain dish cover which my maid had dropped, had or had not been previously chipped, to slip off and make my way to the ironing-room.

The Doll was still there, sure enough, and they hadn't found time to dust her yet. Her white satin frock, with little *ruches* at the hem, and her short bodice, had turned grey with engrained dirt; and her black fringed kerchief was almost red. The poor white silk mittens and white silk stockings were, on the other hand, almost black. A newspaper had fallen from an adjacent table on to her knees, or been thrown there by some one, and she looked as if she were holding it. It came home to me then that the clothes which she wore were the real clothes of her poor dead original. And when I found on the table a dusty, unkempt wig, with straight bands in

353

front and an elaborate jug handle of curls behind, I knew at once that it was made of the poor lady's real hair.

"It is very well made," I said shyly, when the old woman, of course, came creaking after me.

She had no thought except that of humouring whatever caprice might bring her a tip. So she smirked horribly, and, to show me that the image was really worthy of my attention, she proceeded in a ghastly way to bend the articulated arms, and to cross one leg over the other beneath the white satin skirt.

"Please, please, don't do that!" I cried to the old witch. But one of the poor feet, in its sandalled shoe, continued dangling and wagging dreadfully.

I was afraid lest my maid should find me staring at the Doll. I felt I couldn't stand my maid's remarks about her. So, though fascinated by the fixed dark stare in her Canova goddess or Ingres Madonna face, I tore myself away and returned to the inspection of the dessert set.

I don't know what that Doll had done to me; but I found that I was thinking of her all day long. It was as if I had just made a new acquaintance of a painfully interesting kind, rushed into a sudden friendship with a woman whose secret I had surprised, as sometimes happens, by some mere accident. For I somehow knew everything about her, and the first items of information which I gained from Orestes—I ought to say that I was irresistibly impelled to talk about her with him—did not enlighten me in the least, but merely confirmed what I was aware of.

The Doll—for I made no distinction between the portrait and the original—had been married straight out of the convent, and, during her brief wedded life, been kept secluded from the world by her husband's mad love for her, so that she had remained a mere shy, proud, inexperienced child.

Had she loved him? She did not tell me that at once. But gradually I became aware that in a deep, inarticulate way she had really cared for him more than he cared for her. She did not know what answer to make to his easy, overflowing, garrulous, demonstrative affection; he could not be silent about his love for two minutes, and she could never find a word to express hers, painfully though she longed to do so. Not that he wanted it; he was a brilliant, will-less, lyrical sort of person, who knew nothing of the feelings of others and cared only to welter and dissolve in his own. In those two years of ecstatic, talkative, all-absorbing love for her he not only forswore all society and utterly neglected his affairs, but he never made an attempt to train this raw young creature into a companion, or showed any curiosity

as to whether his idol might have a mind or a character of her own. This indifference she explained by
her own stupid, inconceivable incapacity for
expressing her feelings; how should he guess at her
longing to know, to understand, when she could not
even tell him how much she loved him? At last the
spell seemed broken: the words and the power of
saying them came; but it was on her death-bed. The
poor young creature died in child-birth, scarcely
more than a child herself.

There now! I knew even you would think it all
silliness. I know what people are—what we all are—
how impossible it is ever *really* to make others feel
in the same way as ourselves about anything. Do you
suppose I could have ever told all this about the Doll
to my husband? Yet I tell him everything about
myself; and I know he would have been quite kind
and respectful. It was silly of me ever to embark on
the story of the Doll with any one; it ought to have
remained a secret between me and Orestes. *He,* I
really think, would have understood all about the
poor lady's feelings, or known it already as well as
I. Well, having begun, I must go on, I suppose.

I knew all about the Doll when she was alive—I
mean about the lady—and I got to know, in the
same way, all about her after she was dead.

Only I don't think I'll tell you. *Basta:* the

husband had the Doll made and dressed it in her clothes, and placed it in her boudoir, where not a thing was moved from how it had been at the moment of her death. He allowed no one to go in, and cleaned and dusted it all himself, and spent hours every day weeping and moaning before the Doll. Then, gradually, he began to look at his collection of medals and to resume his rides; but he never went into society, and never neglected spending an hour in the boudoir with the Doll. Then came the business with the laundress. And then he sent the Doll into a wardrobe? Oh no; he wasn't that sort of man. He was an idealizing, sentimental, feeble sort of person, and the amour with the laundress grew up quite gradually in the shadow of the inconsolable passion for the wife. He would never have married another woman of his own rank, given *her* son a stepmother (the son was sent to a distant school and went to the bad); and when he *did* marry the laundress it was almost in his dotage, and because she and the priests bullied him so fearfully about legitimating that other child. He went on paying visits to the Doll for a long time, while the laundress idyl went on quite peacefully. Then, as he grew old and lazy, he went less often; other people were sent to dust the Doll, and finally she was not dusted at all. Then he died, having quarrelled with his son and got to live like a feeble old boor, mostly in the kitchen. The son — the Doll's son—having gone to the bad, married a rich widow. It was she who refurnished the boudoir and sent the Doll away. But the daughter of the laundress, the illegitimate child, who had become a kind of housekeeper in her half-brother's palace, nourished a lingering regard for the Doll, partly because the old Count had made such a fuss about it, partly because it must have cost a lot of money, and partly because the lady had been a *real* lady. So when the boudoir was refurnished she emptied out a closet and put the Doll to live there; and she occasionally had it brought out to be dusted.

Well, while all these things were being borne in upon me there came a telegram saying my friend was not coming on to Foligno, and asking me to meet her at Perugia. The little Renaissance coffer had been sent to London; Orestes and my maid and myself had carefully packed every one of the Chinese plates and fruit dishes in baskets of hay. I had ordered a set of the "Archivio Storico" as a parting gift for dear old Orestes—I could never have dreamed of offering him money, or cravat pins, or things like that—and there was no excuse for staying one hour more at Foligno. Also I had got into low spirits of late—I suppose we poor women cannot stay alone six days in an inn, even with *bric-a-brac* and chronicles and devoted maids—and I knew I should not get better till I was out of the place. Still I found it difficult, nay, impossible, to go. I will confess it outright: I couldn't abandon the Doll. I couldn't leave her, with the hole in her poor cardboard head, with the Ingres Madonna features gathering dust in that filthy old woman's ironing-room. It was just impossible. Still go I must. So I sent for Orestes. I knew exactly what I wanted; but it seemed impossible, and I was afraid, somehow, of asking him. I gathered up my courage, and, as if it were the most natural thing in the world, I said—

"Dear Signor Oreste, I want you to help me to make one last purchase. I want the Count to sell me the—the portrait of his grandmother; I mean the Doll."

I had prepared a speech to the effect that Orestes would easily understand that a life-size figure so completely dressed in the original costume of a past epoch would soon possess the highest historical interest, etc. But I felt that I neither needed nor ventured to say any of it. Orestes, who was seated opposite me at table—he would only accept a glass of wine and a morsel of bread, although I had asked him to share my hotel dinner—Orestes nodded slowly, then opened his eyes out wide, and seemed to frame the whole of me in them. It wasn't surprise. He was weighing me and my offer.

"Would it be very difficult?" I asked. "I should have thought that the Count——"

"The Count," answered Orestes drily, "would sell his soul, if he had one, let alone his grandmother, for the price of a new trotting pony."

Then I understood.

"Signor Oreste," I replied, feeling like a child under the dear old man's glance, "we have not known one another long, so I cannot expect you to trust me yet in many things. Perhaps also buying furniture out of dead people's houses to stick it in one's own is not a great recommendation of one's character. But I want to tell you that I am an honest woman according to my lights, and I want you to trust me in this matter."

Orestes bowed. "I will try and induce the Count to sell you the Doll," he said.

I had her sent in a closed carriage to the house of Orestes. He had, behind his shop, a garden which extended into a little vineyard, whence you could see the circle of great Umbrian mountains; and on this I had had my eye.

"Signor Oreste," I said, "will you be very kind, and have some faggots—I have seen some beautiful faggots of myrtle and bay in your kitchen—brought out into the vineyard; and may I pluck some of your chrysanthemums?" I added.

We stacked the faggots at the end of the vineyard, and placed the Doll in the midst of them, and the chrysanthemums on her knees. She sat there in her white satin Empire frock, which, in the bright November sunshine, seemed white once more, and sparkling. Her black fixed eyes stared as in wonder on the yellow vines and reddening peach trees, the sparkling dewy grass of the vineyard, upon the blue morning sunshine, the misty blue amphitheatre of mountains all round.

Orestes struck a match and slowly lit a pine cone with it; when the cone was blazing he handed it silently to me. The dry bay and myrtle blazed up crackling, with a fresh resinous odour; the Doll was veiled in flame and smoke. In a few seconds the flame sank, the smouldering faggots crumbled. The Doll was gone. Only, where she had been, there remained in the embers something small and shiny. Orestes raked it out and handed it to me. It was a wedding ring of old-fashioned shape, which had been hidden under the silk mitten. "Keep it, signora," said Orestes; "you have put an end to her sorrows."

E. M. FORSTER

Edward Morgan Forster (1879–1970) published five
novels during his lifetime, of which the best known
are *Howards End* (1910) and *A Passage to India*
(1924). *Maurice* was written in 1913–14 but published posthumously in 1971 because of its
homosexual content. He was a member of the
Bloomsbury Group and interested in recreating
realist writing. Forster's works were strongly influenced by his travels in Greece and Italy, and later in
Egypt, Germany and India. He was a conscientious
objector during the First World War and took alternative service as a searcher, tracking missing
servicemen for the Red Cross in Egypt. In the inter-
war years, he was a popular broadcaster and
supported Radclyffe Hall's defence of *The Well of
Loneliness*. In 1909, he published an important science fiction novella called 'The Machine Stops', and
in 1911 a collection of fantastical stories titled
The Celestial Omnibus and Other Stories.

The Celestial Omnibus

The boy who resided at Agathox Lodge, 28, Buckingham Park Road, Surbiton, had often been puzzled by the old sign-post that stood almost opposite. He asked his mother about it, and she replied that it was a joke, and not a very nice one, which had been made many years back by some naughty young men, and that the police ought to remove it. For there were two strange things about this sign-post: firstly, it pointed up a blank alley, and, secondly, it had painted on it, in faded characters, the words, "To Heaven."

"What kind of young men were they?" he asked.

"I think your father told me that one of them wrote verses, and was expelled from the University and came to grief in other ways. Still, it was a long time ago. You must ask your father about it. He will say the same as I do, that it was put up as a joke."

"So it doesn't mean anything at all?"

She sent him up-stairs to put on his best things, for the Bonses were coming to tea, and he was to hand the cake-stand.

It struck him, as he wrenched on his tightening trousers, that he might do worse than ask Mr. Bons about the sign-post. His father, though very kind,

363

always laughed at him—shrieked with laughter whenever he or any other child asked a question or spoke. But Mr. Bons was serious as well as kind. He had a beautiful house and lent one books, he was a churchwarden, and a candidate for the County Council; he had donated to the Free Library enormously, he presided over the Literary Society, and had Members of Parliament to stop with him—in short, he was probably the wisest person alive.

Yet even Mr. Bons could only say that the signpost was a joke—the joke of a person named Shelley.

"Of course!" cried the mother; "I told you so, dear. That was the name."

"Had you never heard of Shelley?" asked Mr. Bons.

"No," said the boy, and hung his head.

"But is there no Shelley in the house?"

"Why, yes!" exclaimed the lady, in much agitation. "Dear Mr. Bons, we aren't such Philistines as that. Two at the least. One a wedding present, and the other, smaller print, in one of the spare rooms."

"I believe we have seven Shelleys," said Mr. Bons, with a slow smile. Then he brushed the cake crumbs off his stomach, and, together with his daughter, rose to go.

The boy, obeying a wink from his mother, saw

them all the way to the garden gate, and when they had gone he did not at once return to the house, but gazed for a little up and down Buckingham Park Road.

His parents lived at the right end of it. After No. 39 the quality of the houses dropped very suddenly, and 64 had not even a separate servants' entrance. But at the present moment the whole road looked rather pretty, for the sun had just set in splendour, and the inequalities of rent were drowned in a saffron afterglow. Small birds twittered, and the breadwinners' train shrieked musically down through the cutting—that wonderful cutting which has drawn to itself the whole beauty out of Surbiton, and clad itself, like any Alpine valley, with the glory of the fir and the silver birch and the primrose. It was this cutting that had first stirred desires within the boy— desires for something just a little different, he knew not what, desires that would return whenever things were sunlit, as they were this evening, running up and down inside him, up and down, up and down, till he would feel quite unusual all over, and as likely as not would want to cry. This evening he was even sillier, for he slipped across the road towards the sign-post and began to run up the blank alley.

The alley runs between high walls—the walls of the gardens of "Ivanhoe" and "Belle Vista" respectively.

It smells a little all the way, and is scarcely twenty yards long, including the turn at the end. So not unnaturally the boy soon came to a standstill. "I'd like to kick that Shelley," he exclaimed, and glanced idly at a piece of paper which was pasted on the wall. Rather an odd piece of paper, and he read it carefully before he turned back. This is what he read:

S. AND C. R. C. C.

Alteration in Service.

Owing to lack of patronage the Company are regretfully compelled to suspend the hourly service, and to retain only the

Sunrise and Sunset Omnibuses,

which will run as usual. It is to be hoped that the public will patronize an arrangement which is intended for their convenience. As an extra inducement, the Company will, for the first time, now issue

Return Tickets!

(available one day only), which may be obtained of the driver. Passengers are again reminded that *no tickets are issued at the other end,* and that no complaints in this connection will receive consideration from the Company. Nor will the Company be responsible for any negligence or stupidity on the part of Passengers, nor for Hailstorms, Lightning, Loss of Tickets, nor for any Act of God.

FOR THE DIRECTION.

Now he had never seen this notice before, nor could he imagine where the omnibus went to. S. of course was for Surbiton, and R. C. C. meant Road Car Company. But what was the meaning of the other C.? Coombe and Malden, perhaps, or possibly "City." Yet it could not hope to compete with the South-Western. The whole thing, the boy reflected, was run on hopelessly unbusiness-like lines. Why no tickets from the other end? And what an hour to start! Then he realized that unless the notice was a hoax, an omnibus must have been starting just as he was wishing the Bonses good-bye. He peered at the ground through the gathering dusk, and there he saw what might or might not be the marks of wheels. Yet nothing had come out of the alley. And he had never seen an omnibus at any time in the Buckingham Park Road. No: it must be a hoax, like the sign-posts, like the fairy tales, like the dreams upon which he would wake suddenly in the night. And with a sigh he stepped from the alley—right into the arms of his father.

Oh, how his father laughed! "Poor, poor Popsey!"

he cried. "Diddums! Diddums! Diddums think he'd walky-palky up to Evvink!" And his mother, also convulsed with laughter, appeared on the steps of Agathox Lodge. "Don't, Bob!" she gasped. "Don't be so naughty! Oh, you'll kill me! Oh, leave the boy alone!"

But all that evening the joke was kept up. The father implored to be taken too. Was it a very tiring walk? Need one wipe one's shoes on the door-mat? And the boy went to bed feeling faint and sore, and thankful for only one thing—that he had not said a word about the omnibus. It was a hoax, yet through his dreams it grew more and more real, and the streets of Surbiton, through which he saw it driving, seemed instead to become hoaxes and shadows. And very early in the morning he woke with a cry, for he had had a glimpse of its destination.

He struck a match, and its light fell not only on his watch but also on his calendar, so that he knew it to be half-an-hour to sunrise. It was pitch dark, for the fog had come down from London in the night, and all Surbiton was wrapped in its embraces. Yet he sprang out and dressed himself, for he was deter-mined to settle once for all which was real: the omnibus or the streets. "I shall be a fool one way or the other," he thought, "until I know." Soon he was shivering in the road under the gas lamp that guarded the entrance to the alley.

To enter the alley itself required some courage. Not only was it horribly dark, but he now realized that it was an impossible terminus for an omnibus. If it had not been for a policeman, whom he heard approaching through the fog, he would never have made the attempt. The next moment he had made the attempt and failed. Nothing. Nothing but a blank alley and a very silly boy gaping at its dirty floor. It *was* a hoax. "I'll tell papa and mamma," he decided. "I deserve it. I deserve that they should know. I am too silly to be alive." And he went back to the gate of Agathox Lodge.

There he remembered that his watch was fast. The sun was not risen; it would not rise for two minutes. "Give the bus every chance," he thought cynically, and returned into the alley.

But the omnibus was there.

II

It had two horses, whose sides were still smoking from their journey, and its two great lamps shone through the fog against the alley's walls, changing their cobwebs and moss into tissues of fairyland. The driver was huddled up in a cape. He faced the blank wall, and how he had managed to drive in so

neatly and so silently was one of the many things
that the boy never discovered. Nor could he imagine
how ever he would drive out.

"Please," his voice quavered through the foul
brown air, "Please, is that an omnibus?"

"Omnibus est," said the driver, without turning
round. There was a moment's silence. The policeman passed, coughing, by the entrance of the alley.
The boy crouched in the shadow, for he did not
want to be found out. He was pretty sure, too, that
it was a Pirate; nothing else, he reasoned, would go
from such odd places and at such odd hours.

"About when do you start?" He tried to sound
nonchalant.

"At sunrise."

"How far do you go?"

"The whole way."

"And can I have a return ticket which will bring
me all the way back?"

"You can."

"Do you know, I half think I'll come." The driver
made no answer. The sun must have risen, for he
unhitched the brake. And scarcely had the boy
jumped in before the omnibus was off.

How? Did it turn? There was no room. Did it go
forward? There was a blank wall. Yet it was moving—
moving at a stately pace through the fog, which had

turned from brown to yellow. The thought of warm bed and warmer breakfast made the boy feel faint. He wished he had not come. His parents would not have approved. He would have gone back to them if the weather had not made it impossible. The solitude was terrible; he was the only passenger. And the omnibus, though well-built, was cold and somewhat musty. He drew his coat round him, and in so doing chanced to feel his pocket. It was empty. He had forgotten his purse.

"Stop!" he shouted. "Stop!" And then, being of a polite disposition, he glanced up at the painted notice-board so that he might call the driver by name. "Mr. Browne! stop; O, do please stop!"

Mr. Browne did not stop, but he opened a little window and looked in at the boy. His face was a surprise, so kind it was and modest.

"Mr. Browne, I've left my purse behind. I've not got a penny. I can't pay for the ticket. Will you take my watch, please? I am in the most awful hole."

"Tickets on this line," said the driver, "whether single or return, can be purchased by coinage from no terrene mint. And a chronometer, though it had solaced the vigils of Charlemagne, or measured the slumbers of Laura, can acquire by no mutation the double-cake that charms the fangless Cerberus of Heaven!" So saying, he handed in the necessary ticket, and, while the boy said "Thank you," continued: "Titular pretensions, I know it well, are vanity. Yet they merit no censure when uttered on a laughing lip, and in an homonymous world are in some sort useful, since they do serve to distinguish one Jack from his fellow. Remember me, therefore, as Sir Thomas Browne."

"Are you a Sir? Oh, sorry!" He had heard of these gentlemen drivers. "It *is* good of you about the ticket. But if you go on at this rate, however does your bus pay?"

"It does not pay. It was not intended to pay. Many are the faults of my equipage; it is compounded too curiously of foreign woods; its cushions tickle erudition rather than promote repose; and my horses are nourished not on the evergreen pastures of the moment, but on the dried bents and clovers of Latinity. But that it pays!—that error at all events was never intended and never attained."

"Sorry again," said the boy rather hopelessly. Sir Thomas looked sad, fearing that, even for a moment, he had been the cause of sadness. He invited the boy to come up and sit beside him on the box, and together they journeyed on through the fog, which was now changing from yellow to white. There were no houses by the road; so it must be either Putney Heath or Wimbledon Common.

"Have you been a driver always?"

"I was a physician once."

"But why did you stop? Weren't you good?"

"As a healer of bodies I had scant success, and several score of my patients preceded me. But as a healer of the spirit I have succeeded beyond my hopes and my deserts. For though my draughts were not better nor subtler than those of other men, yet, by reason of the cunning goblets wherein I offered them, the queasy soul was ofttimes tempted to sip and be refreshed."

"The queasy soul," he murmured; "if the sun sets with trees in front of it, and you suddenly come strange all over, is that a queasy soul?"

"Have you felt that?"

"Why yes."

After a pause he told the boy a little, a very little, about the journey's end. But they did not chatter much, for the boy, when he liked a person, would as soon sit silent in his company as speak, and this, he discovered, was also the mind of Sir Thomas Browne and of many others with whom he was to be acquainted. He heard, however, about the young man Shelley, who was now quite a famous person, with a carriage of his own, and about some of the other drivers who are in the service of the Company. Meanwhile the light grew stronger, though the fog did not disperse. It was now more like mist than fog, and at times would travel quickly across them, as if it was part of a cloud. They had been ascending, too, in a most puzzling way; for over two hours the horses had been pulling against the collar, and even if it were Richmond Hill they ought to have been at the top long ago. Perhaps it was Epsom, or even the North Downs; yet the air seemed keener than that which blows on either. And as to the name of their destination, Sir Thomas Browne was silent.

Crash!

"Thunder, by Jove!" said the boy, "and not so far off either. Listen to the echoes! It's more like mountains."

He thought, not very vividly, of his father and mother. He saw them sitting down to sausages and listening to the storm. He saw his own empty place. Then there would be questions, alarms, theories, jokes, consolations. They would expect him back at lunch. To lunch he would not come, nor to tea, but he would be in for dinner, and so his day's truancy would be over. If he had had his purse he would have bought them presents—not that he should have known what to get them.

Crash!

The peal and the lightning came together. The cloud quivered as if it were alive, and torn streamers of mist rushed past. "Are you afraid?" asked Sir Thomas Browne.

"What is there to be afraid of? Is it much farther?"

The horses of the omnibus stopped just as a ball of fire burst up and exploded with a ringing noise that was deafening but clear, like the noise of a blacksmith's forge. All the cloud was shattered.

"Oh, listen, Sir Thomas Browne! No, I mean look; we shall get a view at last. No, I mean listen; that sounds like a rainbow!"

The noise had died into the faintest murmur, beneath which another murmur grew, spreading stealthily, steadily, in a curve that widened but did not vary. And in widening curves a rainbow was spreading from the horses' feet into the dissolving mists.

"But how beautiful! What colours! Where will it stop? It is more like the rainbows you can tread on. More like dreams."

The colour and the sound grew together. The rainbow spanned an enormous gulf. Clouds rushed under it and were pierced by it, and still it grew, reaching forward, conquering the darkness, until it touched something that seemed more solid than a cloud.

The boy stood up. "What is that out there?" he called. "What does it rest on, out at that other end?"

In the morning sunshine a precipice shone forth beyond the gulf. A precipice—or was it a castle? The horses moved. They set their feet upon the rainbow.

"Oh, look!" the boy shouted. "Oh, listen! Those caves—or are they gateways? Oh, look between those cliffs at those ledges. I see people! I see trees!"

"Look also below," whispered Sir Thomas. "Neglect not the diviner Acheron."

The boy looked below, past the flames of the rainbow that licked against their wheels. The gulf also had cleared, and in its depths there flowed an everlasting river. One sunbeam entered and struck a green pool, and as they passed over he saw three maidens rise to the surface of the pool, singing, and playing with something that glistened like a ring.

"You down in the water—" he called.

They answered, "You up on the bridge—"

There was a burst of music. "You up on the bridge, good luck to you. Truth in the depth, truth on the height."

"You down in the water, what are you doing?"

Sir Thomas Browne replied: "They sport in the mancipiary possession of their gold"; and the omnibus arrived.

III

The boy was in disgrace. He sat locked up in the nursery of Agathox Lodge, learning poetry for a punishment. His father had said, "My boy! I can pardon anything but untruthfulness," and had caned him, saying at each stroke, "There is *no* omnibus, *no* driver, *no* bridge, *no* mountain; you are a *truant*, a *guttersnipe*, a *liar*." His father could be very stern at times. His mother had begged him to say he was sorry. But he could not say that. It was the greatest day of his life, in spite of the caning and the poetry at the end of it.

He had returned punctually at sunset—driven not by Sir Thomas Browne, but by a maiden lady who was full of quiet fun. They had talked of omnibuses and also of barouche landaus. How far away her gentle voice seemed now! Yet it was scarcely three hours since he had left her up the alley.

His mother called through the door. "Dear, you are to come down and to bring your poetry with you."

He came down, and found that Mr. Bons was in the smoking-room with his father. It had been a dinner party.

"Here is the great traveller!" said his father grimly. "Here is the young gentleman who drives in an omnibus over rainbows, while young ladies sing to him." Pleased with his wit, he laughed.

"After all," said Mr. Bons, smiling, "there is something a little like it in Wagner. It is odd how, in quite illiterate minds, you will find glimmers of Artistic Truth. The case interests me. Let me plead for the culprit. We have all romanced in our time, haven't we?"

"Hear how kind Mr. Bons is," said his mother, while his father said, "Very well. Let him say his Poem, and that will do. He is going away to my sister on Tuesday, and *she* will cure him of this alley-sloping." (Laughter.) "Say your Poem."

The boy began. "'Standing aloof in giant ignorance.'"

His father laughed again—roared. "One for you, my son! 'Standing aloof in giant ignorance!' I never knew these poets talked sense. Just describes you. Here, Bons, you go in for poetry. Put him through it, will you, while I fetch up the whisky?"

"Yes, give me the Keats," said Mr. Bons. "Let him say his Keats to me."

So for a few moments the wise man and the ignorant boy were left alone in the smoking-room.

"'Standing aloof in giant ignorance, of thee I dream and of the Cyclades, as one who sits ashore and longs perchance to visit—'"

"Quite right. To visit what?"

"'To visit dolphin coral in deep seas,'" said the boy, and burst into tears.

"Come, come! why do you cry?"

"Because—because all these words that only rhymed before, now that I've come back they're me."

Mr. Bons laid the Keats down. The case was more interesting than he had expected. "*You?*" he exclaimed. "This sonnet, *you?*"

"Yes—and look further on: 'Aye, on the shores of darkness there is light, and precipices show untrodden green.' It *is* so, sir. All these things are true."

"I never doubted it," said Mr. Bons, with closed eyes.

"You—then you believe me? You believe in the omnibus and the driver and the storm and that return ticket I got for nothing and—"

"Tut, tut! No more of your yarns, my boy. I meant that I never doubted the essential truth of Poetry. Some day, when you have read more, you will understand what I mean."

"But Mr. Bons, it *is* so. There *is* light upon the shores of darkness. I have seen it coming. Light and a wind."

"Nonsense," said Mr. Bons.

"If I had stopped! They tempted me. They told

me to give up my ticket—for you cannot come back if you lose your ticket. They called from the river for it, and indeed I was tempted, for I have never been so happy as among those precipices. But I thought of my mother and father, and that I must fetch them. Yet they will not come, though the road starts opposite our house. It has all happened as the people up there warned me, and Mr. Bons has disbelieved me like every one else. I have been caned. I shall never see that mountain again."

"What's that about me?" said Mr. Bons, sitting up in his chair very suddenly.

"I told them about you, and how clever you were, and how many books you had, and they said, 'Mr. Bons will certainly disbelieve you.'"

"Stuff and nonsense, my young friend. You grow impertinent. I—well—I will settle the matter. Not a word to your father. I will cure you. To-morrow evening I will myself call here to take you for a walk, and at sunset we will go up this alley opposite and hunt for your omnibus, you silly little boy."

His face grew serious, for the boy was not disconcerted, but leapt about the room singing, "Joy! joy! I told them you would believe me. We will drive together over the rainbow. I told them that you would come." After all, could there be anything in the story? Wagner? Keats? Shelley? Sir Thomas Browne? Certainly the case was interesting.

And on the morrow evening, though it was pouring with rain, Mr. Bons did not omit to call at Agathox Lodge.

The boy was ready, bubbling with excitement, and skipping about in a way that rather vexed the President of the Literary Society. They took a turn down Buckingham Park Road, and then—having seen that no one was watching them—slipped up the alley. Naturally enough (for the sun was setting) they ran straight against the omnibus.

"Good heavens!" exclaimed Mr. Bons. "Good gracious heavens!"

It was not the omnibus in which the boy had driven first, nor yet that in which he had returned. There were three horses—black, gray, and white, the gray being the finest. The driver, who turned round at the mention of goodness and of heaven, was a sallow man with terrifying jaws and sunken eyes. Mr. Bons, on seeing him, gave a cry as if of recognition, and began to tremble violently.

The boy jumped in.

"Is it possible?" cried Mr. Bons. "Is the impossible possible?"

"Sir; come in, sir. It is such a fine omnibus. Oh, here is his name—Dan some one."

Mr. Bons sprang in too. A blast of wind immediately slammed the omnibus door, and the shock jerked down all the omnibus blinds, which were very weak on their springs.

"Dan . . . Show me. Good gracious heavens! we're moving."

"Hooray!" said the boy.

Mr. Bons became flustered. He had not intended to be kidnapped. He could not find the door-handle, nor push up the blinds. The omnibus was quite dark, and by the time he had struck a match, night had come on outside also. They were moving rapidly.

"A strange, a memorable adventure," he said, surveying the interior of the omnibus, which was large, roomy, and constructed with extreme regularity, every part exactly answering to every other part. Over the door (the handle of which was outside) was written, "Lasciate ogni baldanza voi che entrate"— at least, that was what was written, but Mr. Bons said that it was Lashy arty something, and that baldanza was a mistake for speranza. His voice sounded as if he was in church. Meanwhile, the boy called to the cadaverous driver for two return tickets. They were handed in without a word. Mr. Bons covered his face with his hand and again trembled. "Do you know who that is!" he whispered, when the little window had shut upon them. "It is the impossible."

"Well, I don't like him as much as Sir Thomas Browne, though I shouldn't be surprised if he had even more in him."

"More in him?" He stamped irritably. "By accident you have made the greatest discovery of the century, and all you can say is that there is more in this man. Do you remember those vellum books in my library, stamped with red lilies? This—sit still, I bring you stupendous news!—*this is the man who wrote them.*"

The boy sat quite still. "I wonder if we shall see Mrs. Gamp?" he asked, after a civil pause.

"Mrs.—?"

"Mrs. Gamp and Mrs. Harris. I like Mrs. Harris. I came upon them quite suddenly. Mrs. Gamp's bandboxes have moved over the rainbow so badly. All the bottoms have fallen out, and two of the pippins off her bedstead tumbled into the stream."

"Out there sits the man who wrote my vellum books!" thundered Mr. Bons, "and you talk to me of Dickens and of Mrs. Gamp?"

"I know Mrs. Gamp so well," he apologized. "I could not help being glad to see her. I recognized her voice. She was telling Mrs. Harris about Mrs. Prig."

"Did you spend the whole day in her elevating company?"

"Oh, no. I raced. I met a man who took me out beyond to a race-course. You run, and there are dolphins out at sea."

"Indeed. Do you remember the man's name?"

"Achilles. No; he was later. Tom Jones."

Mr. Bons sighed heavily. "Well, my lad, you have made a miserable mess of it. Think of a cultured person with your opportunities! A cultured person would have known all these characters and known what to have said to each. He would not have wasted his time with a Mrs. Gamp or a Tom Jones. The creations of Homer, of Shakespeare, and of Him who drives us now, would alone have contented him. He would not have raced. He would have asked intelligent questions."

"But, Mr. Bons," said the boy humbly, "you will be a cultured person. I told them so."

"True, true, and I beg you not to disgrace me when we arrive. No gossiping. No running. Keep close to my side, and never speak to these Immortals unless they speak to you. Yes, and give me the return tickets. You will be losing them."

The boy surrendered the tickets, but felt a little sore. After all, he had found the way to this place. It was hard first to be disbelieved and then to be lectured. Meanwhile, the rain had stopped, and moonlight crept into the omnibus through the cracks in the blinds.

"But how is there to be a rainbow?" cried the boy.

"You distract me," snapped Mr. Bons. "I wish to meditate on beauty. I wish to goodness I was with a reverent and sympathetic person."

The lad bit his lip. He made a hundred good resolutions. He would imitate Mr. Bons all the visit. He would not laugh, or run, or sing, or do any of the vulgar things that must have disgusted his new friends last time. He would be very careful to pronounce their names properly, and to remember who knew whom. Achilles did not know Tom Jones—at least, so Mr. Bons said. The Duchess of Malfi was older than Mrs. Gamp—at least, so Mr. Bons said. He would be self-conscious, reticent, and prim. He would never say he liked any one. Yet, when the blind flew up at a chance touch of his head, all these good resolutions went to the winds, for the omnibus had reached the summit of a moonlit hill, and there was the chasm, and there, across it, stood the old precipices, dreaming, with their feet in the everlasting river. He exclaimed, "The mountain! Listen to the new tune in the water! Look at the camp fires in the ravines," and Mr. Bons, after a hasty glance, retorted, "Water? Camp fires? Ridiculous rubbish. Hold your tongue. There is nothing at all."

Yet, under his eyes, a rainbow formed, compounded not of sunlight and storm, but of moonlight and the spray of the river. The three horses put their feet upon it. He thought it the finest rainbow he had seen, but did not dare to say so, since Mr. Bons said that nothing was there. He leant out—the window had opened—and sang the tune that rose from the sleeping waters.

"The prelude to Rhinegold?" said Mr. Bons suddenly. "Who taught you these *leit motifs*?" He, too, looked out of the window. Then he behaved very oddly. He gave a choking cry, and fell back on to the omnibus floor. He writhed and kicked. His face was green.

"Does the bridge make you dizzy?" the boy asked.

"Dizzy!" gasped Mr. Bons. "I want to go back. Tell the driver."

But the driver shook his head.

"We are nearly there," said the boy. "They are asleep. Shall I call? They will be so pleased to see you, for I have prepared them."

Mr. Bons moaned. They moved over the lunar rainbow, which ever and ever broke away behind their wheels. How still the night was! Who would be sentry at the Gate?

"I am coming," he shouted, again forgetting the hundred resolutions. "I am returning—I, the boy."

"The boy is returning," cried a voice to other voices, who repeated, "The boy is returning."

"I am bringing Mr. Bons with me."

Silence.

"I should have said Mr. Bons is bringing me with him."

Profound silence.

"Who stands sentry?"

"Achilles."

And on the rocky causeway, close to the springing of the rainbow bridge, he saw a young man who carried a wonderful shield.

"Mr. Bons, it is Achilles, armed."

"I want to go back," said Mr. Bons.

The last fragment of the rainbow melted, the wheels sang upon the living rock, the door of the omnibus burst open. Out leapt the boy—he could not resist—and sprang to meet the warrior, who, stooping suddenly, caught him on his shield.

"Achilles!" he cried, "let me get down, for I am ignorant and vulgar, and I must wait for that Mr. Bons of whom I told you yesterday."

But Achilles raised him aloft. He crouched on the wonderful shield, on heroes and burning cities, on vineyards graven in gold, on every dear passion, every joy, on the entire image of the Mountain that he had discovered, encircled, like it, with an everlasting stream. "No, no," he protested, "I am not worthy. It is Mr. Bons who must be up here."

But Mr. Bons was whimpering, and Achilles trumpeted and cried, "Stand upright upon my shield!"

"Sir, I did not mean to stand! something made me stand. Sir, why do you delay? Here is only the great Achilles, whom you knew."

Mr. Bons screamed, "I see no one. I see nothing. I want to go back." Then he cried to the driver, "Save me! Let me stop in your chariot. I have honoured you. I have quoted you. I have bound you in vellum. Take me back to my world."

The driver replied, "I am the means and not the end. I am the food and not the life. Stand by yourself, as that boy has stood. I cannot save you. For poetry is a spirit; and they that would worship it must worship in spirit and in truth."

Mr. Bons—he could not resist—crawled out of the beautiful omnibus. His face appeared, gaping horribly. His hands followed, one gripping the step, the other beating the air. Now his shoulders emerged, his chest, his stomach. With a shriek of "I see London," he fell—fell against the hard, moonlit rock, fell into it as if it were water, fell through it, vanished, and was seen by the boy no more.

"Where have you fallen to, Mr. Bons? Here is a procession arriving to honour you with music and torches. Here come the men and women whose names you know. The mountain is awake, the river is awake, over the racecourse the sea is awaking those dolphins, and it is all for you. They want you—"

There was the touch of fresh leaves on his forehead. Some one had crowned him.

★

ΤΕΛΟΣ

From the *Kingston Gazette, Surbiton Times,* and *Raynes Park Observer.*

The body of Mr. Septimus Bons has been found in a shockingly mutilated condition in the vicinity of the Bermondsey gas-works. The deceased's pockets contained a sovereign-purse, a silver cigar-case, a bijou pronouncing dictionary, and a couple of omnibus tickets. The unfortunate gentleman had apparently been hurled from a considerable height. Foul play is suspected, and a thorough investigation is pending by the authorities.

AVRAM DAVIDSON

Avram Davidson (1923–1993) was an American author and editor, born in New York. He served in the US Navy in the Second World War and then as a medic with the Israeli forces in the 1948–9 Arab–Israeli war. He began publishing in the American science fiction and fantasy magazines in the 1950s, particularly in *The Magazine of Fantasy and Science Fiction*, which he went on to edit from 1962 to 1964. He won a Hugo Award (the longest-standing award in the science fiction and fantasy field) for his story 'Or All the Seas with Oysters' in 1958, and won one for editing in 1963. He produced novels and short stories, not only in science fiction and fantasy but also in detective and mystery fiction. He still has many devoted fans, but in his lifetime his erudition and increasingly ornate style restricted his popularity.

The Golem

The gray-faced person came along the street where old Mr. and Mrs. Gumbeiner lived. It was afternoon, it was autumn, the sun was warm and soothing to their ancient bones. Anyone who attended the movies in the twenties or the early thirties has seen that street a thousand times. Past these bungalows with their half-double roofs Edmund Lowe walked arm-in-arm with Leatrice Joy and Harold Lloyd was chased by Chinamen waving hatchets. Under these squamous palm trees Laurel kicked Hardy and Woolsey beat Wheeler upon the head with codfish. Across these pocket-handkerchief-sized lawns the juveniles of the Our Gang Comedies pursued one another and were pursued by angry fat men in golf knickers. On this same street—or perhaps on some other one of five hundred streets exactly like it.

Mrs. Gumbeiner indicated the gray-faced person to her husband.

"You think maybe he's got something the matter?" she asked. "He walks kind of funny, to me."

"Walks like a *golem*," Mr. Gumbeiner said indifferently.

The old woman was nettled.

"Oh, I don't know," she said. "*I* think he walks like your cousin."

The old man pursed his mouth angrily and chewed on his pipestem. The gray-faced person turned up the concrete path, walked up the steps to the porch, sat down in a chair. Old Mr. Gumbeiner ignored him. His wife stared at the stranger.

"Man comes in without a hello, goodbye, or how-areyou, sits himself down and right away he's at home . . . The chair is comfortable?" she asked. "Would you like maybe a glass tea?"

She turned to her husband.

"Say something, Gumbeiner!" she demanded. "What are you, made of wood?"

The old man smiled a slow, wicked, triumphant smile.

"Why should *I* say anything?" he asked the air. "Who am I? Nothing, that's who."

The stranger spoke. His voice was harsh and monotonous.

"When you learn who—or, rather, what—I am, the flesh will melt from your bones in terror." He bared porcelain teeth.

"Never mind about my bones!" the old woman cried. "You've got a lot of nerve talking about my bones!"

"You will quake with fear," said the stranger. Old

Mrs. Gumbeiner said that she hoped he would live so long. She turned to her husband once again.

"Gumbeiner, when are you going to mow the lawn?"

"All mankind—" the stranger began.

"*Shah!* I'm talking to my husband . . . He talks *eppis* kind of funny, Gumbeiner, no?"

"Probably a foreigner," Mr. Gumbeiner said, complacently.

"You think so?" Mrs. Gumbeiner glanced fleetingly at the stranger. "He's got a very bad color in his face, *nebbich*. I suppose he came to California for his health."

"Disease, pain, sorrow, love, grief—all are nought to—"

Mr. Gumbeiner cut in on the stranger's statement.

"Gall bladder," the old man said. "Guinzburg down at the *shule* looked exactly the same before his operation. Two professors they had in for him, and a private nurse day and night."

"I am not a human being!" the stranger said loudly.

"Three thousand seven hundred fifty dollars it cost his son, Guinzburg told me. 'For you, Poppa, nothing is too expensive—only get well,' the son told him."

"*I am not a human being!*"

"Ai, is that a son for you!" the old woman said, rocking her head. "A heart of gold, pure gold." She looked at the stranger. "All right, all right, I heard you the first time. Gumbeiner! I asked you a question. When are you going to cut the lawn?"

"On Wednesday, *odder* maybe Thursday, comes the Japaneser to the neighborhood. To cut lawns is *his* profession. *My* profession is to be a glazier—retired."

"Between me and all mankind is an inevitable hatred," the stranger said. "When I tell you what I am, the flesh will melt—"

"You said, you said already," Mr. Gumbeiner interrupted.

"In Chicago where the winters were as cold and bitter as the Czar of Russia's heart," the old woman intoned, "you had strength to carry the frames with the glass together day in and day out. But in California with the golden sun to mow the lawn when your wife asks, for this you have no strength. Do I call in the Japaneser to cook for you supper?"

"Thirty years Professor Allardyce spent perfecting his theories. Electronics, neuronics—"

"Listen, how educated he talks," Mr. Gumbeiner said, admiringly. "Maybe he goes to the University here?"

"If he goes to the University, maybe he knows Bud?" his wife suggested.

"Probably they're in the same class and he came to see him about the homework, no?"

"Certainly he must be in the same class. How many classes are there? Five *in ganzen*: Bud showed me on his program card." She counted off on her fingers. "Television Appreciation and Criticism, Small Boat Building, Social Adjustment, The American Dance . . . The American Dance—nu, Gumbeiner—"

"Contemporary Ceramics," her husband said, relishing the syllables. "A fine boy, Bud. A pleasure to have him for a boardner."

"After thirty years spent in these studies," the stranger, who had continued to speak unnoticed, went on, "he turned from the theoretical to the pragmatic. In ten years' time he had made the most titanic discovery in history: he made mankind, *all* mankind, superfluous: he made *me*."

"What did Tillie write in her last letter?" asked the old man.

The old woman shrugged.

"What should she write? The same thing. Sidney was home from the Army, Naomi has a new boy friend—"

"He *made* ME!"

"Listen, Mr. Whatever-your-name-is," the old woman said; "maybe where you came from is different, but in *this* country you don't interrupt people the while they're talking . . . Hey. Listen—what do you mean, he *made* you? What kind of talk is that?"

The stranger bared all his teeth again, exposing the too-pink gums.

"In his library, to which I had a more complete access after his sudden and as yet undiscovered death from entirely natural causes, I found a complete collection of stories about androids, from Shelley's *Frankenstein* through Capek's *R.U.R.* to Asimov's—"

"Frankenstein?" said the old man, with interest. "There used to be Frankenstein who had the soda-*wasser* place on Halstead Street: a Litvack, *nebbich*."

"What are you talking?" Mrs. Gumbeiner demanded. "His name was Franken*thal*, and it wasn't on Halstead, it was on Roosevelt."

"—clearly shown that all mankind has an instinctive antipathy towards androids and there will be an inevitable struggle between them—"

"Of course, of course!" Old Mr. Gumbeiner clicked his teeth against his pipe. "I am always wrong, you are always right. How could you stand to be married to such a stupid person all this time?"

"I don't know," the old woman said. "Sometimes

I wonder, myself. I think it must be his good looks."
She began to laugh. Old Mr. Gumbeiner blinked,
then began to smile, then took his wife's hand.

"Foolish old woman," the stranger said; "why
do you laugh? Do you not know I have come to destroy you?"

"What!" old Mr. Gumbeiner shouted. "Close
your mouth, you!" He darted from his chair and
struck the stranger with the flat of his hand. The
stranger's head struck against the porch pillar and
bounced back.

"When you talk to my wife, talk respectable, you
hear?"

Old Mrs. Gumbeiner, cheeks very pink, pushed
her husband back in his chair. Then she leaned forward and examined the stranger's head. She clicked
her tongue as she pulled aside a flap of gray, skin-
like material.

"Gumbeiner, look! He's all springs and wires
inside!"

"I *told* you he was a *golem*, but no, you wouldn't
listen," the old man said.

"You said he *walked* like a *golem*."

"How could he walk like a *golem* unless he *was*
one?"

"All right, all right . . . You broke him, so now fix
him."

AVRAM DAVIDSON

"My grandfather, his light shines from Paradise, told me that when MoHaRaL—Moreynu Ha-Rav Löw—his memory for a blessing, made the *golem* in Prague, three hundred? four hundred years ago? he wrote on his forehead the Holy Name."

Smiling reminiscently, the old woman continued, "And the *golem* cut the rabbi's wood and brought his water and guarded the ghetto."

"And one time only he disobeyed the Rabbi Löw, and Rabbi Löw erased the *Shem Ha-Mephorash* from the *golem*'s forehead and the *golem* fell down like a dead one. And they put him up in the attic of the *shule* and he's still there today if the Communisten haven't sent him to Moscow . . . This is not just a story," he said.

"*Avadda* not!" said the old woman.

"I myself have seen both the *shule and* the rabbi's grave," her husband said, conclusively.

"But I think this must be a different kind *golem*, Gumbeiner. See, on his forehead: nothing written."

"What's the matter, there's a law I can't write something there? Where is that lump clay Bud brought us from his class?"

The old man washed his hands, adjusted his little black skullcap, and slowly and carefully wrote four Hebrew letters on the gray forehead.

"Ezra the Scribe himself couldn't do better," the

398

old woman said, admiringly. "Nothing happens," she observed, looking at the lifeless figure sprawled in the chair.

"Well, after all, am I Rabbi Löw?" her husband asked, deprecatingly. "No," he answered. He leaned over and examined the exposed mechanism. "This spring goes here . . . this wire comes with this one . . ." The figure moved. "But this one goes where? And this one?"

"Let be," said his wife. The figure sat up slowly and rolled its eyes loosely.

"Listen, Reb *Golem*," the old man said, wagging his finger. "Pay attention to what I say—you understand?"

"Understand . . ."

"If you want to stay here, you got to do like Mr. Gumbeiner says."

"Do-like-Mr.-Gumbeiner-says . . ."

"*That's* the way I like to hear a *golem* talk. Malka, give here the mirror from the pocketbook. Look, you see your face? You see on the forehead, what's written? If you don't do like Mr. Gumbeiner says, he'll wipe out what's written and you'll be no more alive."

"No-more-alive . . ."

"*That's* right. Now, listen. Under the porch you'll find a lawnmower. Take it. And cut the lawn. Then come back. Go."

"Go . . ." The figure shambled down the stairs. Presently the sound of the lawnmower whirred through the quiet air in the street just like the street where Jackie Cooper shed huge tears on Wallace Beery's shirt and Chester Conklin rolled his eyes at Marie Dressler.

"So what will you write to Tillie?" old Mr. Gumbeiner asked.

"What should I write?" old Mrs. Gumbeiner shrugged. "I'll write that the weather is lovely out here and that we are both, Blessed be the Name, in good health."

The old man nodded his head slowly, and they sat together on the front porch in the warm afternoon sun.

Permissions Acknowledgements

'The Princess of the Hither Isles' from *Darkwater* by W. E. B. Du Bois. First published by Harcourt, Brace and Company 1920 © W. E. B. Du Bois 1920, 1999, 2016. Reproduced with permission of Verso through PLSclear

'The Celestial Omnibus' by E. M. Forster reprinted by permission of Peters Fraser & Dunlop (www.petersfraserdunlop.com) on behalf of the Estate of E. M. Forster

'The Golem' by Avram Davidson reprinted by permission of the Estate of Avram Davidson. For more information visit www.avarmdavidson.com

MACMILLAN COLLECTOR'S LIBRARY

Own the world's great works of literature in one beautiful collectible library

Designed and curated to appeal to book lovers everywhere, Macmillan Collector's Library editions are small enough to travel with you and striking enough to take pride of place on your bookshelf. These much-loved literary classics also make the perfect gift.

Beautifully produced with gilt edges, a ribbon marker, bespoke illustrated cover and real cloth binding, every Macmillan Collector's Library hardback adheres to the same high production values.

Discover something new or cherish your favourite stories with this elegant collection.

**Macmillan Collector's Library:
own, collect, and treasure**

Discover the full range at
macmillancollectorslibrary.com